FOLKLORIC

BOOK ONE OF THE FOLKLORIC SERIES

KARENZA GRANT

L'Ours

A L'OURS BOOKS ebook

Ebook first published in 2024 by L'Ours Books

Copyright © Karenza Grant

Cover: Deranged Doctor Design

Copyediting: Toby Selwyn

Map: Melissa Nash

ISBN (ebook) 978-1-915737-03-8

ISBN (paperback) 978-1-915737-04-5

www.karenzagrant.com

To Octavia

FOLKLORIC

Book One of the Folkloric Series

Written in British English

www.karenzagrant.com

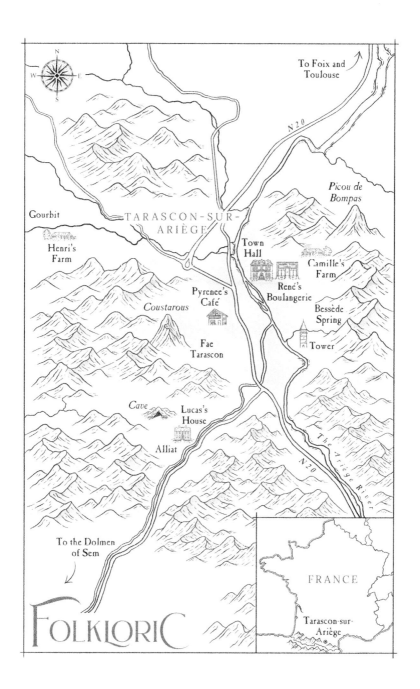

To Foix and
Toulouse

N 20

Picou de
Bompas

Gourbit

TARASCON-SUR-
ARIÈGE

Henri's
Farm

Town
Hall

Camille's
Farm

Pyrenee's
Café

René's
Boulangerie

Coustarous

Bessède
Spring

Fae
Tarascon

Tower

Cave

Lucas's
House

Alliat

The Ariège River

N 20

To the Dolmen
of Sem

FOLKLORIC

FRANCE

Tarascon-sur-
Ariège

CHAPTER 1

FOLKLORE MATTERS. PERIOD.

It's not a load of old stories, done and dusted, or a lot of creepy tales to frighten kids, and it's definitely not some guy in authority choosing the latest version of history for the textbooks. It's the long-term memory of everyday people brought to life—it's the survival of everything *we* like to remember best.

Society couldn't function without folklore, and truth be told, I couldn't function without it either. It was my fascination, my obsession, the thing I loved most of all. Maybe it was my way of making small-town France and my even smaller life a little more interesting, or perhaps it was my method of understanding the world. In any case, it explained why after having just finished my exhausting shift at the café, I was still there, sitting opposite Tarascon's most odious jerk, attempting to get his story for my folklore research paper.

Max Legrand ran his fat fingers over his greasy face,

squishing chubby cheeks and messy stubble. My phone lay on the table by Max's tea, recording the conversation.

"Well... I was coming around the side of the barn, helping Henri with a sack of feed." Max's voice filled the café from the beams in the vaulted ceiling to the cosy wood walls. The scent of his sweat spoiled the aroma of freshly baked bread. There was just too much of him—his width three times that of Henri sitting alongside, grinning in eagerness to hear the story again. Henri was always up for one of Max's recitations, although he was way too nice to be friends with the guy.

"And it was getting late," Max continued. "Dusk had settled and mist rolled in from the top of the mountain. I can tell you, it was a mite strange out there. I couldn't help looking over my shoulder. I'd call it eerie, I would."

Henri nodded enthusiastically, thinning hair bouncing above bright eyes. "Yep, it was some kind of eerie, alright."

"Yeah." Max's shirt buttons strained as he sat back and ran a hand over his buzz cut. "Eerie. Creepy, like." He grinned, peering around to make sure the room was listening. He wasn't telling this story for me, he was telling it for the attention.

Everyone stared at him, including the Dungeons & Dragons geeks secluded away in their nook. They'd actually stopped rolling dice—a minor miracle as they made the most of every moment after school. Gabe, the lanky one who dressed as an elf, ear tips included, gawked at me. Félix the dungeon master and the others watched with peculiar fascination, as though I was a lamb being led to the slaughter. Maybe they were right. With Max, anything was possible.

The town's new doctor sat opposite pretending not to listen, although casting the occasional glance in our direction. The rest of the café weren't being so subtle. They were on the edge of their seats.

I shifted, scraped back the espresso locks that had escaped my messy bun and attempted to loosen the apron tied tight over my jeans. I was much too hot in the late-May heat. Alice caught my eye from behind a counter stacked with the best patisserie for miles. She glared at me and shook her head, clearly code for "This guy is such a jerk. Don't waste your time". She was right, as always. She had that kind of sense that... made sense.

I focussed on Max. Boy, was he taking his time. "What happened then?" I pressed my lips together and nodded my encouragement.

Max sat back and narrowed his eyes. "Are you sure you want to hear this, Camille? I mean, it's just some stupid thing that happened the other day. It's not important, like."

The tease was clear in his eyes. It was important to me, and Max knew it. The research I'd amassed for my paper, *Recent Experiences of Ancient Folkloric Phenomena*, was rock solid. There was no way it wouldn't be published. I just needed a couple more case studies, and Max had been telling his cronies all week about a dark airborne figure he'd seen at Henri's.

I found it fascinating how people assigned paranormal origins to experiences they couldn't understand. There was always an explanation, of course. They just couldn't see it, so the paranormal stuck. Max truly believed his experience was real. And as much as I wanted to believe in monsters and fairies and everything in between, that kind of folklore sprang from the collective beliefs of the community.

The figure in Max's story was already being linked to the death of an old woman who'd lived nearby. She'd been ninety-seven and had died of old age, but it was intriguing how she'd become mixed up in this—the primeval fear of death rankling everyone. I got that—I hated death and dead things. But it was what shaped fear into story that interested me, and I needed a proper recording of Max's tale, rather than hearing second-hand snippets here and there.

"It would be extremely useful for my research, as you know." I fiddled with my necklace, chaining my fingers with silver then releasing them in an attempt not to show the tension creeping through me. "So I would be very grateful if you could continue." I was impressed with myself. I never sounded that patient.

He knocked back his tea. He'd be holed up in a bar if he didn't have to stay sober for driving his cab. Pyrenee's café was not his natural environment, but then, this was the second home to half the town. It was the cosy, take-your-time armchairs, and the brioche. Definitely the brioche.

"Oh, and I saw your grandfather the other day," he said.

I groaned inside. Here it came.

"He was talking about his goats, you know…?"

Don't respond, Camille. Don't respond.

"I heard old Delphine is missing," Henri put in. "She's

been such a super queen to that herd. Did he manage to find her?"

"Nope, still missing," I said, distracted by the mischievous glint in Max's eye.

"Well, at least the old man can talk about *Delphine...*" Max laughed uproariously. "Can't talk about anything else. Mad as a hatter, that one. Good cheese, though."

The customers either shifted uneasily in their seats or snickered. I wanted to shout. I wanted to wring Max's neck and kick the sneer off his bloated lips whilst yelling that Grampi was one of the kindest, most decent people I knew. Way out of Max's league. But I wanted the story more, so I kept quiet, his words twisting me up.

For everyone else, Grampi *did* appear as mad as a hatter. The only thing that came out of his mouth were vague references to his herd of goats. Nothing else at all—ever—which made him a prime target for bullies like Max. But deep inside, he was one hundred percent compos mentis.

Not getting a rise, Max deflated. "Alright, now, where was I? Oh yes, the animal feed. And it was creepy out there—"

"And getting dark," Henri added.

Max nodded. "So, I'm carrying this sack of feed around the side of the barn, and I hear a sound. A kind of shrill wailing, and then a deep moaning born on the gale. Unearthly, I'd say. Not human, for sure."

This was really interesting. There had been many historic reports of evil creatures riding the wind to do mischief in the valley.

"It grew louder and louder," he continued, his eyes comically wide. "The shrieking piercing my ears, the atmosphere so damn bad I can't describe it, and the smell... like dead flesh rotted twenty times over."

And there were tales of fairy-like creatures only recognisable by their terrible odour. This fitted with two other local stories I'd collected. "And...?" I asked.

"By this time, I was rooted to the spot. And the wind grew, roaring around, whining through the barn. And then..." He paused dramatically, the café silent in anticipation. Gabe scratched his elf ear tip. It fell off and dropped into his cup.

"The boards of the little shed at the back shook like they'd be torn off the frame," Max boomed. "The screeching was coming from inside." He took a well-timed breath. Whatever else I thought of him, he was a master storyteller. "I didn't know what to do. I had a choice. Run away or confront the wailing." He puffed out his chest. "So I strode forward and threw open the shed door." Max glanced around at the expectant faces, then homed in on me. "And do you know what I saw, Camille?" he said in a theatrical whisper.

"Go on." Curiosity burned, despite myself.

"It was Henri!" Max raised his arms and gestured to the guy. "It was Henri on the john, groaning and wailing like nothing I'd heard before. He must have been in some pain." Max bellowed with laughter and slapped Henri on the back. The café broke out in howls. "Yep, that was it. Groaning like a good 'un, the poor lad."

Henri's mouth hung open for a moment, then he joined the uproar.

I stared at Max, unable to process what he'd said. Then it sank in. He'd made a joke of me and everything I loved, not to mention his opinions about Grampi. My insides twisted as anger spiked through me. He hadn't told me the real story— he'd been going on about a dark, ghostly figure all week. Was it really so difficult for him to tell me the same thing? He knew how much I wanted this.

I rose and snatched up my phone. "Max Legrand, you're a devious, conniving jerk who would rather get a laugh than help anybody." I leant toward him. "And one of these days, I'm going to pay you back for this so damned hard."

"Come on, Camille. I'm just having a jest." He ogled down my top. I flinched back. "I mean," he added, "it's not like you're one of them academics, or anything fancy like that. You're never going to get published, and you know it."

And there it was. The proverbial slap in my face, worse than his stupid joke, worse than his ogling, worse than anything else at all.

Chapter 2

I needed to get out of there—quickly. Before I did some serious harm to Max. But his words cut deep because they were true, and I couldn't deny it.

I headed behind the counter and into the corridor, pulled off my apron and found my bag. When I came back out, the café had returned to its usual chatter. Everyone had moved on, Max included, but not me.

Alice placed her hand on my arm. "He's not worth it. He's an ignorant troll who enjoys making fun of people—when he's not sexually harassing them."

Her warm eyes and round, sweet face peered out amidst her messy bob, the petals of her rose tattoo just visible on her collarbone. She was a comforting contrast to the intensity I saw in the mirror. "Everyone was laughing," I said. "Not just at Max's story. Laughing at my ridiculous attempts to do something serious with my research. As he said, I'm not an academic, and I never will be. My work won't be accepted."

"You know more about the folklore of the area than any old, balding scholar," she replied softly. "And I wasn't laughing."

I raised my brow. That wasn't enough.

"And the D&D guys, they weren't laughing," she tried. "And the doctor—he kept a straight face through all of it."

"Why were you looking in the doctor's direction?" I couldn't help the tease despite it all.

"Just admiring. Nothing more." She reached over and tucked an escaped strand of hair behind my ear, something she'd done since we were knee high. "Sweetie, you don't usually care about what people think. What's going on—?"

Someone cleared their throat from the other side of the counter. Félix the dungeon master stood there, all chubby, fluffy-teen cheeks and caramel curls. Gabe was next to him, the hood of his elven cloak drawn over his head, hiding his missing ear tip and casting his badly shaved deep-bronze skin into shade. The other two members of the team peered over their shoulders.

"Umm," Félix attempted, shifting uneasily. "We wanted to say that we honour and respect the High Warrior of the Borders: Protector and Holder of the Knowledge of Free Men and Fae." He meant me, his expression earnest. The others nodded in agreement.

For some unknown reason, they'd started addressing me like that a few months ago, and it always caught me off guard. They seemed to be my greatest fans. I guessed they immortalised me in their game, which was more than a little creepy. It was probably because I knew my way around a sword, thanks to Grampi. Or perhaps on some deep level they detected I was a true nerd, just like them.

Félix scratched his nose. "And we think Max is a complete jerk."

"I... appreciate that, guys," I said, touched. "Thank you." But Max was still much too close, and I really couldn't be there any longer. "Gotta go," I said to Alice.

She tilted her chin, assessing me from the corner of her eye as she rewrapped the tie of her apron over her dungarees. "You going to be okay?"

"Of course." I pasted on a grin. But I was so completely far from fine. "I'm going to leave my truck and walk home. I need to clear my head." Letting her know meant she wouldn't worry about my abandoned vehicle in the car park. I kissed her on the cheek. "Love you."

Outside the back door, a bundle of rags huddled on the path, a messy beard and hawk nose just visible in its midst. Roux was sleeping off whatever he'd been drinking. Alice would be out soon with a coffee. He hated being disturbed for any other reason—when he was sober enough to notice.

I stepped quietly past and almost slid my foot into a bloody mess. A mangled mouse carcass lay on the path, its body torn, its features set with terror, its skull visible on one side.

"Damn it, Fifi," I muttered, fighting a retch and looking away, which did nothing to remove the images of broken flesh strobing through my head. If only she wouldn't deposit lifeless bodies everywhere. It was hideous... revolting... like all dead creatures.

Roux grunted at the disturbance, and the rest of the world came back—the flank of Coustarous looming behind the café, its slopes bathed in the afternoon sun, the meadow below lush green.

It was always the same—my complete overreaction to death. Wounds and blood weren't too great either. And I really couldn't take it after Max and the café filled with laughter—laughter at my utter failure to achieve anything in life.

I needed something to ease the pain.

———

From my secluded corner at the back of Brasserie le Saint Roch, I peered out at the world, my hands wrapped protectively around my Bourbon, the bottle on the table emptying more quickly than was healthy.

The French doors that usually extended across the front of the bar had been drawn open to allow in the sun, and the traffic of the N20 thundered past—lorries of tomatoes from Spain, heading to Northern Europe on one of the few half-decent routes through the Pyrenees mountains.

Life strolled past on the pavement, shadows growing long as the evening progressed. A few customers stepped inside. The doctor had come in a half hour after me and was sitting at the front, gazing out. He was already a good way down his second bottle of wine. Looked like I wasn't the only one with problems.

My idea was that if I got completely plastered, I would

forget all about my research, the paper and Max's smug, conceited face. Things were getting fuzzy around the edges. It was working. If I kept at it, I wouldn't remember a thing, and tomorrow, I'd be too preoccupied coping with the hangover to care about anything else. Such a great plan and not at all self-destructive. Never say I didn't face my problems.

My phone buzzed again. Yet another text from Alice to check I was okay. I reassured her, but the inclusion of the straw-hat-with-a-little-bow emoji might have been a mistake. I'd meant to press the smiley.

Raised voices at the bar drew my attention. It was much better to tune in to someone else's life than think about mine. "And he was in Gourbit," the guy on the bar-stool said. "You know, that farm out the other side of the village."

"Know the place," Ren the barman replied gruffly as he polished a glass.

"Well, Max heard a wailing and a shrieking, some kind of demon born on the wind—"

I covered my ears and groaned as my failure rose up like that blasted demon and slapped me once again. "Forget. Forget. Forget. Forget. Forget," I murmured. When they appeared to have moved on to other things, I poured another measure and tipped it back, then poured again. The sweet, sweet liquid sank in, and my vision blurred some more. Through the haze I made out the doctor heading over.

"Hey," he said as he walked past for the bathroom. I struggled to think of a response. *Hey to you too, my life is shit,* came to mind, but it didn't seem appropriate, so I attempted a smile that felt more like a wonky grimace. When he returned, he went to his table, gathered his bottle and glass, and stepped over. I wasn't sure if it was my vision or him, but he appeared to be swaying a little.

"Camille, isn't it?" he asked in a low voice. I could already tell he had a good bedside manner.

"Yep, that's me. Folklore research failure and butt of Max's jokes." A positive introduction always made a good impression.

He chuckled. "Mind if I join you?"

"Nope. Go ahead." I gestured to the empty chair, happy for any kind of distraction from... me.

"Can I get you a glass?" he said, placing the bottle down.

The thought of mixing wine with Bourbon flipped my stomach. "No, I'm good."

He settled at the table, his broad mouth slanted in a grin, his straight, swept-back hair a dark umber mess. As he studied me, his eyes narrowed, accentuating the angles in his face. I'd guess he was a few years older than me and, all in all, I could see what had caught Alice's eye. Truth be told, he'd already caught my attention too.

"So, Max is an asshole," he said.

I stared at him for a moment. I had the idea that doctors were honour bound not to insult their patients—with a code of ethics or something. Then it struck me that Max wasn't a conversation I wanted to be having. But I couldn't help the words escaping. "He's the most abysmal abomination of an absolute ass that ever stepped into this town." I took a mouthful of Bourbon, and actually, I kind of felt better for letting my irritation out.

"Yep." He took a sip of wine, turning his head. A scar ran from under his ear, disappearing into his open shirt collar. "That was pretty evident. The guy is a complete and utter jerk."

My lips tugged upwards. "Do all doctors talk like that?"

He shook his head, his face lit with something I couldn't put my finger on. Shrewdness, perhaps. "Only the ones who've had way too much to drink." Then his expression settled. "But I was wondering, earlier in the café... You're really into folklore, right?"

"Absolutely."

"Then, if you don't mind me asking, why don't you go study at uni or something?"

I had to laugh. "Going straight for the jugular? I would've thought Max had sent you if you'd not been so insulting about the guy." I'd wanted to shove every part of my life into a dumpster for the night, and now this. But confronting everything might do me good. Not my usual approach, but maybe it would help to talk the damned thing through.

I met his assessing gaze. "Well, I was going to. At least, I got as far as the interview for Toulouse. But the professor didn't appreciate my argument with his theories about the morphing of Pyrenean gods into Christian saints. He was clearly incorrect."

The doctor's lips drew together as if he was trying not to smile. Even so, the corners of his eyes creased.

"I wasn't going to put up with his rubbish," I continued, "and he didn't like that, so I didn't get the place. But you know, two years later"—I sat up and smirked—"my arguments were proven correct."

"I do know that," he replied.

"What? How? Very few people know anything about the subject—other than folklore nerds, of course."

He leant forward, his elbows on the table, his glass in his hands. "I, uh, have an interest in folklore."

I gawked at him. He'd just uttered the ultimate chat-up line of my dreams, the one I'd fantasised about a cute guy in a bar saying before... Well, let's not go there. His proximity brought the scent of cedarwood and maybe rosemary, the natural fragrance drawing me more than any overpriced, chemical rubbish. I shook myself, making the room sway.

I needed to get a grip. Talking about folklore was in no way suggestive to anyone in the world but me. Although his body language, leaning in as he was, did indicate a degree of interest. Damn. I was way too plastered to assess the situation properly.

"So why don't you apply to a new uni?" he added.

I glanced outside. Twilight was unfurling, the lights of the traffic too bright. "I chose to stick around and care for my grandfather when my parents moved away. They wanted to put him in a home, but he's completely functional apart from..."

"The goat thing?"

"Yep, the ol' goat thing." He needed a middleman for communication. And anyway, money was tight. The farm had endless bills.

I swirled my glass, spinning the Bourbon. In the years

since I'd unsuccessfully applied for uni, I'd studied every aspect of local folklore I could get my hands on. I'd read every paper, I'd done piles of my own research. Now, I wasn't certain the lightweight syllabus of a degree taking three years of my time was worth it. But how else would I get acceptance as an academic?

"You know," he said, "I sometimes wonder if scholars in universities are the best people to record what belongs to a living population. It takes someone who knows the mountains, who feels the pulse of the valleys within them."

I studied him. My thoughts exactly. There was a case for the objective observer, but bringing in a researcher from outside a community always caused problems. He met my gaze, neither of us looking away. He really was hot, and it wasn't just the folklore. Then it dawned on my addled brain —he was a complete mystery. I didn't even know his first name. "You're Doctor Rouseau, right?"

"Sorry." He sat back and dragged his hands over his face. "I think I left my manners behind with the fifth glass. It's Lucas. Lucas Rouseau."

"So, what's your story?" I asked. "What brings you in here nursing more than one bottle? Can't be much worse than having to deal with Max."

"It's bad. It's really bad." There was something grim in his eyes, then he broke into laughter. "I mean, we all have stuff, right? Work stuff, family stuff, life stuff. I guess it's just stuff."

An eloquent answer. I nodded. "The curse of stuff. It beats being a self-absorbed rejected folklorist."

He bit his lip then glanced at me. "You know that story of Max's—the real story, not the one with the john?"

"How could I not? Everyone is talking about it."

He wrapped both hands around his glass, his face serious, as though this was a grave moment. "It's real—the thing he saw. Completely real."

My lips pursed, a smile attempting to escape, but he appeared so solemn, I couldn't let it. "Yeah?" I managed, but the smile won. It broke its bounds and I guffawed.

His expression broke too, and he roared with laughter. "And hobgoblins—real too," he added, cracking up.

I loved his silliness and I wanted to play. "And sinagries—giant spectral dogs—you'd better watch out for them."

Ren came out from behind the bar and strode to our table. "Right, you two, there's no way you're driving home. Keys."

Lucas and I looked at each other and burst out laughing again. I shifted for access to my pocket and had to grab the table to stop myself falling off the chair, stoking a new volley of giggles. Once I'd clambered back on, I just about managed to detach my car key from its ring, then I cast it onto the table. Lucas did the same. Ren gathered them up with a shake of his head. "I'm glad I'm not you two tomorrow morning," he said before retreating hastily.

"And elves, and gnomes, and dwarves, and dracs, and nymphs are all completely real." Lucas didn't miss a beat.

I snorted repeatedly, tears beading in the corners of my eyes. Lucas gathered himself, his lips stilling into a small smile. He drew his hand to mine and traced my knuckles in and out. His touch sent shivers through me, replacing the hilarity with something carnal.

I matched his gaze, and we grinned, then I turned my hand and took his fingers into mine, playing with his smooth skin. I liked this guy very much. Ha! I'd been right. Despite my inebriated state, I'd interpreted his flirting correctly. I mean, folklore, right? The ultimate chat-up line.

He raised his hand to my cheek, his thumb brushing my lower lip, his glance following as though he was having a hard time restraining himself.

"Oh, and unicorns... got to be so real," I said, relishing his attention.

"Yeah, but they're pretty rare. I've only seen one, and that was from a distance."

My eyes settled on his broad, straight mouth. "Okay. I have to admit, I don't know much about unicorns."

He drew up my chin so my eyes met his, his touch something else. "I can't show you a unicorn, but I know a way we can lose ourselves that will be even better than drink." His eyes sparkled, his gaze devouring me—a complete turn-on.

I ignored the voice screaming—no, caterwauling—*think of the morning*, and *he's the only doctor for miles. What about the next time you need medical assistance?* But that was stupid. I'd be fine. It was the perfect way for two adults to drown their problems.

I pulled out my phone to call a cab. "Your place or mine?"

CHAPTER 3

I EMERGED FROM THE DEEPEST SLEEP I'D ENJOYED IN A long time, my eyes still heavily closed, although light glowed beyond. I was so dreamily relaxed, I wasn't going to move. In any case, today was Sunday, my day off.

The bed felt strangely comfortable—more comfortable than usual—and the morning shone brighter. I turned onto my side, pulling the covers up to my neck and hauling open an eye just a crack.

Oh, no, no, no, no.

Not possible.

Yet undeniably, I lay in a stranger's bed. I forced my eyes fully open and propped myself up, nausea rising, my brain bouncing painfully in my skull. Lucas wasn't here. The room was large and airy, the walls white, the floorboards bare, the furniture understated and elegant. The breeze swayed the curtains and carried the scent of roses, the aroma too much in my state. My stomach turned and bile rose in my throat. It wasn't like I ever did this sort of thing. Well, not very often.

I grasped for memories. The taxi ride. Pulling Lucas's shirt off and the sculpted furrows underneath—dang, that chest. Then laughing. Falling over—at least twice. And... nope. As hard as I tried, I couldn't remember anything else. I only had the faint impression of a very pleasurable few hours. Although how we'd managed anything at all as drunk as we were was beyond imagining.

And look at me. I didn't know where I was, and I hadn't let anyone know where I was going. But, no. I didn't need to panic. There was nothing wrong with this sort of thing. I was sorted for contraception and I was a woman enjoying her body. But it wasn't that. It was the state I'd been in when I'd left the café—the state we'd both been in.

Anyway, he was the town doctor. He had a reputation to maintain. He wouldn't abduct strangers—I hoped. Positive thinking was the preferred attitude. But... I didn't even know the guy.

There was one way I could learn about him, though. I leant across to the bedside cabinet and opened the door. People always kept their secrets there. A medical journal and a box of tissues. Damn. He was either Mr Perfect or he hid his true self in a different cupboard.

Clanging rang out from below—the noises of the kitchen. I could snoop through Lucas's room, but there were better ways of getting to know him—like talking. I shuddered at the thought of the conversation we were going to have.

Another scent caught my attention—something herbal. A

steaming tisane stood on the cabinet to my side. That was sweet. Next to it lay *The Folklore of Roussillon: A Study* by E Durand. I picked it up and leafed through the pages. The book was rare. I'd wanted to get my hands on it for years. Would I even be in the position to ask if I could borrow it now? What kind of position were we in, anyway? We'd been totally hammered, and it had been a stupid mistake. I needed to get out of here, and quick, before things got awkward.

I drew the mug into my ever so slightly shaking fingers and sipped the tea. It was hot and soothing. Tension drained from me with my exhale. A vague memory came back of Alice saying the doctor had moved to Allict, and a glance out the window at the flank of a mountain confirmed my rural location. I was a ten-minute drive from town. Lucas didn't have his car, so I needed a ride.

Wrapping the sheet around me, my head feeling as if it was bulging, I rose and headed for my jeans. They'd been neatly folded with my T-shirt, bra and knickers on a chair by the open window, my bag strung across the back. I fished in the pocket for my phone and dialled Alice.

"Hey, sweetie." She sounded muzzy. It was her day off too. "You better today?"

"Did I wake you?" I asked, avoiding the question.

"No, I was relaxing in bed. What's up?"

"Is there any chance you can give me a lift this morning?"

"Something wrong with your car?"

"It's a long story. Tell you later."

"Mine is still at the garage. They hadn't finished it yesterday."

"Okay, hon." I kept my voice cheery. "That's no problem. I'll sort something out. Love you." I ended the call.

Hell. My only other option was a cab. I took a deep breath and rang the one firm in town. Luckily, there were few houses in Alliet, so they knew the doctor's place. "No problem," the voice came back. "Max is just on a call. He'll be with you straight after."

My stomach sank, nausea redoubling. We'd been lucky last night. Another guy had driven us. But now, Max. The whole town would know about this. It wasn't a walk of shame, it was a taxi of doom.

But I wouldn't let Max get to me. This was the twenty-first century. People did this kind of thing, and he could go jump. Plus, I would deal with Lucas properly, not slink away like I had something to be ashamed of.

More clangs sounded from below. I definitely didn't want him to cook me breakfast. As quickly as my head would allow, I pulled on my clothes, found the en suite and freshened up, then grabbed my bag and headed into the corridor.

The elegant decor continued in the landing with high ceilings and broad, sweeping stairs, a tasteful mix of original artwork here and there. I walked down as quietly as I could, nerves building. I had no idea what I would say. Probably, *Sorry, it was a complete drunken mistake. You're a nice guy, but I don't know you from Adam.* No doubt he thought the same.

I followed the clattering to the rear of the house, past an open door. Inside, chemistry equipment sat on a large table, shelves lined the walls, stacked with filled jars and books, and a low-grade herby smell drifted out, mingling with the aroma of coffee. The whole thing looked like an alchemy lab.

Drawing a long breath, I made my way toward the kitchen. The clattering had stopped, so perhaps he was sitting down. Although my shoulders were back, my nails dug into my palms. But I could deal with this.

I drew open the door and the room lay empty. A long farmhouse table stood in the centre with a chair and a cup recently abandoned. There was no sign of Lucas or breakfast.

The back door was open. I walked past the stove and peered out. The most stunning herb garden lay beyond, the blossoms abundant—spears of rosemary, echinacea and mint. Roses trailed over the hedge and up the house walls, and a small lake sat to one side with a stand of alders. It was a piece of cultivated heaven amidst the rugged slopes. And a little way off, climbing the foothill, was Lucas, his shirt off, his toned back shining a deep gold in the warm sunlight.

This wasn't good. Or maybe it was very good. Perhaps he'd left me in the house alone to creep away. Then we could delude ourselves the night had never happened. But that was silly. We needed to clear the air and my taxi would be here soon.

"Lucas," I called, but the wind had risen, sending my words adrift. He hadn't paused and was almost out of sight. I hooked my bag over my head and hurried after.

Away from the shelter of the high hedges, the wind grew stronger, blustering about. I called again and again to no effect. Keeping Lucas in sight, I strode over close-cropped grass and scooted around the occasional boulder, queasiness slinking through me at the exertion when I should have been tucked up in bed.

Lucas took a sharp left and disappeared behind a rocky outcrop. Hurrying on, I reached the rocks and rounded the corner. The path ended at the opening to a cave. He had to be inside.

"Lucas?" I tried again, tentatively.

Scuffling came from within. Bears were a possibility, or wolves. I backed away. Why had he even wandered off with me upstairs in his home?

"Camille," came his voice from the depths. "Come, see. There's amazing prehistoric rock art in here. Magdalenian or older."

That piqued my interest. But he could have asked before the trek. I stepped into the darkness.

Water dripped somewhere, and I drew in damp, chalky air. It took my eyes a few seconds to adjust. A beam of light grew visible, descending from an opening in the roof along the passage, but I couldn't see any sign of him, and it was too weird.

"Lucas, come on. This is creepy." He could keep his prehistoric drawings to himself. I was going back to wait for my cab.

I made to turn around, but a dark bulk shifted into the light.

CHAPTER 4

SOMETHING HUNCHED ON THE GROUND BEFORE ME. A leathery creature crouched in the shaft of light, all sinewy limbs and taut skin over bone. Its head was little more than a skull with a slight attempt at a nose and lips, and its mouth hung open, filled with saw-like teeth.

My breath caught and cold sweat prickled over my back. I had piles of research about this kind of beast. A drac—clear as anything—an evil incubus that lured victims into rivers or ponds to devour them. Ask one for a favour and it would steal your soul. They were manifestations of folk memory—ancient spirits of waterways. The only trouble was, dracs didn't exist. This... thing didn't exist. I wanted to step back, to edge away, but I couldn't move.

It pulled something into the light and sat on it. An animal... a goat... dead and upturned. The drac tore at the thing, opening its chest and cracking its ribs. It sank its maw into the flesh, feet and horns splaying as it guzzled. My stomach heaved.

The beast gripped one of the legs. Blood stained the white hair that was patterned with three distinct black spots. Above the pattern, a hoof extended with a small twist to it. There was only one goat with that patterning on her misshapen limb. Delphine. The drac was eating Grampi's favourite goat, the one we'd bottle-fed from a kid, the one who'd grown strong to lead the herd.

My muscles tightened, disbelief coursing through me— disbelief and revulsion at the torn carcass—at death. And the dead thing was our dictatorial and stately queen—Grampi's *pet*. My nausea tripled.

The drac devoured Delphine with unearthly rapidity. Then it raised its head, blood smeared over its face, a severed leg in its claw. It met my gaze.

"Camille," it growled. I jumped back with a yelp. That tone... even through the growl... it was familiar. And that expression, intelligent and astute... "It's me," it said, its voice unmistakably Lucas's.

"No." I almost laughed the word. The whole situation was beyond belief. I'd drunk too much, for sure. "I'm either still drunk or I've got alcohol poisoning, or... you spiked my tea and you're a figment of my drug-addled imagination." I sounded more certain than I felt.

"I'm real, and you know it," it replied.

Hysterical laughter bubbled from my chest. "I don't know anything of the sort. Dracs don't exist, therefore you don't exist. Perfect logic."

He took a bite of the leg then threw it away. I flinched, my eyes wide. Delphine was worth more than this.

"Bit of a chewy breakfast," it said. "Nothing on the legs." It pulled itself up to standing, managing to look haughty despite the blood oozing down its desiccated body. "I'm just showing you the real me. Women like that sort of thing—seeing the inner man, all his darkest secrets."

That was the last time I looked in a bedside cabinet.

It drew a claw to its head and rubbed. "This hangover is killing me." Rasping echoed around the cave as it hauled in a lengthy, grating breath. As it did so, the creature's skin stretched, the colour lightening, puffing, filling with muscle, form and colour. And before me stood Lucas, his golden skin and ripped torso naked, all apart from a generous smearing of blood and gore.

I shook my head. "This is absurd." The delusion was getting worse. I'd not told anyone where I was going, and now look at the mess I was in. But I'd called a cab, and it would be here any minute. It might even be here now. I had to run. If I didn't, I'd be his next meal.

I darted toward the cave entrance. Lucas shot past faster than humanly possible, and stood on the threshold. I drew up short, trembling. I was trapped.

He raised his palms, a sign for me not to move. "I'm not going to hurt you. Give me a moment to explain." His voice rang with confidence and steadiness, as though I was in his consulting room.

I couldn't pull my eyes from the blood and sinew smeared over his face and down his chest. A chest... a body that I'd... Nope. I couldn't go there. My gaze flicked to the view of the valley at Lucas's side and the house below, but there was no sign of the taxi.

"Dracs seduce people and devour them," I blabbered. "That's what you did—what you're doing. You used some kind of fairy magic to get me into the sack and now you're going to eat me." There was one problem with my reasoning. It would mean dracs and fairy magic were real—and didn't dracs lure their victims to death by drowning?

Then it struck... "I'm not your first victim, am I? You move from town to town, enticing innocent women to their deaths, then you relocate to cover your tracks."

He raised his brow, amusement in his eyes. "I don't have any victims at all, and I didn't seduce you. I was completely smashed yesterday, just like you. I'd had a terrible day, and you were at the bar looking"—he flicked gore off his finger— "reasonably hot. And if I have consent, and only then, I have trouble resisting temptation as much as the next guy... drac. To tell you the truth, you weren't too difficult to get into bed."

Bastard.

"I did put something in your tea, though," he added. "But not what you think."

I glowered at his arrogant, conceited face, every part of me clenching. He'd spiked my drink. That explained everything. "Don't you get how completely out of line that is?"

"Of course I do, but I needed to show you reality." His eyes widened, as though he could convince me of his sincerity. "The herbs in the tea allow you to see the world as it really is."

"I can't believe you're using some hippy mumbo-jumbo to justify your actions."

He shook his head and the corners of his mouth twitched. "No, it's folklore—everything you've researched. I told you last night, it's all real, but you can't normally see it."

He was attempting to talk around the fact he'd spiked my drink by using more folklore seduction. What a slime. Over his shoulder I caught a glint of sunlight on metal. The taxi.

I studied him, wondering what he'd do if I ran. With his speed I'd have no chance. I opted for fake confidence—not that it would do any good if he did want to eat me. Striding forward, I shoved him in the chest.

He stumbled back.

"You ate Delphine," I yelled, and stormed down the hill.

CHAPTER 5

"CAMILLE," LUCAS SHOUTED.

I didn't stop.

"I was going to offer you a lift," he yelled.

Incredulity seeped from every pore as I turned around. "You have to be freaking joking? Not to mention, you don't have your car."

"Oh, shit, I forgot." He stood by the rocky outcrop, his hair and junk swaying in the wind, blood staining most of him. Even from here, I could see the smirk plastered across his face. "One more thing... now you've had the tea, you might see things you've not experienced before. I've put my number in your phone if you need help."

"How did you—"

"Face recognition. You open your eyes occasionally when you're sleeping." He laughed. After all of this, he actually laughed. The sod. "If you want me, just call."

I couldn't believe my ears. I turned and pelted down to

the taxi, yanked open the door and dropped inside, locking it behind me. Max's beady eyes studied me in the mirror. "Take me to Brasserie le Saint Roch," I managed, my breath heaving. I needed to pick up my keys and then my truck. "And don't say a damned thing."

He pulled away and drove in silence. My adrenaline spike petered a little and the full force of my hangover descended, the roar of the engine splitting my skull, the stone-studded foothills rushing past too fast. Max's stench of old sweat turned my stomach over and over. And through it all, I could see Lucas's hideous form as he guzzled Delphine. The man was a psycho. I'd get a blood test and report the monster. Then I'd sleep off whatever he'd given me, and the world would return to normal. I opened the window and clutched my throat, certain I'd hurl.

Max threw a bag into the back. I ignored his offering and breathed through the urge. It would only add fuel to Max's fire if I vomited in his cab along with everything else. Max shifted, casting glances in the rear-view mirror, barely able to restrain himself. He never could shut up.

"Look, Camille..." Here it came. The world according to Max. "You're a nice girl. You have this ridiculous idea about folklore and stories and the like"—I tried to ignore him—"but you serve coffee okay—apart from that time you spilled it all over Henri, and that time Jean's brioche landed on his glasses, and the incident when you tripped on Alf's gouty foot." He scratched his bulbous chin. "Actually, you're a terrible waitress, but we won't hold that against you—"

"Save it for someone who's interested." I winced from the

glare as the sun bore through the glass. For a moment, Max seemed to expand—his neck, his thick head, all of him bulging. I closed my eyes in defiance of the hallucination.

He was silent for a minute, and then, "A pretty little lady like yourself with good"—he cleared his throat—"attributes, shouldn't go distracting a good man like the doctor. Not to mention, promiscuity of any kind is not becoming in a female."

I glared at the back of his spotty neck, unable to believe what spewed from his mouth.

"The doctor has important work to do," he continued, "saving lives and looking after the sick. It's difficult for a hot-blooded male to resist enticement, and he doesn't need distraction. So best you let him concentrate on his work."

"What the..." I rubbed my hands over my eyes. "It's none of your goddamned business, Max. And are you that much of a knucklehead not to realise what you just said, or even to register that it's the twenty-first century?" My voice rose. "The asshole doctor—or any man, for that matter—has as much responsibility for his actions as any *female*."

Max drew up outside Brasserie le Saint Roch. "Now then. There's no need to get all worked up by a little sensible advice." He shook his head as though I was a small fluffy animal that could never understand a man's needs.

I scanned my card on the payment machine and hauled myself from the cab. "You can take your advice," I growled, "and shove it where the sun doesn't shine."

With careful steps, I headed to the back door and hammered. Max pulled away, and I released a breath. He wasn't worth the aggro. But I damned as hell was going to sort out that scumbag Lucas. Ren came out with my key, his head shaking. I thanked him then stalked to the café car park, climbed into my truck and slammed the door, my skull fragmenting at the thunk.

I turned the ignition and pulled out. The last thing I needed right now was a police interview and a blood test, but I wasn't going to let Lucas get away with it. He was the town's doctor, for heaven's sake—he had a position of trust.

For the station, I needed to take a left out of the car park. I raised my fingers to click the indicator, but no matter how hard I tried, my hand wouldn't respond. I attempted to turn the wheel left, but I couldn't make my body react. Then, as though on autopilot, I indicated right and headed home.

CHAPTER 6

I HUDDLED ON MY SOFA, A BLANKET WRAPPED AROUND me, my phone clasped in my hand. I'd tried all day to dial the police, but my fingers had other ideas—they wouldn't shift an inch. What was wrong with me? I'd driven straight back to the farm desperate to about-turn and report Lucas, but I hadn't been able to force myself. And now I couldn't even make a phone call.

Perhaps a different tactic. I clicked on messages. I wanted to text to Alice, *Think my drink was spiked*, but try as I might, my fingers wouldn't obey. This had to be a complication of whatever Lucas had given me, but I'd not heard of a drug having such a specific action.

I tried again, this time wanting to write, *Hope you're having a lovely Sunday, hon.* My fingers obliged. Text sent. In a second, my phone pinged. *You too, sweetie. Put your feet up xxx.*

With a will of iron, I tried to dial the police again, my

grip tightening around the case, my thumbs trembling. Nope, I couldn't do it. I couldn't make myself report Lucas. I threw my phone into the cushions, my head spinning. I needed to figure out what was going on, but the internet had revealed nada, and I had no idea what to do next.

That was the last time I was going to get trashed. I should have spent the day refining my folklore paper. I really needed to do some work on it. But as Max had succinctly stated, there was no point.

Closing my eyes, Lucas filled my head again, his teeth tearing into Delphine, blood covering his hideously taut features. I was deluded—completely deluded. But he was a doctor, a respected member of the community—if he went round spiking drinks, what else did he get up to? And that laboratory of his. He had the equipment to make who knew what. One thing was certain, he was an arrogant prick. Although he *had* risked his career by admitting what he'd done. That didn't make sense.

Nothing made sense.

Perhaps there was some other explanation. Lucas admitted spiking my drink, but he'd also said his hideous drac-man guise wasn't my imagination. Of course, it had been, so what if all of it had been a hallucination? The drac, the goat and Lucas. That made sense. Then perhaps I had some weird sickness like ergot poisoning. I rummaged for my phone and tried to dial the hospital. Nope. I couldn't even do that. I had to admit, I was getting pretty freaked out.

Through the French windows, something shifted in the yard—something other than a goat. My spacious studio loft was the converted top floor of the old limestone barn, the lower level still used for storage. It gave me a good view across the yard to the farmhouse where Grampi lived, and out over the town below and the mountains beyond.

I scanned the yard, hoping to see Grampi. After morning milking, he headed out most days, walking on the foothills, but he always returned for evening milking at the latest. He was perfectly capable of taking care of himself, despite what others thought. Even so, I liked to check in on him at least once a day, usually more.

The herd milled about, all brown shagginess and horns, back from roaming the slopes of Picou de Bompas behind the farm. But something larger stood where the bushes met Grampi's house, close to where Rose munched grass. It was definitely goat-like, but taller and more human. I rose with a wince and peered out for a better look.

The thing had huge curling horns with a goat's head and legs, but it had the chest and arms of a man, and it stood like one. My stomach swayed. It was Aherbelste, one of the ancient Pyrenean deities, protector of herds and homes. Then Rose ambled into the bushes, and he was gone.

I rubbed my eyes and swallowed. The substance in my system had warped Rose's sweet face, that was all. It wasn't her fault Christians of old had decided her curly horns, horizontal irises and long, triangular face heralded the devil incarnate. And now I was seeing him too.

Grampi emerged from the trees and headed into the house, his step vigorous, his shoulders a little hunched with age. Time I had some fresh air and checked on him. I threw the blanket off and made my way gingerly downstairs, managing pretty well. The day on the sofa and pints of water had done wonders. Now I only needed to stop hallucinating.

Outside, goats milled around, one on the roof of the milking barn attempting to nibble a particularly out-of-reach branch, another eating an old cleaning rag. I pulled the cloth out of its muzzle and it gave me a gentle butt.

Rose trotted over, ever protective of me. "Hello, old girl." I scratched behind her ears and she nuzzled my pocket. "Nothing in there. Sorry." A glimmer of disappointment filled her narrowed eyes, a little gesture she used to snaffle more than her fair share of carrots goats were as communicative as dogs, if not more. "Not going to work this time. I don't have any." She walked away scornfully. But, bless her, she was doing a great job as replacement queen, organising the herd, unsettled as they had been with Delphine gone.

Delphine... How was I going to tell Grampi? But I shouldn't say anything. Not yet. I could've imagined the whole thing, and I wasn't going to upset him until I was certain.

The farmhouse door swung open with a crash, my head letting me know it really wasn't completely better yet. Grampi stood there, his full white beard and eyebrows bristling, a dangerous sparkle in his bright blue eyes, a glinting medieval knightly sword in his hand. He wanted to spar, but of all the days he could have picked...

He glared at me for a moment, then charged. I sprang across the yard and into the trees by the loft, flinging myself behind the nearest trunk. "Not now!" I yelled, my voice much too loud for my senses. "I guess you could say I've not had the best morning."

Slam. The flat of his blade struck the tree right by my head. Grampi stepped into view, ridiculously agile for his eighties. The strike had been a warning. I twisted away and ran for the next trunk.

"Hoof rot hasn't been a problem this year, but Tulip has a bit of a limp," he shouted, as if that explained it all. "And Daffodil is off her food."

My theory was that Grampi understood everything, but something went wrong when he tried to speak or write. There was no connection with what he said to reality—other than the information about goats. He couldn't speak my name, and even the nods and shakes of his head weren't reliable. Generally, I found it best to ignore the actual goat conversation and guess what a normal person would say in his place.

I took this update on Tulip and Daffodil to mean *you have to be prepared in any situation*. A guess based on how he'd behaved before the goat-speak started. I also went by the look in his eye—the most accurate measure of how he was feeling at any given time. Right now, his eyes sparkled with mischief. Best guess—he'd noted I'd been out, presumed I'd been drinking, and was playing with my hangover. Great.

"Yes. Alright, I admit it, I have the hangover from hell. But now is really not a good time." I needed to get on with finding out what was wrong with me.

Clang. That blow had been too close to my fingers. Grampi was great for his age, but he'd become a little trembly lately. No matter the hangover, I wasn't going to risk losing a digit. I dove to the loft door at the side of the barn, grabbed my sword from inside and sprang out, brandishing it before me, its weight reassuring in my grip.

My head throbbed, but Grampi meant business. He came at me and we exchanged blows, the force of steel on steel streaking through my poor body, the clatter scattering the goats. His mischievous look continued, confirming he was laughing at my self-inflicted state. His moustache twitched under his long nose as he struck again. I parried, sidestepping amidst the trees, purposefully on the defensive.

"Plenty of milk this morning," he shouted. I knew from his tone that he wanted me to attack. But I was good with the blade these days, very good, and although Grampi had been a master, now he was too frail for my full force. We carried on, and as I got into it, my hangover relinquished its hold. I sprang behind a low branch and Grampi dove under, striking beneath. To say he was sprightly was a total understatement.

Despite myself, I actually smiled for the first time today. The exercise was doing me good—it always had, even when I'd been barely old enough to support the weight of the blade. I'd goaded Grampi to teach me, loving every minute of it. It wasn't until my twentieth birthday that I surpassed his skill level. That and him getting older meant he wasn't a challenge anymore, but he enjoyed it so much, it was my turn to repay the favour.

The edges of the blades had been rounded, so neither of us could do much harm, but these days, I worried that the jarring of my blows might be enough to fracture fragile bones. Although when he came at me like just now, I didn't have any choice.

He thrust again and stumbled as I dodged. I sprang forward and caught his arm. "You okay?"

"Daisy has precocious udder," he replied through breaths, trembling a little as he lowered his sword. "Going to produce a lot of milk, that one."

I nodded. "Yep, that's enough." I put my blade under my arm and guided him back to the house. If he'd disagreed, he would've stood his ground.

Inside, I laid my sword on the kitchen counter, then tucked Grampi up on the couch in the corner and pulled the blanket over him. "A fine young nanny is that Daisy," he muttered contentedly.

"Rest up for a few minutes," I said, and kissed his head. He closed his eyes, clasping his hands across his chest. But his hands... the wrinkled and age-spotted skin... it appeared darker than usual, his fingertips a dirty green as though they were rotten, tendrils of decay twining along his fingers and across his wrists.

I was seeing things again... but what if I wasn't?

In the gap between Grampi's trousers and socks, a similar tendril wound up his leg. He'd kicked his shoes off at the door and his socks hung loose. I slipped one off. His feet were like his hands—spiralling threads of an unhealthy growth extending along his arch, the tips of his toes gangrenous. I'd never seen anything like it.

CHAPTER 7

IT WAS ANOTHER HALLUCINATION. AFTER ALL, THE ROT on Grampi's fingers didn't look real. It looked... inhuman was the best description I could think of. My stomach twisted. I had to do something about my mental state, but incapable as I was of asking for help, I had no idea what to do.

Grampi was already asleep. I pulled his sock back on and tucked the blanket over his feet, then scanned the old wooden kitchen as though I could find an answer there. Countless mementos of Grampi's military travels hung everywhere. The vase that had been my grandmother's stood out on the sideboard as the only floral decor—a keepsake of someone unknown to me. She'd died years before I was born. Out of the window, Rose and the others milled around the yard.

Oh, crap. Grampi's escapade meant he would sleep through milking. I'd have to do it. A small voice in my head said that an octogenarian shouldn't have to milk a herd of goats. Another voice griped that if he insisted on keeping a herd, he could damned well milk it himself. When I'd suggested it might be time to reduce goat numbers, the fire in his eyes maintained that such a thing was completely unacceptable. Usually, he was more than fit enough to manage. But not this evening.

Hangover and all, I hauled myself out to the milking barn between the farmhouse and the loft. The swordplay had done me good, and although my tongue had grown fur, grit had found permanent residence at the back of my eyeballs and a faint buzzing filled my ears, I was... alive.

I filled the feed bucket and hooked it onto the milking stand. Rose hopped on and I closed the metal bar to keep her secure. The buzzing in my ears rose a little. Best I got on with the job and had an early night. Whatever had happened today, sleep was no doubt the ideal solution.

Working through the herd took forever. Well, not forever, maybe an hour. But forever in my state. And the buzzing became more persistent, as if I had my own personal swarm of mosquitoes.

Once done, I flexed my sore fingers—I hadn't built up calluses like Grampi's—then carried the milk into the farmhouse and stowed it in the cheese fridge. Grampi had gone up to bed. Nothing would wake him until morning, and the long sleep would do him good.

I grabbed my sword and strode back to the loft entrance, then hung the blade with my coats, kicked off my shoes and headed upstairs. The buzzing grew. It came from below, near my feet, and as I made the top step, ants swarmed over the wooden boards. I drew a sharp breath and shifted to the side. I wasn't silly about bugs, but I didn't want them inside.

The ants hurried about, swelling. I rubbed my head. I was seeing things again—ants couldn't expand like that. They marched through the sitting area, into the kitchen, still growing. Shaking my head, I stepped backward into the corner by the sofa and slid down the wall, tears of frustration and desperation welling up. "This isn't real. This isn't real. This definitely and absolutely isn't real." I wrapped my arms around my legs, buried my head and rocked. All I had to do was wait. The hallucinations would go. It was only a matter of time. And didn't people see insects when they got high?

But the kitchen clattered, and the floorboards shook with thudding from the bedroom area. I didn't want to look— really, I didn't—but it sounded like the loft was being trashed. Bracing myself, I opened my eyes. My jaw dropped. Swarming around were hundreds of small men speeding past in brown, foot-high streaks.

The men were everywhere and into everything—tossing sofa cushions, invading the fridge, bathing in the sink. A group were breaking eggs into the frying pan, another lot were emptying the cupboards. Some were raiding the wardrobe and drawers, and a few blighters were hurling books. I shook my head—not the books, they couldn't damage my books.

This. Could. Not. Be. Happening.

I wouldn't have a place left if I didn't do something. But it was all a hallucination, right? Hell, my brain was addled.

There were whoops, catcalls, yells and battle-cries. A

man standing on the desk hauled up my laptop. He ran to the edge and lifted it above his head to throw it off the side.

All my research was in there. "Nooooo," I yelled, and dashed over.

He put it down behind him and peered up sheepishly, his shaggy beard twitching. He was dressed in animal skins roughly sewn into a tunic and thick trousers, sinews tied around his legs. He was a Man of Bédeilhac—a type of fairy that had lived in the cave of Bédeilhac since the flood. They were amiable but very dangerous if angered, and then they'd go on the warpath. Likely, they personified our prehistoric ancestors.

They definitely weren't real.

The Man of Bédeilhac tittered, inching sideways. I made to grab him, but he sprang to the floor and bolted off. I stuck my laptop into its padded rucksack and hooked it over my shoulders, nice and safe.

The cacophony persisted, the contents of every cupboard sprawled about, bed linen billowing, burning wafting from the kitchen. The nearest Man of Bédeilhac was attempting to eat a tube of toothpaste. I dove for him, but he dashed off.

I turned to a group casting cushion feathers into the air and launched toward them. They scattered. I ran at the posse around the saucepan, black smoke rising dangerously. They disappeared under the units—the little critters. I turned off the stove. I wasn't having this—I wasn't going to have my whole place torn up by a bunch of prehistoric hallucinations.

I pelted down the stairs, grabbed my blade and stormed back up to the centre of the loft. The sword felt like home as I swung it, barely missing the furniture. With a blade in my hand, I could handle anything. "Right!" I yelled above the din. "Who wants to play?"

They paused in unison, silence descending, feathers swaying gently to the ground. If it hadn't been so alarming that I was hallucinating on a grand scale, it would've been funny. Then, with a cry from one of them, they continued the destruction.

The nearest one sprinted across the floor. I swung my blade at him then stopped short. What was I going to do? Kill him? Grampi and I were so controlled when we crossed swords that nicking skin was a rarity, thankfully, as I couldn't walk past a dead mouse without the urge to vomit. The thought of ending the Man of Bédeilhac's life, of facing his limp, mangled body, drew bile to my throat. I pressed my hand over my mouth. Yep, I was doing a great job of sorting this whole situation out.

I hauled a breath. There had to be another way.

One of them ran out from under my bed. He couldn't see where he was going as he had my best pair of knickers on his head. The little beast wore a skin cloak. I shot over and thrust my blade through the leather and into the floorboard, pinning him to the ground. Quick as a flash, I grabbed him, his cloak tearing free. I wrestled the knickers around his head and body a few times, securing him tight. He was well and truly trapped. I tucked him into a headlock under my arm, then yanked my blade from the boards and pressed it against his throat.

"Alright!" I yelled. "Either stop what you're doing, or the knicker thief gets it."

Silence. Hundreds of wide eyes gazed from me to the wiggling bundle. I wasn't going to hurt the guy—but they didn't know that.

In the hush, one of them stepped forward, his chestnut beard impressively bushy, his eyes bright and keen. He held an axe made of wood and stone tied with sinew, which he swung at my bare toe, slicing the skin.

I hopped on one leg at the sting. "What the hell are you doing?"

He drew the axe back, the others gawking at the spectacle.

"No way." I pressed the blade closer to the squirmer. "You do that again and Mr Knickers will be the first to die."

"Oh, drat," the Man of Bédeilhac said as he lowered his axe. "We're just doing our job. There's no need to be getting all threatening like that."

"Your job?" I screeched. "Your job is trashing my loft?" He hung his head, having the grace to look ashamed. "What right do you have to come in here and—"

The Man of Bédeilhac's eyes grew wide as he stared at something behind me.

"And," I continued, "destroy everything I love?" He wasn't listening. "Damn it, will you please pay attention?"

He shuffled his feet. "I would, miss, but it's just that there's... ummm... something behind you."

The oldest trick in the book. Yet now he'd said it, my

neck prickled. Thuds of falling bottles echoed from the bathroom at my back.

I turned slowly and screamed.

Filling the bathroom door, stooping a little—if that thing could stoop—was a giant-sized man's foot and lower leg with, where should have been a knee, a massive eye. A came-cruse —a Pyrenean creature of fear—a thing that rushed down mountains to scare nocturnal travellers. It definitely, completely and utterly wasn't real.

It joggled and I stepped back, the Man under my arm squirming, the rest of them, including the one with the axe, staring on. Then something occurred to me. If all of this wasn't real—which it definitely wasn't—there would be no harm in killing the came-cruse, or any of them. In fact, it might be therapeutic—killing my demons. I withdrew my sword from the knicker guy and charged at the came-cruse.

As I stormed forward, its one massive eye grew even wider. The whole thing shrank in on itself as much as its bulk could, and it began to tremble. I stilled my blade millimetres from its flesh. Its trembling grew, and a solitary tear beaded in its eye then spilled out, trailing down its hairy leg. The thing was terrified. Boy, did I feel like a jerk.

But, come on. These creatures were storming my loft and trashing my possessions. Before one of them made a move again, I returned the blade to Mr Knickers's throat, and the Men of Bédeilhac collectively drew a breath.

How was I going to get rid of them? Or, more to the point, how was I going to stop this hallucination that, if I admitted it to myself, felt completely real? I needed help, and there was only one option I could think of.

I shuffled to the sofa, Men of Bédeilhac shifting out my way as one—like a school of fish, all apart from the cries of "get off my toe" and "mind my personal space, you great oaf".

The sofa was bare, the cushions either in pieces or scattered across the room. I dug down the back of the seat and pulled out my phone. My traitorous fingers seeming completely happy with the task, I tapped on Lucas.

CHAPTER 8

I WAITED FOR LUCAS. ALL THE WHILE, THE LITTLE critter under my arm begged for mercy, the came-cruse trembled in the bathroom and all the Men of Bédeilhac stood stock still, not daring to move in case Mr Knickers bit the dust by my blade.

A car drew up minutes later and Lucas let himself in. He emerged from the stairwell dressed for work, a huge grin on his face. "Having a good time, Camille?"

I shouldn't have called him. He was my tormentor. Perhaps it was Stockholm syndrome, although there was no way I had any kind of bond with this guy. But I needed answers, and he was the only one who could provide them. Plus, I was the one holding the sword. "What did you do to me? I couldn't even phone for medical help. What kind of a sick doctor are you?"

He appeared almost... distressed for a moment, then it was gone, replaced by nonchalance. "The kind showing you everything you want to see, everything you want to believe is true. I included the binding potion that stopped you asking for help as an addition to the other herbs in your tea because..." He let out a breath and rubbed his head, looking tired. "I've only just started my new job, and I don't want to lose it."

"But you can't go around drugging people." I jostled Mr Knickers as he squirmed particularly hard. "At least tell me what you gave me, so I can get some help."

He glanced at the destruction, ignoring me. "Slaughter?"

"Yes, governor." The one with the axe zoomed over and saluted beneath Lucas, almost too close for him to see.

"I thought I said no mess?"

"Your exact words were, gov, 'Shake things up a bit and give her a fright, but don't break anything.'"

Lucas picked up a handful of feathers. "Well, what's this?"

Slaughter shrank back. "The lads do get a little excited..."

"Wait." His words sank in. "You told them to do this to me? To my loft?" But then it clicked. He hadn't done this to my loft because it was all in my head. Mr Knickers poked his pointy feet into my side. I gave him a shake. "Will you just stop it."

Lucas continued to ignore me. "Get this place cleaned up. Now! And why did you bring him in on it?" He nodded to the came-cruse. "You know he's not up to the job."

"Scare factor," Slaughter said meekly. "Until he started crying, that was."

"Well, return him to Fae. And make sure he's alright."

"Yes, sir!" Slaughter bellowed to a comrade, and an old Man of Bédeilhac with a long grey beard appeared. "Wrench, take the came-cruse home. The rest of you, get on with it!"

I watched with incredulity as Slaughter and the other whirling dervishes reverse-destroyed my loft. At least, I hoped that was what they were doing—it currently looked like additional destruction. Wrench jumped on the came-cruse's foot and the two hopped past. The came-cruse gave me an awkward wink, which seemed to mean, "Sorry for the fright." Despite myself, I sent it a reassuring smile.

Something poked my foot. Slaughter stood beneath me. "Could we have that one back, miss? I expect Snigger can hardly breathe wrapped up in your knickers."

Lucas raised an eyebrow, his lips pursed.

I lowered my blade, put Snigger down and pulled the knickers off him, stuffing them in my pocket with a glare at Lucas. Snigger spun around and collapsed on the floor. "Is he alright?"

"Completely fine," Slaughter said. "He's not been so close to a lady's underwear before. It'll take him a few minutes to recover." Two Men of Bédeilhac stretchered him away on my hardback edition of *The Great Encyclopedia of Faeries*.

"I want that back," I yelled.

Remembering I had a lethal weapon in my hands—well, if you didn't count the blunt blade—I strode to Lucas. The corners of his mouth twitched and his eyes creased—that shrewdness assessing me. He remained motionless as I pressed the point into his shirt at the neck. "Answers. Now."

He raised his chin, took the blade in his hand and pushed it away. "Such an impressively sharp weapon."

"I'm serious. It may be as blunt as a butter knife, but I know how to use it, and I'll do whatever damage I can to you if you don't tell me what you've done to my head." I glanced at the Men of Bédeilhac. "None of this is real and I'm having the worst trip of my life."

He raised his hands in acquiescence. "It's not a trip. You've had verity, that's all. And I want you to know, I don't go around spiking drinks." He smirked. "Except yours."

He was so conceited. "Explain 'verity'."

"Alright." He inclined his head to the cushions piled by the window. "Mind if I take a seat? I've been called out four times today on top of clinic."

"You have to be joking. Have you seen this place?"

He narrowed his eyes, not understanding.

"You caused this." I raised the blade. "Get tidying. You can explain while you work."

He shook his head, undid a shirt button and pulled his collar loose, then picked up a pile of books. "Verity shows you what's really there. Nothing more. It's not a hallucinogen. It's the reverse, in fact."

"That doesn't make sense. Come on, Doctor." The sarcasm dripped from my voice. "You can do better." I kept my sword up.

He eyed the blade. "Alright, but hear me out."

I nodded. "And keep working."

He stacked the books, the Men of Bédeilhac a whirr of activity around us. "The world has two distinct realms—the human realm and the fae realm." He gathered a couple of hardbacks. "They're two sides of the same coin. They balance and complement each other. Humans need the intuition, emotion and inspiration of Fae, and fae need the logic, structure and materiality of the human realm. Simple."

I scoffed. He was utterly deluded.

"Here, in the Pyrenees," he continued, "this area in particular, we live on the borderlands between the two realms. There are other borders in other places, but this one is, let's say, important."

It was a load of rubbish. Even so, the folklore part of my brain was curious. Lucas appeared to be sincere. Either he believed what came out of his mouth, or he was a damn good liar. It astounded me how one man could be so utterly crazy.

All about us, the Men moved faster than humanly possible—a hive of activity. The place was beginning to look a little tidier. "Then how come people don't know fairies... fae, are real?" I asked, amusement in my voice. I prodded the blade in Lucas's direction. "Don't stop tidying."

"Usually, it's because humans don't want to know. Even if there's a story going around like Max's, they don't really want to accept the truth. It's just a curiosity." He picked up a bed sheet and shook it out. "That's how human minds work these days. Stick a came-cruse in front of one, and their brain wouldn't accept its reality. And since humankind developed horrendous weapons and polluted the world, fae are completely happy to keep themselves secret. That kind of stuff is poison to most of us."

"Hmmm, sounds like fae are sensitive creatures. Not the types to eat anyone's goat."

He folded his sheet, studying me. "To keep separate, we strengthen our disguises with a little glamour where necessary, but mostly we don't need to. All verity does is ease away the blockages to seeing fae. We're careful who we give it to, though. If someone isn't receptive, they can go mad."

"You don't say?"

"You'll be fine," he said.

"What makes you think that?" Despite my fitness, my arm was starting to ache from holding the sword still.

He gathered a few more books, shelved them, then leant against the bookcase. "You're open to it. Probably through studying folklore, or maybe from growing up on the borders. Sometimes that helps."

"And you're a drac," I said, unable to resist finding out how far his ridiculous story went. "An incubus—an ugly, disgusting vampire thing."

He shrugged. "Pretty much sums me up. Not particularly the vampire thing, though. That was Uncle Estruch and the affair at Chateau Llers. It started the whole vampire business in the twelfth century. He was a bad egg."

"Count Estruch was your uncle?" That tale was Europe's oldest fleshed-out vampire myth, much older than the Vlad the Impaler myths linked to Dracula. Were there any limits to this man's fabrication? Not to mention that he and his uncle would have to be rather decrepit by now.

"I'm not proud of it. I don't eat people or suck their blood."

Slaughter appeared from nowhere. "It's true. He's got a terrible family, but he's alright in himself. Nice, even. Does all kinds of healing stuff."

Lucas nodded and folded his arms, looking much too self-satisfied.

"Folklore states that dracs are either wicked or mischievous," I said. "And you're definitely—"

"Mischievous." His eyes glinted. "I just can't help myself." That hadn't been the option I was going for.

"Rest of them are wicked, though," Slaughter added. Lucas shoved him away with his foot.

"Let me get this right." He obviously knew about local folklore and was drawing from it. "Dracs are shifters—you can change form from that hideous thing to a man—but if I remember rightly, dracs can also shift into gold cups or donkeys." I couldn't hold back the laugh. "Very impressive."

He glared at me. "Actually, I can shift into pretty much anything. Only it's hard, very hard, so I don't." I had him on the defensive. "The donkey thing was just a phase dracs went through for a while. It was easy to capture children if we offered them a ride. Quite a cunning idea, actually."

"Sick, more like." My turn to be defensive. But really, kids?

He saw the look in my eyes. "What? I told you, I don't eat people. Anyway, most of the time I'm in this, my secondary form. I can only easily shift into my true self, and that's just for feeding."

"And that makes things so much better?"

He added another book to the case.

I attempted to see the world from his twisted point of view. "You're a fae drac who ate Delphine, the Men of Bédeilhac and the came-cruse are fae, and I'm not hallucinating. Oh, and Grampi has mouldy green fingers and toes."

His brow knitted. "Really?"

"Yep."

"Sounds like a fae curse. If it's just at his fingers and toes, it should be years before it's serious. Plenty of time to treat it."

His skills at make-believe were outstanding. And despite everything he'd said, I still had no idea how to deal with what he'd given me.

"You lot!" Lucas shouted at a group of Men running toward the stairs with my frying pan. "Where do you think you're going?"

"It's burnt, gov," one of them said. "We don't like washing up... We're going to dump it."

"Get to the sink and polish it until it shines."

"So, why me?" I asked. "Why drug me and pull me into your warped world?"

"Now we're getting to the good part. We—that means you and me—have been asked to take on the role of Keepers of the borderlands between the fae and human realms."

I grinned. "Well, how lovely. A partnership with the man who drugged me and ate my goat."

"I thought, if we're going to be partners, you should see

the real me." His brow bumped, augmenting the glint in his eye. "Anyway. It wasn't your goat."

"How the hell do you know?" I seethed the words. It definitely had been. Each goat had individual markings. I'd know Delphine's anywhere.

He turned to the bookcase and carefully aligned the spines. If it wasn't for the goat-eating, drink-spiking psycho delusional drac thing, I might have been impressed.

"The partnership"—he glanced back at me—"is always between one human and one fae who work together to keep the realms bound and fae hidden. I have been asked as the fae, and you have been offered the task as the human."

This was getting even more ridiculous. I couldn't help calling him out. "Knowing all this in advance, you got me into bed when I was plastered. What a nice move."

He winced. "That wasn't the most sensible thing I've ever done. I didn't plan it that way—I was completely trashed. To tell you the truth, I can't remember it."

I glared at him. Apart from a few vague impressions, I couldn't remember either. I guessed we were even on that count. "And me not being able to call the police on you?" I shoved the blade a little closer.

He ignored it. "The binding potion will wear off in a few days."

"Oh, joy. What about the other one—the hallucinogen?"

"Camille, I told you, you haven't had a hallucinogen. And the effects are not going to wear off. You'll be seeing tiny prehistoric men for the rest of your life."

The Men of Bédeilhac were putting the last cushions

into place. One of them extracted a lump of wax from his ear. I shook my head. "No way. Absolutely, no way."

The clothes were back in the drawers, the kitchen was spotless, everything had been placed exactly as before—even the feathers were gone. It was impressive. Half an hour ago, I thought I'd have to move out. A small pile of broken items lay in the centre of the room. A book, a few cushions, a saucepan and some other bits and pieces.

"You lot need to sort replacements for all that," Lucas said to a bunch of Men. They shrank back and trembled.

"We will, gov. Mark my word," Slaughter replied on their behalf.

"So." Lucas met my gaze. "The place is done—all tidy and back to normal. Well, most of it. What do you think?"

"What do I think? Hmmm, let me see." I tapped my finger on my lips. "What I think is that you are utterly crazy. A completely deluded madman who spikes women's drinks with extremely dangerous substances. I think I want you and your band of Men—who don't even exist—to get the hell out of my loft and never, ever return." I waved the sword at him in the least professional but most threatening way possible.

He pressed his lips together in a restrained smile. "Alright. But you know where to find me." Then he turned and walked away, the Men of Bédeilhac following with countless pattering feet.

"Thought that went pretty well, boss," came Slaughter's voice as they descended the stairs.

"Much better than expected," Lucas replied.

CHAPTER 9

PULLING ONTO THE N20, I FOCUSSED ON THE ROAD ahead and nothing else. I'd seen Aherbelste again in the farmyard, and I wanted to avoid anything that might trigger another trip. But when I slowed into the Pyrenee's car park, that idea shot out of the window.

The café stood on the edge of town. It benefited from its position on the route nationale, set a little way from the town centre and most of the houses, its chalet-style quaintness with shutters at the windows lending an inviting air. To the rear stood meadows dotted with fruit trees, and beyond, the slopes of Coustarous swept upward. At least, that's what the area normally looked like. But not today.

I climbed out, reluctantly abandoning my blade in the footwell. I'd slept with it last night, wanting it by my side constantly after yesterday, but taking it into the café wouldn't go down well with Alice or her mother. Clutching my bag, I slammed the door and turned to my latest hallucination.

Instead of meadows, the footpath that ran alongside the car park opened out into a cobbled lane. Either side stood timber-framed shops painted in bright colours, the storeys of each broadening as they rose, until they culminated in steeply sloping roofs. A whole medieval town sprawled under Coustarous.

Unable to resist my own delusion, I took the back gate out of the café's property and stepped into the lane. Trees grew everywhere. Vines, roses and geraniums climbed the shopfronts, the plant life a part of the buildings, the scent of blossoms heady. To my side rose an ironmonger's and a florist's, across the street stood an apothecary and a tavern. More shops lay beyond, but I couldn't make them out.

Ahead, a group of creatures approached. An ogre leered then ducked inside the florist's. The others appeared human, although there was definitely something different about them. A sarramauca—a black cat-like creature, its fur radiating in all directions like a huge pompom—crossed the lane, then a cluster of goblins fell out the tavern door and brawled on the floor.

Dumbstruck, I returned to the café and headed through to the main kitchen. Alice was there, dressed in her trademark Alice skirt, spiked cuffs on her wrists.

She hugged me. "What's wrong, hon. You look terrible." Warmth radiated from the huge commercial oven, the heat and the surroundings comforting. Alice's mother, Inès, had arranged the professional kitchen to look just like home, with old-style units and pans hung from the walls.

Inès came over, her curly grey hair restrained by a spotted headscarf, her hands covered in dough. She kissed my cheeks, being careful not to get dough on me, then examined my face. "You do look pale, Camille. Are you alright?"

I'd tell them everything—that's what I'd do. They'd think I was crazy and take me to hospital. Somehow, I'd make sure they didn't call Lucas, and then I'd get that blood test. "I... I'm... I..." They peered at me in concern. "I..." Nope. The words wouldn't come. I sagged.

Alice shot Inès a "give us space" glance.

Inès nodded with an encouraging smile. "If you need anything, I'll be over here." She returned to her baking at the other end of the kitchen.

Alice drew out a stool, worry wrinkling her brow. It wasn't like me not to be able to speak. "Come on, sit down," she said. "I'll make you a drink."

By the time she'd brewed me a noisette, I'd pulled myself together. Fairy town or no, I wasn't going to let the doctor's psycho actions ruin my life. First up, I needed Alice not to worry. "Sorry," I said, my voice composed. "Yesterday was really stressful."

She squeezed my hand. "Grampi?"

I shook my head. But then, his fingers and toes had been green. "Partly." I tipped back my noisette.

"Is he worse?"

"A little bit. But, Alice, I'm fine. The coffee is doing me good."

She examined me for a moment, her astute eyes rimmed

in their usual black, then said, "I'll tell you something to take your mind off Grampi." Thankfully, she'd cottoned on that a change of subject was needed. "I saw that guy I like, Raphaël, on Saturday night. The one with the curly hair."

"Oh yeah?" I forced my voice steady. "He's cute."

She nudged my shoulder and shot me an unladylike wink. "We're going on a proper date next week."

"Customers!" Guy yelled from behind the counter, antsy after his early baking session. "Am I supposed to handle everything alone?"

———

Resolutely ignoring the roofs of the fae town that were visible through the kitchen window, I folded the slice of brioche loaf over a stick of Inès's homemade dark chocolate, then placed a strawberry on top and pinned it all with a wooden stick. Some more strawberries, a swirl of crème fraîche and a few mint leaves added to the side finished it off. Inès's brioche goûter was one of Pyrenee's most popular dishes, and customers came from far and wide for it, often stopping en route to Spain or when driving to ski resorts in the winter. In particular, it drew the after-school crowd.

The kitchen was still, the staff elsewhere. I relaxed my shoulders and released a sigh as I finished making up the last of the plates. About this time in the afternoon, weariness from being on my feet settled in. But I only had a couple of hours, then maybe I could do something to get out of my drug-addled mess. I'd tried to call the hospital several times with no success.

A shape caught my eye in the back yard. Roux was settling down. I'd take him out a coffee in a bit.

That was four plates made up. I fitted three and cutlery onto the tray and made my way out. Regulars and a few new faces chatted over coffee and patisserie, sitting at tables or huddling in armchairs. I headed to the D&D gang in their nook. They gathered up their multifaceted dice as I handed the plates around and managed to slide the contents of one onto the table. I nudged it back onto the plate with the side of my hand.

"There you go, guys. The other is just coming." I smiled at them, but they were either staring down at their drinks or shooting each other subversive glances. It was so unlike them. Alice had given the guys permission to game at the café for as long as they liked each day as they'd had various problems using their homes. Ever grateful, they usually beamed at the staff. But not today. I followed a flick of Gabe's eyes to a group of teen girls stationed in the armchairs by the fireplace.

The girls were giggling. The one with straight ebony hair and immaculate make-up said, "What an absolute dork. I wonder how long he takes in the morning sticking his ears on?" They burst into giggles—the kind of giggles that sounded far from funny. Girls could be so mean.

Shame filled Gabe's face, a red blush extending from his neck.

I strode over to the girls, sporting my best no-nonsense expression. "Do you have a problem with some of our customers?" I asked the mouthy one... Nora, if I remembered rightly. She shrank back, her own blush blooming. "If you girls can't be civil, then get the hell out."

I went to the nook for my tray. "High Warrior of the Borders—" Gabe began, not so loud that the girls would hear.

"Gabe," I replied. "Save it. Just today. You wouldn't believe what a weekend I've had."

"Umm... well... thanks, then," he said.

"No trouble." I went back for the other plate.

"Good call with the girls," Alice said from the espresso machine, a pen tucked behind her ear from her stint in the office taming the accounts.

"Tell me we were never that bad," I said as I passed.

She grinned. "Only sometimes."

"No," Guy added, his blond hair flopping over his eyes, "you girls were terrible—and at it all the time. I barely escaped school with my masculinity..."

I bumped his shoulder.

As I headed to the kitchen, I glanced into the office, where Inès was sleeping in an armchair. She worked too hard —she was a perfectionist, that was the trouble. Although she'd managed to hand over much of the bread to Guy and the patisserie to José—only after years of training them both meticulously—she couldn't find anyone to help out with the brioche and the viennoiserie—the yeast-baked pastries that were her speciality. It wasn't that we were short of staff, at least not normally, it was just that no one ever met her standards in that department. But with her chronic fatigue, she barely managed.

I entered the kitchen and stopped short. Standing on the counter with its back to me was a small goblin about a foot high, the last brioche roll in its hand.

I dove for it. It dropped the brioche and spun around, its bulbous eyes wide in its wrinkled face. I grabbed it with both hands. It squirmed and squealed, desperate to get away.

"You critter," I growled, fully aware I was talking to a hallucination, although it appeared so completely real. All of it did—the fae town, Aherbelste and yesterday's little men. It wasn't like my vision was distorted or I felt high. And there certainly hadn't been a comedown.

The hallucination cowered in my hands. "So... So... Sorry... so sorry..." it jabbered.

I studied its wrinkled bluish-grey skin, the wisp of hair on its head, its short, ragged trousers. It was an osencame, a mischievous goblin that hid household objects. "This isn't the first time, is it?" Cakes went missing occasionally. Although Fifi was not allowed in the kitchen, ever, disappearances were generally blamed on her. But now—

"Oh! What have you got there?" Alice cried as she entered. "A lovely little dragonfly!"

The osencame struggled with all its might. "So," I said slowly, "tell me exactly what you're seeing, when you say 'dragonfly'."

She sent me a mock scowl. "Wings. Long thin body. Blue. Pretty. Is that good enough for you?"

The osencame nodded. "A lovely little dragonfly. Yep, that's what Mushum is. Just blue and pretty."

"Oh, it's buzzing," Alice said. "I think it wants to go out. I've heard they bite, though. Be careful."

One hundred percent proof I was utterly deluded. "I'll put this nice little dragonfly that doesn't look anything like a goblin out the window, then."

"You're nuts." Alice laughed, grabbed a stack of brioche à tête and left the room.

A pretty accurate diagnosis.

"Mushum only wants a little patisserie," the osencame managed between wiggles.

"You're gonna have to pay, like everyone else," I said as I carried it to the door.

"Yes, Mushum will pay. Pay in information, Mushum can. Only Mushum must have patisserie. Whatever you want to know, Mushum can tell you in exchange for macarons, choux à la crème, or chouquettes... especially chouquettes." Its brow rose in hope, drawing its bulging eyes together.

"Oh, yeah?" I threw it out back and slammed the door.

I repaired the brioche roll and took it out to the nook, hoping goblin hands weren't too unhygienic. "Thanks." Gabe grinned.

A few people had left and tables stood empty, scattered with used crockery. I grabbed a tray from the counter and began stacking, tension rippling through me, my palms sweaty. The hallucinations were showing no sign of stopping.

René Thierry pushed through the entrance and strode up to the counter, his canvassing leaflet bag strung over his shoulder, his badly dyed mousy hair neatly combed back, an officious look on his face. As Tarascon's mayor, he'd decided it was his job to strut around with his chest extended, his belly secured by a much too tight belt. Did it hurt his back, walking like that? No one else behind the counter, I went over with the laden tray of dirties.

"How can I help you, René?" I asked as I slid the tray onto the worktop.

He stared down his nose. Despite the fact our families had known each other for the last few hundred years, if not more, I was an inconsequential waitress not worth the time of day. "I'd like to speak to Inès. It's a matter of importance."

"She's sleeping, and I don't want to disturb her."

"Well, I've got an important issue to discuss," he blustered. "It can't wait." His longstanding feud with Inès was common knowledge, and he was never satisfied unless he'd managed to rile her before leaving.

The problem was, Inès was a better baker than he would ever be, and he hated that. His boulangerie over by the town hall was alright, his baguettes perfectly acceptable, but they just didn't have the wow factor, and everyone knew it. His trade existed of people who didn't have time to walk over here, and unsuspecting tourists who hadn't yet learnt of Pyrenee's delights.

"If you have anything important to say, best say it to the manager." I glared at him before shouting, "Alice!"

"What's up?" She hurried in and stopped short on seeing the mayor. "That's what's up," she muttered, then put on her best smile. "René. How lovely. Can I help you?"

He let out a frustrated breath, no doubt hating having to speak to someone with spiked cuffs. He pulled his shirt down, shot a glance at the D&D nook, making Gabe cower, then turned back to Alice. "As mayor, I've been informed that the gas pipework in this building needs updating urgently."

"What concern is that of yours?" Alice scowled at him. "It's all under control."

"The completion paperwork hasn't yet been lodged with the town hall, despite the fact the situation is clearly a danger to everyone." He was a little too loud, and the closest customers exchanged anxious glances. "A gas explosion could cause loss of life."

The nearest couple headed out in a hurry.

"There's no reason to worry," Alice said. "The engineers are booked in, and we're well within our allotted time. Plus, there's actually no problem with the pipework. It's just a formality."

"Even so," he replied, "a reputable business would have sorted the whole thing out months ago. It's a disgrace."

Every muscle in Alice's body locked tight. I rearranged the patisserie in the glass counter, there for backup, just in case.

"The fact that you are mayor, René," she said through gritted teeth, "does not give you the right to take confidential information into your own hands and use it against someone you have a petty rivalry with." Well said that girl.

Somehow, he managed to puff his chest out further. "I'll have you know, it's my duty as mayor to do whatever I can to keep the people of this town safe from unscrupulous traders. Make sure you get the work done. And quickly."

He turned to the D&D nook. "Don't be late home," he barked at Gabe, then strode out the door.

The demon girls tittered quietly. Gabe gawked at the table—the poor guy. Though I had to hand it to him, there were many ways to rebel against parents—drink and drugs and staying out late were perfectly productive, but with a father like René, dressing up as an elf each day was so much more effective. Gabe may have been hiding trembling fingers, but underneath it all, he was made of stronger stuff.

"What a wanker." Alice plated up an order.

"My thoughts exactly," I said, doing her cappuccinos.

As René left, Max stomped in, and my heart sank. Was he going to start blabbing? I hadn't told Alice I'd slept with Lucas. I wasn't even sure I could.

Max lumbered across the room and bent down to talk to a guy seated at a table. I stifled a gasp. It was Max, yes, but different. He was hulking and heavy-set—a lot more than normal. I couldn't tell if it was muscle or fat or both, but he was massive... and he had huge pointed ears pinned flat on the sides of his now completely bald head.

"Troll," I said flatly. It made sense. After all, I'd always had a feeling he was one. I shook myself. It was a hallucination—the third one today counting the fae town that continued to lurk outside. I closed my eyes. I had to do something about this.

"The most trollish troll that ever lived," Alice replied as she drew boiling water for a tea.

"Wait. You can see him?"

She tilted her chin. "Of course I can."

"I mean... the difference... the ears."

"Yes, I can see his ears. Camille, you're worrying me."

I took her hand in mine, her warmth an extension of what a damn sweet person she was. "Just tell me, what shape are his ears?"

"Hon, come on. Something is up. You've been acting strangely all day. You know you can talk to me."

"Seriously, Alice. Tell me the shape of his ears."

She shrugged. "Round, short, small lobes. I don't know how to describe ears. They're just ears."

"No points?" They clearly had points. Not dubious, undefined points, but sharp pointy points. Pointier than Gabe's silicone.

She shook her head. "Nope, no points."

Max came over. "A chausson aux pommes, little ladies. I've got a call, so don't leave a man waiting."

Alice rolled her eyes and delivered her order to its table. I barely took my gaze off Max as I packaged his viennoiserie and tapped the order into the till.

"Feeling better after your little jaunt yesterday?" He chortled. "Young ladies shouldn't go out—"

"You're a troll." The words fell from my mouth before I could help myself.

His eyes grew wide, then the usual unintelligent leer settled back in. "And what are you going to do about it?" he whispered as he scanned his card.

I flinched. He'd admitted it.

"And don't you go telling anyone, now. People get silly ideas about trolls. We've got a reputation, see. Being bigots and stupid, that sort of thing. And it's not nice. It's prejudice. I'm living a quiet life, and I don't want any trouble." He took his package and strode out.

I gaped at his back, vaguely wondering who he expected me to tell. Then I ran after him.

He'd left his cab in the car park and was heading up the footpath into the fae town. The place was busier than this morning. Slender elves and stout dwarves as well as goblins of all sizes roamed around. I caught up with Max by the florist and tugged his shirt.

He turned and scowled. "I'm a busy man, Camille. What do you want?"

I needed to know more, but I could only blurt, "You're not a man. You're a troll."

He shook his head. "Don't go on about it, now. I asked you not to. A good girl like you should respect a man's needs."

I bit back a remark and focussed, struggling for words. "But you really are a troll, aren't you? I mean, this florist, this town... you. I'm not seeing things?"

He smirked. "You've had verity, and it doesn't take much to guess who gave it to you. Although, why on earth the doctor would—"

"You know about verity?" I shot back.

He looked at me as though I was an alien, and maybe, in this place, I was. "Everyone knows about verity. Every fae, at least." He laughed and lumbered into the shop.

I stared at the door as it swung shut behind him. Max was many things, but I doubted he'd lie—he had his own set of principles, even if they were warped. Of course, I could've hallucinated the whole conversation. But if I had, I'd be standing in a field, talking to a tree, and someone would've called me out on it.

Turning around, I absorbed the bizarre life that thronged the street. Even though the idea was utterly bonkers, perhaps I had to admit the possibility that all of this might just be real.

CHAPTER 10

"FAIRIES ARE REAL. FAIRIES ARE FREAKING REAL," I muttered over and over as I wrenched the gears on the truck and settled into a slow trundle up Picou de Bompas. Like this morning, I had the niggling impression there were all kinds of things hidden in the bushes. And even though that asshole of a doctor might not have been lying about fae, it didn't mean I wasn't struggling massively with the whole thing. It was better if I didn't look.

I parked up on the edge of the farmyard and headed to the house. Grampi had been a little woozy earlier, and I wanted to keep my eye on him. The goats were nowhere to be seen, probably still foraging.

"Grampi," I called as I entered the kitchen. No reply. He could've been out walking, although he was sensible about staying in if he felt wobbly.

The door to the rest of the house was open and I made my way in. Glancing through to the bedroom, I could see the edge of a shoe on its side. I ran in, my heart thrashing. Grampi lay splayed out on his front.

He lifted his head. "Got to check the herd for lice. It's time I treated them again."

I let out a breath, relieved he was conscious and talking. He'd fallen and was stuck, but it hadn't happened before, and my chest panged to see him like this. He'd always been so strong. "Did you hurt yourself?" Even though I wouldn't get a sensible response, he could hear me.

His eyes glimmered and creased at the corners—a positive sign—and he appeared to be alright apart from his arms. The mouldy green that had coloured his fingertips now extended almost to his elbows, with tendrils reaching under his rolled-up shirtsleeves. It looked nasty.

"Okay. We're going to get you up." I dragged a chair across. "Can you get onto your hands and knees?"

He tucked his hands under him and pushed up, then managed to gather his knees forward. "That's not such a large wattle," he said, then used the chair to draw himself upward. I supported his arm as he stood up straight then wobbled precariously.

"Whoaa there." I took his weight as he stumbled to his old double bed and lay down. He released a slow breath then a volley of damp hawking.

I felt his head. Hot. Too hot. "I'll get you some water."

In the kitchen, I dialled Lucas, irritated I didn't have another option. I still couldn't phone the hospital, and anyway, I wanted answers.

"Camille." He picked up immediately. "What a wonderful surprise."

"Cut the crap. That green stuff on my grandfather is now halfway up his arms, and he's not well."

"I'll be there in five." He hung up. Damn it—I wasn't happy about having him here. Giving him the benefit of the doubt about fae, he'd still trashed my loft, spiked my drink and eaten Delphine.

I helped Grampi with his water and tucked him in, then I retrieved his sword from its mounting on the kitchen wall and strode outside. After a few minutes, Lucas pulled up in a swanky black Mercedes SUV.

He jumped out, bag in hand, looking way too dishy, his hair falling over his forehead. "Where is he?"

I was caught off guard by the concern in his face. But after yesterday, I wasn't taking any chances. I thrust the blade at his chest. "Firstly, three things."

He raised his eyebrows.

"One, no eating the goats." He glanced at Rose, who was leading the herd into the yard. She paused, sensing a predator.

"I don't eat goats all the time," he said with mock offence. I stepped closer with the blade. "*Alright.* No goats."

"Two, no spiking anything, and no medication without agreement."

He nodded.

"And lastly, no fairy raids. Agreed?"

"Agreed. I honestly didn't think the Men would do quite

so much damage." Such a sincere voice. If it wasn't for the smirk, I might have believed him.

"That way." I pointed with the blade to the farmhouse door, then followed him in, giving directions to the bedroom.

Lucas strode to Grampi's bed. "Monsieur Amiel, I'm Lucas, the new doctor. I'm going to check you over."

Grampi's eye sparkled. "Marigold is getting plump. I'm not sure how to stop her eating."

I rubbed my head. If only I had a way to prevent Grampi informing Lucas about his next tasty snack.

"That's the goat thing?" Lucas whispered over his shoulder.

"Yes. And don't go getting ideas."

His lips formed a devil of a grin, then he turned back to Grampi. He worked efficiently, checking Grampi's temperature, pulse and blood pressure, listening to his heart and chest, and examining him visually. And to give the monster credit, he did all of it with patience and care. Finished, he zipped up his bag, and we headed to the kitchen.

"So, how is he?" I asked.

He sucked in a breath. "It's definitely a standard fae curse, and the goat-speech may be part of it. There's no indication of the cause, and I don't understand why he's so much worse than yesterday." Butterflies spiralled in my middle. It wasn't exactly the "he's absolutely fine" I wanted, not to mention I was struggling with the fae causation.

He met my eyes, his face unnaturally devoid of conceit —a far cry from yesterday. "Camille, I'll give you some medicine to slow the symptoms, and I may be able to brew something more specific for the curse rot. But we need to find out who did this to him and how, otherwise he won't have long."

"Not long?" What was he saying?

He looked away before meeting my gaze again. "Maybe a few weeks. A couple of months at best."

I swallowed. "No, I don't believe you... I mean, how can I after everything you've done?"

"You've seen the rot. And if you get a second opinion, a normal doctor will only pick up on a red rash and a temperature, and you'll lose him anyway."

A ball of panic rose in my throat. "So what do I do...? What can I do? There has to be something." No way was I going to lose Grampi. I could hear his words from long ago. "Camille," he'd say when I lost one of our spars, as usual. "I'm proud of you, chérie. You keep trying, and that's what makes the best of people." His voice had been steady—his words always meant something, and he never spoke out of turn. Because of it, people listened—I listened. He'd been a rock, unlike Papa, absorbed with projects and proposals, and Maman busy with everyone but me. I didn't know then that I'd miss his meaningful words—miss the sound of my name on his lips.

Lucas drew a bottle from his bag and placed it on the side. "This should help. Five mils twice a day."

How could I trust him? But the rot...

"There is something else you can do," he added.

"Oh?" Anything for Grampi.

"Work with me as a Keeper of the Bounds. You'll be in

the perfect position to find the culprit and a cure, and I'll do whatever I can to help."

"I can't shift the idea that you could be making all of this up, although"—my voice tightened—"I've been to the fae part of town... and seen Max."

Lucas smiled softly. "I'm sure that was a lovely surprise —" His phone rang and he glanced at it. "I have to take this."

I returned to the bedroom with the medicine and sat on the bed, studying the blank bottle. It certainly didn't look like standard medication. There hadn't been any complaints in town about Lucas as a doctor, but how could I give Grampi something provided by the person who'd drugged me?

Grampi peered at the bottle.

"Just wondering if it's alright," I said lamely. He scratched his nose, bringing the curse rot into clear view. It looked terrible. How could I risk not giving him the medicine? I poured a dose out into a plastic dispensing cup and sniffed it. The aroma was sweet and herby.

A keen gleam twinkled in Grampi's eye. I wanted to tell him what was going on and why I didn't trust his doctor, but how could I? I inclined my head to the cup. "I... I don't know what to do," I stammered.

Grampi shrugged, snatched the cup from my fingers and downed it in one.

I gawked at him. He'd taken the decision out of my hands, literally. And even though he didn't know half of what was going on, it was his decision to make. I hoped with every fibre of my being it was the right choice.

"Wattles and horns," Grampi mumbled contentedly, his eyes already closed.

I rose, straightened the blankets and kissed him. "Sleep well," I whispered, but he was already gone.

I entered the kitchen as Lucas ended his call. "It was about Henri." He pocketed his phone. "You know, Max's friend?"

"I sure do." Much too well after the other day.

"He's seriously ill, and it's fae related, which means it involves both of us as Keepers of the Bounds. Besides, it may have something to do with the curse." He fixed me with a solemn gaze. "Camille, I have to go—every second counts. But come with me. I'll tell you the details on the way, and perhaps we can sort this mess out."

I studied him, my fingers twisting my necklace. He'd spiked my drink, he was a creature from hell, and this was all so ridiculous—so utterly beyond belief. But I'd never live with myself if I didn't at least try to help Grampi.

Chapter 11

Lucas turned the SUV, scattering goats. As we sped off, I rang a friend of Grampi's, who agreed to do the milking and keep an eye on him. That sorted, I adjusted the blade by my knee so it wouldn't scuff the leather upholstery, then wondered why I'd bothered. Lucas deserved far more than his seats being scuffed.

"I'd like to see you swing that in here," he said.

"It's staying by my side. I'm not taking any risks." Actually, I was in a car with a psycho drac. It was a huge risk, but it was one I was willing to take if I could help Grampi. The thought of him... Nope, I wasn't going there. I'd do something about it.

"Henri's wife has called an ambulance," he said, his eyes on the narrow lane that we pelted down much too fast. "But I think we'll make it there first."

"What happened?"

"You know old Madame Bonnet, the one whose death got linked to Max's story?"

"Yeah, sort of. I mean, I never heard the full story in the end."

"I don't know what she died of, but from the symptoms, it was fae related. Henri has the same signs, and they sound pretty far advanced."

"I hope he's alright. He's the sweetest guy."

"Yep." He glanced at me briefly. "And Camille, I know you're struggling to trust me, but I truly don't go around drugging innocent people. Dark fae and criminals might be another matter..." His voice faded as though he was thinking better of explaining. I wasn't sure I wanted to know. "Anyway, I was charged with administering the verity so you could take on the task of Keeper. I have to say, I felt like shit doing it. I just didn't think you'd be up for it any other way."

I ran through the conversation we would've had if he'd offered it to me. Nope. I truly wouldn't have gone there. Mind you, I was so drunk that night, I would've taken anything. Good space to be in, Camille.

He glanced at me again.

"What?" I said. "And please concentrate on driving." We were going much too fast, but he seemed comfortable with the speed—and comfortable heading to a critically ill patient. I guessed he did it all the time, but my stomach churned.

"You certainly are," he said.

"Are what?"

"Concentrating." He'd noticed. "Why are you staring at nothing but the dash? You look catatonic."

"There are... things I'm not sure I'm ready to see." I really didn't want to know what lurked in the bushes.

He laughed. "They won't bite—actually, they might. But they're not especially great at climbing into moving vehicles. You don't have to worry."

I ventured a glance to the right. A massive spectral dog stood by the side of the road, its fur the colour of night, saliva dripping from its jaws. "Hmmm, sinagries are real too. Completely not worrying at all." What appeared to be a peirotu, a type of hobgoblin, disappeared into the undergrowth ahead. I shivered. "Are there this many fae everywhere?"

He shook his head. "Nope. There are more here on the borders, the area where the two realms influence each other. Out in the human realm, there are some, but not many. Actually, we could do with a bit more integration. It strengthens the link between realms, but most fae aren't keen, and most humans can't accept that fae exist." We entered town and sped through, crossing the river and passing Lucas's consulting room. Lucas pounded the horn here and there as we dodged traffic, then we took the Gourbit lane and hurtled along.

I couldn't deny, the folklore part of me was intensely curious about getting up close and personal with so much myth. I glanced sideways at Lucas—too up close and personal. I could barely comprehend that I was sitting in an SUV with a drac. Should I record his life experiences or run for my life?

He seemed primal... feral yet completely restrained, and

there was that shrewdness. What did he know that I didn't? Well, right at this moment, pretty much everything. "So, who the hell thought it was a good idea that I do this job you're proposing... this Keeper thingy?"

"It's arranged by mutual agreement of fae. The place doesn't have the same officious structure as the human realm, but there is an assembly, a meeting of minds, and they offered us the roles as partners."

I snorted. "Partners? With you? Let me see, so apart from drugging me, you're still a hideous, vicious drac who ate Delphine." A drac I slept with. Bile rose in my throat as I saw his grotesque form in the cave. Way to choose men, Camille.

He grinned. "Hundred percent drac—but not the Delphine bit. It wasn't one of yours."

"I'd recognise Delphine anywhere," I snapped. "Just to be clear, no more eating goats from our herd."

"I told you, I didn't—"

A large boar rushed out in front of us. "Oh, it's Baeserte, the boar god!" I followed his trajectory as he scampered into the bushes on the other side of the road. Unbelievable—right before my eyes, the Pyrenean god of not only boar but wine and hunting.

"Nope." Lucas's lip twitched. "Just a normal, everyday boar."

I glared at him as he tried not to laugh. "It's not funny. How should I know what I'm looking at?"

He chortled to himself.

"Anyway," I said, "why did this assembly choose me?" I

drew myself up. Camille, the chosen one. It was a pretty self-aggrandising idea, I had to admit.

"You weren't exactly chosen."

"What do you mean?"

"Well, I guess you were, in a way. Just like any employer chooses their staff. You ticked the required boxes and were... adequate." His lips twitched again. When did this guy stop sniggering at his own jokes? But it was an improvement on the arrogance.

"What kind of boxes?"

"The most important is knowledge of folklore—it's a biggie. There aren't many people who have that anymore. Plus, you know the area well, and you're pretty fit." I winced at the opportunity I'd given him to find that out. But what with the swordplay and 10K a couple of times a week when I wanted to unwind, I supposed it was true.

"And swordsmanship is essential," he added. "A weapon is handy in Fae, and again, hardly anyone wields a blade in the human realm these days." He steered the car around a hairpin bend. "The council didn't have many options. To tell you the truth, there wasn't anyone else."

Not so special then. Kind of fitted the pattern of my life. But I liked the idea that folklore had gotten me the job. So far, it had given me reams of fascination and enjoyment, but in terms of money and career—nada.

"Actually, I think you'll be well suited to the job," Lucas said.

"Considering I have no idea what it entails, I don't know what to think about that statement. All I want to do is help

Grampi. I can't see me becoming your partner and doing some kind of fae enforcement."

"Just give it a chance."

"I'm here, aren't I?"

We grew quiet as we rushed through Gourbit. Please let Henri be alright. Please let Grampi be alright, for that matter, too. Lucas turned into the farmyard and we screeched to a halt by the door. We jumped out and headed into the house without knocking, Lucas clutching his bag.

"In here," came a shrill call. I followed Lucas as he strode through to a bedroom.

Madame Dumas was at the door. "Please help him. I don't know what to do." Henri convulsed on the bed.

"Not to worry, Madame Dumas." Lucas assessed Henri's quaking form. "Step back with Camille and I'll see what I can do. The ambulance will be here in a few moments."

Madame Dumas folded in on herself, her body shaking, tears streaming. I wrapped my arms around her and she leant into me, sobbing. Over her smooth grey head, I watched Lucas haul Henri into the recovery position and check his airway. He filled a syringe and drove its contents into Henri's arm.

All the time, dear old Henri shook, his eyes rolled back. The sight was so all-consuming that I didn't notice Henri's skin at first. He wore pyjamas, but where Lucas had pushed up the sleeve, his arm was covered with deep purple lesions seeping with blood and pus. Despite what Lucas had said in the car, it was a shock to see Henri so sick.

"Come on, Henri. Come on," Lucas muttered. He swabbed one of the lesions.

I was too aware of the room—the soapy lavender scent of Madame Dumas's hair, the odour of incontinence and something rancid coming from Henri. I looked away to the corner, not wanting to see him suffering.

"No, no, no, no." The vehemence in Lucas's voice drew me back. Henri convulsed in a different way, his chest arching, his neck bent unnaturally. Then he was still—too still.

Madame Dumas yelped and hid her face, and the room sank away. Not Henri, not dear sweet Henri.

"Damn it!" Lucas cried. He lifted Henri to the ground and thrust into his chest. "You can do it. You can do it," he murmured as he pumped. He gripped Henri's nose and chin and sent breaths into his throat before returning to his chest, driving his palms down again and again.

CHAPTER 12

ON LUCAS WENT, THRUSTING AT HENRI'S CHEST. THE
room spun and Madame Dumas shook harder. After endless
minutes, footsteps sounded in the corridor and the ambulance crew burst in.

"How long?" one of them asked.

"Fuck knows." Lucas continued on.

One of the crew dove in, ripped open Henri's shirt and
placed pads on his chest. Lucas stepped back and glanced at
his watch. "Ten minutes."

"Analysing rhythm. Stand clear," the machine ordered.
Then, "No shock advised. Resume CPR."

Another of the crew took over from Lucas, pounding at
Henri's heart.

Lucas sank back, cussing quietly, then louder and louder
until he spun around and slammed his fists into the wall, the
plaster cracking. Madame Dumas flinched against me.

He took a breath and stepped over. "Madame Dumas."

She looked up, her face stricken, her cheeks damp.

"Henri's gone," he said. "Right now we're just pumping blood around. We need your permission to let him rest."

I stared at Henri's body over Madame Dumas's head, the corpse swimming before me. There was no breath, no life in him, his body growing cold. My throat constricted and nausea rose up. With all my might, I pulled my eyes away. I had to hold it together for Madame Dumas.

"Leave him be," she managed, meeting Lucas's gaze, her lips trembling. The ambulance crew stilled their activity.

"I'm so sorry for your loss," Lucas said.

She broke away from me, grasped Lucas's hands in hers and squeezed, tears running down her face. "You did everything you could. Anyone could see that. Thank you for trying."

He nodded, pain dulling his eyes.

"I want him here," Madame Dumas said to the crew. "I want him to rest quietly for the night. To say goodbye." The crew lifted Henri back onto the bed and straightened the covers.

"Camille," Lucas said, "we have to leave very soon."

I frowned, grief welling up for Henri, for poor Madame Dumas. This wasn't the time for a hasty exit, but he knew that—he had to have a good reason. I couldn't leave Madame Dumas without support, though. I drew out my phone and, looking anywhere but at Henri, dialled the Dumas's neighbours, a young couple they got on with very well.

While we waited for them to arrive, Lucas questioned Madame Dumas about who she and Henri had interacted with lately and where they'd been, then he paced around the kitchen deep in thought, his eyes wild. All the time my mind was on Henri—and Grampi, that he might end up the same way.

Once the neighbours had taken over, I hugged Madame Dumas, and we drove off. "What the hell happened back there?" I asked as we sped along the lane.

His jaw tightened. "You saw the lesions?"

"Oh, yes."

"They're invisible to most humans, and they're usually a symptom of a body gone wrong by a fae cause rather than any specific disease. Madame Bonnet had them too, but she was so old, I presumed she'd picked up some minor fae malaise that wasn't linked to her death. But now, with Henri..." He slammed his palms on the wheel. "There's clearly something going on, and I should've looked into it."

I had no idea what to say. I couldn't imagine dealing with death like this on a daily basis. And despite whatever else Lucas was, he appeared to be a committed doctor. "If you'd known more, I'm guessing you would've done something," I ventured. "Don't blame yourself."

He shook his head.

"But Henri was fine when we saw him the other day," I added. "If the lesions weren't the source, then what caused his death?" Henri's corpse filled my head. I focussed on a shadowy fae... thing, slinking through the bushes—better that than reliving the last hour.

"I have no idea." Lucas's fingers whitened against the wheel. "I can tell you, though, it seems there's a pattern to the condition—an initial general feeling of tiredness and mild sickness, then a fever with vomiting. At that stage, the lesions develop. Then, at some point in the next forty-eight hours, the patient goes rapidly downhill and develops seizures, then cardiac arrest."

I stared at him. "Do you think it's contagious?"

"Right now, I'm not sure. It could be a bacteria, a virus, a potion or a poison. I'll run some tests. And I'm wondering if I can prepare something that would be a general boost to anyone who might come down with it. As I don't know the cause, it would be the best I could do."

"And Grampi? The lesions didn't look like that green stuff on his skin."

"It's completely different. Your grandfather has a fae curse. And even with its speedy progression over the last day, it's not as deadly."

I bit my lip. "But still deadly?"

He nodded.

But we had time to do something about it. "So what happens now?"

"Now, we go to Fae and find out what caused the deaths."

I dissected his words—*go to Fae*. "The fae town in Tarascon... it's not in Fae?" It had looked different, but I had the impression it was somehow part of the normal town.

"It's a glamoured part of Tarascon—the busiest fae town in the human realm around here. The borders of Fae are a little more remote."

With all the stories and lore I'd accumulated, I honestly

didn't know what to make of going into Fae properly, but there was one thing I wanted to clear up. "When you mentioned 'we'..."

"This is Keeper business. It concerns us both."

I rubbed my temples. "I didn't say I was taking the job." Right now, I couldn't even consider the possibility, and I wasn't going to be shoehorned into it.

"How are you going to know what it entails unless you give it a try?"

He had a point, and I wanted to see Fae. "If it means we investigate Grampi's curse."

"Definitely."

"Then it looks like I'm going to wonderland."

I phoned Grampi's friend and checked everything was okay. Grampi was sleeping peacefully, and the herd had been milked and were content. Even so, I couldn't help worrying.

A few minutes later, we drew up in front of Lucas's house and headed inside, my blade under my arm just in case. The sun had lowered behind the mountains and the temperature was dropping.

"Here again," Lucas said with a crooked grin as he unlocked the back door. I wasn't going to think about the other night.

"Make yourself at home," he added. "And help yourself to a drink or food. I have a couple of things to do in the lab, then we'll get going."

"You eat normal food?"

"I need fresh kill a few times a month, but in between I stock up on everything else."

"Oh," was all I could think to say.

He headed into his laboratory. I propped my blade against the table, found the bathroom and freshened up. Then, unable to eat after earlier, I made tea, carrying one into the lab for Lucas.

He sat on a stool before the table doing something with a petri dish. I gazed around at the alembic, microscope and antiquated flasks. Herbs in glass jars lined the walls—some names I recognised, some I didn't. A skull sat on a shelf with a host of strange brass instruments, and all about stood rows of ragged old tomes.

"I hate to think what you get up to in here." I placed his tea next to him.

He finished what he was doing and grasped the cup. "Potions, mainly. Right this moment, I've cultured the sample I took from Henri's lesions and I have the beginnings of a potion that might be useful if anyone else gets sick." He cradled his tea in both hands. "I took Henri's blood after he passed, and I've had a look at it. There's a configuration of corpuscles that is consistent with potion usage, although there may be other causes. I've asked for his post-mortem to be done as soon as possible, but if the cause is fae, it won't show anything. Oh, and I've sent a text to all my patients requesting they report symptoms similar to Henri and Madame Bonnet's."

And all the while, I'd made put the kettle on. Looks like I'd made myself useful.

"Also"—he indicated a flask at the other end of the bench —"I have something brewing that might help your grandfather on both medical and magical levels." He took a swig of tea.

"Magic? That hasn't been mentioned before."

"One thing at a time." He glanced at his watch. "We need to get into Fae. Give me a moment to change, and we'll get out of here." He rose and headed upstairs with his cup.

I settled at the kitchen table, gazing around his perfectly normal kitchen and sipping the best mint tea I'd ever had. The place was cosy with natural wood everywhere, and pretty tidy for someone who'd moved in a few weeks ago. It didn't exactly reflect his inner drac. A dungeon with torture equipment or a lair filled with demons might be more suited.

A moment later, he entered dressed in dark brown leather trousers and a shirt made of something similar split open halfway down his chest, revealing the ripped sculpture I vaguely remembered through my Bourbon haze. I drew my hand to my mouth to stop myself spitting tea. "Fancy dress party?" But hell, with the pouch on his belt and the sword on his back, he looked like a hot, lithe warrior.

He shrugged, jostling a bundle of leather in his hand. "When going to Rome..."

"So this is the latest fae fashion?"

"It's practical, that's all. I don't have anything for you, but we can get you kitted out in Fae."

"If you did have a wardrobe full of the female equivalent of what you're wearing, I would've been worried. Even more worried than I am, that is."

He threw the bundle at me a little too hard. "Take your

blade with you. Even though it's blunt, it'll be better than nothing."

"There's no chance of me leaving it behind." My folklore brain scanned through a variety of mythic beasts I hoped never to meet as I shook out the straps. It looked like a back scabbard, but I'd only ever used a side version.

"Like this…" He turned around to show me his.

I tucked my arm through one of the loops, obviously getting it wrong. Lucas pulled the scabbard out of my hands, turned it the right way and held it up.

"I could've managed." I shrugged into it.

He drew his arms around my chest to position the straps, his rosemary and cedar scent heady, his breath warm on my neck.

"There you go," he murmured.

I dropped my shoulders, involuntarily melting into him, but a flash of pointed teeth tearing through Delphine put an end to that. The man was a homicidal, maniacal killer. And he was an incubus—I had to keep my wits about me. I pulled out of his arms and turned to face him. "I can manage."

There was that tweak of his lips again. He couldn't help himself. I buckled up then flipped my blade and pushed it into the scabbard.

"Ready?" he asked.

No. Of course I wasn't ready to enter Fae. It was something I'd never thought possible, something beyond my wildest dreams. But I fixed him in the eye. "Let's go."

CHAPTER 13

DUSK DRAWING IN, WE HEADED UP THE FOOTHILL toward the cave where Lucas had eaten Delphine.

"So the entrance to Fae is here, above your house?" That was convenient.

"The whole Pyrenean mountain range consists of border-lands—the area where the fae and human realms affect each other. But the actual meeting of the realms—the entry points to Fae—can be found on most mountains and remote places around here. The borderlands appear pretty much the same no matter which side of the bounds you're on, so it's possible for someone to wander into Fae and not realise it. When that happens, they're ushered back out as quickly as possible."

We passed the cave and carried on up, Lucas's pace relentless. I could feel the incline in my legs, but all I could think of was Henri's lifeless corpse and the rot that wound its way over Grampi's skin. I hoped he was sleeping soundly—and that we'd find a cure.

As we rounded a crest about three-quarters of the way up, the air changed ever so slightly, luminescence coming from all around. I glanced at Lucas, and he nodded. We were in Fae.

It was strange. I could sense the difference on one level, as though I was somewhere else entirely, although at the same time the place felt... familiar. The foothills and the distant snowcapped mountains appeared exactly like the Pyrenees I loved, but at one moment the world seemed more clear, more real somehow, then the next everything was shimmering and ephemeral, as if it might disappear in the wink of an eye. I pulled out my mobile. A few photos of Fae might be nice. It was dead.

We strode on upward, Lucas taking the lead on the narrow path. I ogled the sword strapped to his back. From what I could see, it was a similar type to the medieval knightly swords I'd trained with, but the hilt was finely crafted with gold, copper and steel inlaid in intricate patterns. I longed to get a look at the blade inside the leather sheath. My eyes also caught the butt beneath the swaying sword. Now *that* was a work of art—but I wasn't going there. I averted my gaze.

We rounded another brow and a menhir stood ahead of us.

"There's a word from the old language that fae sometimes use as a mark of respect," Lucas said.

"Andos." It had to be. "The name was associated with many Pyrenean gods, but none specifically. I always wondered if it was a title of respect."

He raised his brow. "I'm impressed. Not many people know that."

"It's curious to find my theory is correct." My folklore knowledge was coming in useful.

"Everything is alive in Fae," Lucas said, "and it's necessary to pay respects to certain things with the greeting."

"That makes sense."

"The menhir is one of them. It's a marker of the ways. Space in Fae isn't continuous like in the human realm, it's more... hyperbolic, plus it can shift and change form. Some places are much bigger than they seem. Some areas border others, even though they couldn't possibly due to their size and shape. We use way markers to travel to distant parts of Fae quickly and easily. There are other methods of travel, but this is the simplest, and it doesn't use any resources."

"Resources?"

"Herbs, minerals, whatever is needed for colludes—magic."

As we approached the menhir, a number of pathways opened up, extending out from the stone into the valley beyond.

Lucas walked past. "Andos." He nodded to the stone.

I centred myself, focussing on the respect I felt for this ancient, sacred place, in a spiritual acknowledgement of the hidden realms of the world, of nature. Summoning reverence from deep within, I placed my hand on the limestone and whispered, "Andos." Then I stepped past.

"You've got to say it louder." Lucas's voice drew me from my reverie. He was already further down the slope.

"What? Why?"

"So the stone can hear." He looked at me as though I was crazy. "You need to say it... now." He glanced around warily.

I didn't get it. "I marked respect in my own way, and I felt a deep connection, which has to mean more than pronouncing the word from the hilltops."

A deep rumble shook the ground. "Look, trust me, Camille... just say it. Right. Now." His brow knitted. "Please?"

I scowled as the wind built to a powerful gust. The weather was changing and we were pretty exposed. The back of my neck prickled as if something was behind me. I turned slowly as a tumult of rain lashed down.

A huge black shadow rose from the menhir, extending and solidifying into a troll-like mass, its skin textured like cracked rock, its bulk as big as a house. My blood ran cold. I'd read tales of stones turning into vicious fairies—tessons, they were called—and it was happening before me. I drew my blade.

The wind howled. Lucas was shouting, but I couldn't make out his words above the storm. He pelted toward me.

In a swift movement, the creature stepped forward and passed me in a stride. It picked Lucas up and dangled him by the feet, flailing him about. He'd managed to draw his blade, but wasn't doing anything effectual with it.

The storm built to a ferocious intensity, water and mud rushing down the mountainside. I had to help Lucas. He was yelling something over and over, but I couldn't understand.

Avoiding its thundering footfalls, I charged at the tesson

and lunged to strike, but all I could see was the creature's stony skin. Was there blood under that? And flesh? Nausea heaved from deep within as a colossal foot headed toward me. I dodged it, then its partner. I had ample opportunity to attack, but I couldn't—I couldn't open flesh to reveal blood and gore. But I was being ridiculous. This thing was more of a boulder than a creature, and one spike in the foot wasn't going to kill it.

I darted from a stomp, willing myself to strike. If I didn't do something, it would be Lucas who was dead, but the thought of broken flesh was too much. I sprang out the way of another footfall, Lucas still yelling as he was flung this way and that. He swung in my direction, missing me by a fraction of an inch. "And—" he yelled as he came close, the word whipped away by the gale.

"And what?" I called. He was still shouting, his face red with it, or possibly with the centrifugal force of all the spinning. Hell, I was pathetic. I had to help him.

Then it clicked. Oh, shit. And—os. "Andos!" I screamed.

The tesson released Lucas, who tumbled into a deep stream of mud. The creature shrank in size to a foot high and stood before the menhir, staring guiltily at the ground, its hands clasped behind its back.

The weather stilled, the clouds dissipated and the placid evening returned. Relief flooded through me. Lucas stalked over, looking like a bog beast. He wiped his face to reveal an evil grimace, his glare skipping between me and the tesson.

"I was the one who said 'Andos'," he yelled at the creature. "She didn't." His look could have scorched the mountainside.

Yes, I should have said it, but I hadn't realised. And his fury should have been from me not helping him, rather than my mistake. What was going on with me? In all the time I'd fought Grampi and occasionally others without protective equipment, absolute control had been paramount. I'd rarely broken flesh—if I did, it made me want to vomit. And now, I couldn't even strike. But it was probably just nerves. So much had happened in the past couple of days, and I needed time to acclimatise to real combat.

"I... I'm sorry, sir," the tesson squeaked. "But she's new. I... thought it would be better if I took it out on you. It is my right, after all." It tried to square its shoulders, but it wasn't much more than a slither of rock. "And you know I can't control it."

"Andos!" Lucas yelled at me. "I said 'say Andos'. How difficult is that? Number one rule of Fae, be nice to stones!" He scraped mud off his arms and chest then flicked it off his hands.

Despite everything, my lip twitched, and I tried not to laugh. "I did say 'Andos', and very reverently."

"You weren't loud enough," the tesson said. "If I can't hear it clearly... well, how am I supposed to control myself?"

Lucas growled—he actually growled like the vicious animal he was—then he wiped his blade on a reasonably unmuddy patch of grass, before sheathing it and storming off down the hill. I glanced back at the tesson.

"Sorry, ma'am," it said. "Didn't mean to frighten you, but rules is rules."

"I'll remember that," I replied, and added clearly, "Andos."

"Much appreciated." Its brittle face cracked into a smile, then it disappeared behind the menhir.

I sheathed my blade and adjusted my soaked clothes, then ran after Lucas, who was already halfway down the hill. "I kind of think the mud suits you," I said as I reached him.

He shook his head, continuing his march as he muttered under his breath.

"Andos," I said as we passed another large rock—not exactly a menhir, but I wasn't taking any chances. The tesson had been more than enough of a shock for one day. Seeing something brought to life that had previously only been a myth was... bewildering.

"Andos," I repeated for the next boulder.

Lucas swung around. "Not now!" he yelled. "There is absolutely no point *now*."

"How am I supposed to know?" We passed another rock. "Andos." Alright, I was enjoying his irritation. Payback for the hell he'd put me through.

Heavy scraping cut through the air as Lucas's teeth grated. The sound really was impressive. I tried to do the same with mine as the path led into woodland, only managing to give myself a nail-down-chalkboard shiver.

"Look, Camille," he said. "Parts of Fae are dangerous. You're going to have to follow my lead."

"Do you really think I don't understand that? But you

have to explain things." My voice rose. "I've been offered this role because I know folklore, but really, I don't know anything about this place, do I? And anyway, we've just hiked all the way up here mostly in silence. You had plenty of opportunity to expound on the dangers of menhirs, but all I got was a brief and very last-minute mention." He stared at me as if trying to think what to say, his jaw locked tight. Not coming up with anything, he looked away.

As we entered the trees, the light changed. In a second, night descended in recondite blue. A plump, almost full moon shone through branches of oaks, acacias and holly, the foliage clear in the silver light. The path extended before us, snaking through the forest. I drew in the peaty scent of moss and fungi.

"What happened?" I asked.

"The way led us into a different part of Fae." The annoyance in his voice was a little less marked. "This is one of the undecided lands, neither bright nor dark. It's a mingling of both."

Something tickled my back. I sprang around. A rowan tree brushed against my shoulder. I hadn't noticed it so close as I'd walked by. I hurried after Lucas. "Why are we here?"

"I have an informant I want to see. He may know something about the deaths. This is a place he frequents, so it will be easier to call him here."

As we carried on, the occasional twig cracked amidst the trees, and in my peripheral vision, dark shadows slunk in the undergrowth, reflecting my building unease. I stumbled over a stone and regained my footing. There hadn't been anything on the path a moment before. I turned to see the rock rise up and scuttle away on tiny legs, the thing giggling faintly.

"Andos," I called, fascinated. The rock halted and the giggling stopped, then it broke into howls of laughter, swaying back and forth before rolling into the bushes. I felt a movement at my back—fingers running up my spine—then a weight lifted from me. I spun around. The spindly fronds of an ash tree held the hilt of my sword and were swinging it gently. I carefully unfurled the fronds and retrieved my blade. Did I say "Andos" to something that was stealing from me? Although I had a sense the tree was curious more than anything. Even so, my unease grew.

I sheathed my blade. Lucas turned around and glared at me again. The remaining mud covering his skin had dried and was cracking off. "Keep your wits about you."

We strode on, my mind whirring. I was in Fae. How the hell should I write about this in my research? It would be difficult to report back on my own experiences with any degree of objectivity. And if I tried, no one would believe me. It left me nowhere. And *Recent Experiences of Ancient Folkloric Phenomena* seemed pointless in the face of everything that shifted and swayed around me.

Eventually, we entered a clearing, the glade stark in the moonlight.

"This will do." Lucas rummaged in his pouch and drew out a bundle of cloth.

"What for?" I asked.

"Fickleturn," he boomed, ignoring my question. "You

two-faced dirty scoundrel. Get your scrawny ass here this minute!"

A wretched-looking goblin, about three feet high and dressed in a jerkin and breeches, appeared before us, his grey skin shivering.

"Lucas," he hissed. "Never a pleasure to see you. I hope you drop down dead and rot in the darkest of dark lands, terror worms eating your insides very slowly." My stomach heaved at the imagery. I pressed my lips together. It would be nice to have a brief break from death and gore for one moment.

Lucas shook the bundle out to reveal a small and dirty pair of breeches. He waved them in the air, a large grin on his face. "Nice to see you too, Fickleturn. Good to see you've found replacement trousers."

"I'm not interested in anything you have to say," the goblin replied. "If you don't mind... I'm going to get as far away from you as possible." He made to move, but only shook, as though he was struggling against himself.

Lucas flapped the fabric again, this time in my direction. "If you have a goblin's trousers, you have power over them. It has to be this particularly nasty type of goblin, though. Not any of the others."

"As if she doesn't know that," the creature said. He probably thought I was a regular in Fae. But then, how many people actually did visit or live here? Lucas stuffed the trousers back in his pouch then headlocked Fickleturn, his blade against the goblin's throat. "You have to do exactly what I say," he growled.

"I knew you'd come sooner or later," Fickleturn crooned, straining ineffectually from Lucas's sword. "Dracs are so predictable, and you are the most predictable of all. Lucas has been such a good little doctor. It's utterly sickening."

"Tell me who's behind the human deaths," Lucas rumbled.

"How should I know? Although it would take powerful magic to do that sort of thing on the bounds."

"And there's been a fae curse," I called out.

Fickleturn's gaze settled on me. "Camille Amiel, how awful that you're here, after all the strife you caused me." He thought I'd caused him trouble? I didn't understand. No doubt it was a mistake, but how had he known my name? Lucas just glowered at the goblin.

"And someone has been cursed?" Fickleturn continued, the amusement clear in his voice. "Tut, tut, tut. Terrible. Terrible. Of course, I wouldn't know anything about *that*."

"You know a whole lot more than you let on," Lucas said.

"You may be able to force my actions with my breeches," he cackled, "but you can't force my speech. And I won't tell you anything."

"I know plenty of other ways to get information." Lucas pressed his blade closer.

"Don't you think I knew you were coming?" Fickleturn said slowly. "Don't you think I made plans...?"

Lucas laughed. "And your plans have been *so* effectual in the past."

"Just because you can control me," Fickleturn snarled as the ground began to shake, earth flying, "it doesn't mean you

can control everyone else. And there are plenty of other creatures that don't like you one little bit."

With his words, the ground exploded and a myriad of
rats the size of small dogs swarmed out and encircled us, their
eyes red, their mouths open, ridiculously large teeth bared. I
drew my blade, a lump forming in my throat. We were
completely outnumbered. And why did everything to do
with fae have very large teeth?

CHAPTER 14

"CHARGE!" FICKLETURN SQUEALED, AND THE RATS pounced.

With complete nonchalance, Lucas said, "Slaughter, sort them out."

Countless Men of Bédeilhac appeared from nowhere, brandishing prehistoric weapons. Slaughter led the way, swinging his axe, and they met the rats head on. Dust flew, and amidst it all limbs, tails and whole furry bodies arced through the clearing, a searing squeaking filling the air. Slaughter obviously hadn't meant business when he'd chopped my toe last night. The men were lethal killing machines.

A rat broke from the throng and charged at me. I swept my blade down to slice off its head, but the thought of killing it... I halted my sword before it struck. Nope, I wasn't there yet.

A Man swept in and decapitated the rat with a couple of

blows of his axe, blood spurting onto my shoes. "Sorry, ma'am," he said. "The little blighter slipped away."

"No trouble," I managed, trying not to heave. Lucas glanced at me, his eyes narrowed. He'd noticed my flakiness.

In moments, the whole place stilled, and the Men were cleaning their weapons, the ground littered with pile upon pile of rat bodies. I would've felt relief if I hadn't felt so sick.

"Honestly, Fickleturn," Lucas said to the goblin, who was cussing lividly in his grip. "I don't know why you bother. It's really quite pathetic."

"Still can't get me to speak, though, can you? Nothing you can do about that."

Lucas strode toward the trees. "Let's go," he called. I picked my way across the mutilated corpses and headed into the forest.

Once clear of the rats, Lucas slammed Fickleturn onto the ground and held out his hand as if expecting someone to give him something. The branches of the beech above shook, and coils of ivy dropped into his palm. "Just in case he finds a way to get out of the trouser binding..." He tied up Fickleturn's hands and feet then slung him over his shoulder by the ankles. "He needs a little persuasion to speak, and I have just the thing."

Lucas headed along a path through the trees, bright moonlight glinting through leafy boughs. I wiped the blood off my shoes and followed him amidst the troop of Men.

Fickleturn shrieked and squealed as he dangled over Lucas's shoulder. "Slaves," he cried. "See how we're all enslaved to him. He uses the lowest tricks to ensure we do his bidding. Never trust a drac."

"Oh, yes," Slaughter agreed happily. "We're all his slaves. Completely bound to his service. Forced to do his every whim."

I studied the back of Lucas's head as he stomped along, Fickleturn's words stirring curiosity. I didn't know anything about Lucas. Well, apart from that he was a drac, a drink-spiking creature that reputedly seduced people to their deaths. But also, he was a doctor who seemed to care about saving lives. And yet Fickleturn and the Men were his slaves...

My head spun. What with this new information and the nausea sitting in my stomach from the carnage, plus Henri earlier, I was more than a little overwhelmed. Oh, and not to forget, I was walking through fairyland.

I just needed to place one foot in front of the other in the hope of finding out something useful about Grampi's curse, then go home and forget about it. Bourbon would do the trick —but, no. Never again. Perhaps red wine this time.

And whilst I was here, Grampi was home alone and sick —the neighbour would have left a while ago. "I have to say," I called ahead to Lucas above Fickleturn's screeching, "I have no idea how long we've been here, and I'm worried about leaving Grampi for too long in his condition." Fairyland was notorious for distorting time.

"He should be fine," Lucas said.

"How do you know? You said that about the curse, and it got much worse."

"Slaughter," Lucas said. "Take some Men and keep an eye on Izak."

"Yes, gov." Slaughter saluted.

"Wait one moment," I said before the little guy could disappear. "Remember the other day... mass destruction of my property? I don't think it's a good idea."

"The Men are bound to do my bidding," Lucas replied. "There's nothing to worry about."

There it was again—they were bound to him. I strode up alongside. "But, slaves. Really?"

Lucas rubbed his neck with his free hand and the last of the mud flaked off.

"Yep, the finest slaves," Slaughter said enthusiastically. "Absolutely obedient. We do everything the master commands without hesitation."

Fickleturn sniggered from behind Lucas.

"Do you really think slaves are my thing, Camille?" He gave Fickleturn a shake.

"Considering I've never met another drac, I don't have a clue."

"I can't get rid of them," he said, his lip twitching, his eyes on the path that wove downward.

"Come on. How hard have you tried?"

He shot daggers at me, then said, "Slaughter, I release you and all Men of Bédeilhac from my service."

Slaughter chortled. "Not like I haven't heard that one before, boss." He swung his axe, knocking over the Man behind him without noticing, then puffing out his chest. "As chief of the Men of Bédeilhac, I declare our willing, loyal and undying slavery to Lucas Rouseau for the rest of our days, or the end of the world... whichever should come first. What do you say, Men?"

An almighty bellow rose up. Lucas raised an eyebrow.

Fae was such a strange place. I'd heard stories about this sort of thing. "But Fickleturn?" He was now jabbering and cackling.

"He's a go-between, and a very knowledgeable one at that. He trades information, and I need to find out what happened with Henri and Madame Bonnet. Things work differently here. You're going to have to trust me on this one."

After everything, benefit of the doubt was all I could manage. I glanced at Slaughter. "Just watch Grampi. No destruction."

"Course not, ma'am. We only did that to your loft because Lucas—"

Lucas struck out his foot, sending Slaughter flying into the trees. In a split second, he was back, a huge grin on his face as though he'd had the best ride of his life. "Sorry, gov." He turned to me. "Promise, ma'am. Absolutely no destruction."

"Alright, then." What was I letting myself in for?

The whole troop of Men swept away, leaving Lucas, Fickleturn and me alone.

"All of them?" I had visions of the farm rampaged.

"They'll be alright."

Fickleturn babbled incoherently. I made out the occasional "despicable" and "revenge".

At the bottom of the hill stood another menhir, the stone

surrounded by hawthorn, the blossom glowing in the moon-light. Paths like spokes led in all directions.

"Andos," Lucas said as he passed, then glared at me.

Surely he didn't think I was going to make the same mistake again? "Andos," I pronounced.

Lucas shook his head and chuckled, taking the right-hand path. I blinked as the land transformed into a stunning summer's day with a blazing azure sky.

"How come it's daytime now?" I said.

"Some lands follow the same astronomical pattern as the human realm, some don't. Some are always summer, like this one, or always night, like before."

We headed through a wheat field, the blades rippling in a warm breeze, the scent of chamomile wafting from below. In the distance, patchwork hills undulated, the place reminding me more of the Vendée or a typical English landscape than the Pyrenees. Fickleturn's incoherent babble rose.

As we neared the edge of the field, a grassy barrow framed by massive menhirs loomed before us, smoke rising from a roughly stacked chimney.

"No! Not in there!" Fickleturn screamed. "Anything but there!"

CHAPTER 15

A BROAD OPENING LED INTO THE MOUND, MASSIVE stones towering either side. I followed Lucas and a screaming Fickleturn inside.

"Wayland," Lucas called.

"Come on in, my friend," came a voice. But... Wayland. Not *the* Wayland—pan-European blacksmith deity. Not Wayland, forger of Charlemagne's Curtana and Joyeuse, and Roland's Durendal—some of the most famous swords of myth and history. Wayland, the Finnish prince who outsmarted King Niðhad. It couldn't be.

The scent of woodsmoke and leather filled the air as we strode through the entrance hall lit with flaming torches. It led into a circular stone chamber. A forge roared at the back, heat blasting out, and a massive anvil stood in the centre. Roughly curtained doorways extended off, leading into darkness.

All about the place hung blacksmithing equipment—

tongs, pokers, bellows and odd-looking things. Shields, swords, daggers and axes were mounted on the walls. Lances and spears were propped up here and there amidst pieces of armour. The theory that fairies hated iron flew out the window—although I should have realised as we'd brought steel blades into Fae.

Wayland stood at the hearth, a hammer in one hand, a sword in the other, massive biceps flexed. A leather apron covered his immense, bronzed chest, and his full beard, like his dark curly locks, radiated outward, giving any Man of Bédeilhac competition.

He placed his work down, strode to Lucas and clasped him in greeting, avoiding Fickleturn. "Andos," he boomed. "Good to see you, Lucas. Very good to see you."

"Andos," Lucas replied. "Good to see you too, my friend. Give me a moment, I'm a little occupied." He stepped away, drew the screeching Fickleturn over his shoulder and flung him onto the floor by the forge.

Wayland met my gaze. "Camille Amiel, Andos. Wonderful to meet you." He bowed his head.

Did everyone in Fae know my name? "Andos," I said. "It's an... honour to meet you." I couldn't believe it. The Wayland. Nope, I was fangirling hard.

"Lucas mentioned you'd be coming." So that was how he knew. He beckoned, his eyes shining as brightly as the hearth. "I have something for you. Come this way."

Leaving Lucas adjusting Fickleturn's ties, I followed Wayland through a curtained doorway, wondering what he had in store. We entered a smaller and cooler chamber lit only by a couple of torches. The place was filled with leather goods strung on the walls and stacked on the ground.

Lucas swept past the curtain and headed to a row of boots. "Mind if I grab some?"

"Help yourself," Wayland said. He turned to me. "Camille, I should have everything you need for your role as Keeper." He gestured about.

I stared at the gear. I was being offered something similar to Lucas's outfit. I wasn't exactly into cosplay, but my clothes were still damp and uncomfortable from earlier. I stepped over to some women's tops and fingered the subtle leather, the workmanship exquisite. "Umm, I have to say, I've not accepted the role yet. To tell you the truth, I don't know much about it."

"I'm working on that," Lucas called as he ducked back out, new boots on.

Wayland ran a hand over his beard. "That's understandable. But know that the role is vitally important—to Fae, but also to the human realm. Both must support each other. They must be bound securely for any form of life to exist. And there are some creatures of Fae who must be kept in check if innocent humans aren't to suffer. It's an honour to be tasked with such an undertaking."

Different to Lucas's take. "Well, I'm here." For Grampi. But... perhaps Wayland could help in that department. "I... uh... hope you don't mind me asking, but my grandfather has a fae curse. Would you by any chance know what might help him?"

He stood like a sentinel, feet planted apart, arms folded

across his chest. His unwavering furnace of a gaze blazed into me. "To help your grandfather, you must focus on what troubles you most."

Right. Gods—never a straight answer. "Um... could you be a little clearer?"

"You dislike death. You find it a challenge to use your blade."

How did he know...? But then, being omnipotent was in his job description. "Uh, yes," I replied. "Blood and flesh... it's revolting."

"And you want to overcome this." It wasn't a question—as his gaze bore in, I felt as if he knew me through and through. Of course, I'd wanted to help Lucas with the tesson, not to mention the rats. But the revulsion was a problem in my daily life too. My reactions were all out of proportion. I even struggled to see gore in films.

"I suppose I do. I've not needed to think about it much until now, but..." But what if there were worse things out there than the tesson?

"Then you need to face what lies beneath your reactions. That will help you most of all."

There was no doubt I needed to get a grip. I had no idea what caused me to react so strongly. Even so, this was way off the point. "But my grandfather—"

"Your reactions, Camille. Sort them out." His words were heavy, as though they measured my life—and as though that was the end of the conversation.

I wasn't going to let it drop. "Are you telling me my revulsion and the curse are connected?"

"Haven't I said as much?"

I tried to find a shred of a link and came up with zero.

"That," he continued, "is my gift to you."

Some gift. I'd hoped for healing magic, if that was even a thing. He was a god—surely he could do better? But it didn't look like I was going to get anything else out of him. "I'll bear that in mind," I murmured.

Wayland's expression broke, a smile lighting his eyes. "Well, what are you waiting for? Even if you're just trying out the job, you'll need some gear." He rummaged in a pile, drew out a pouch and belt and passed them over. "These might be useful."

The pouch appeared to be standard fair, like Lucas's, but the belt... I studied the exquisite patterning of stars carved and stamped into the leather. "It's stunning... I can't." It really was too much.

"This is what I'm here for," he roared. "Now put something on. I've got a job to finish before you go." He strode out, leaving me alone with piles of gear.

I pulled on a top and some trousers and boots to the sound of Wayland's hammer striking metal. The trousers hung low on my hips with a broad waistband that fit perfectly. The top was sleeveless with a V at the throat, and short enough to reveal a slice of midriff. Both were supple and unbelievably comfortable. I could see the appeal.

I fastened Wayland's belt and pouch, then I found a scabbard, crafted with stars like the belt, and hauled it on. It fit like a glove. I had to admit, I felt damned good in the outfit.

Lucas and Wayland's chatter drifted through as Wayland

continued to smith. I stuffed my old clothes and shoes into a sack, picked up my blade and ducked out under the curtain. Fickleturn was jabbering quietly to himself.

Lucas and Wayland turned. They were speechless for a moment, Lucas gaping, then Wayland nodded. "Perfect, Camille. Just perfect."

Lucas cleared his throat. "Yes, very practical," he managed.

Fickleturn's voice rose, screeching obscenities at Lucas.

I dropped the sack and raised my blade to tuck it into the scabbard, but Wayland reached out a palm. "A blade in exchange for a blade."

I peered at him, unsure of his meaning. He gestured with a finger to Grampi's sword. I had no idea why he'd be interested in it—it was a replica, not much more than a blunt toy—but I handed it over anyway. Wayland took it and propped it beside the hearth. Using tongs, he picked up the sword he'd been hammering and plunged it into a vat of water. Steam rose, filling the chamber. Then he rubbed the blade all over with a shammy. Satisfied, he turned it around with care and offered me the hilt. "May it be a blessing in the grimmest of lands."

I raised my brow. Wayland had made a sword for me? "I... couldn't possibly..."

He nodded in encouragement.

Words escaped me. With utter reverence, I clasped the warm metal and peered at its exquisite form, its blade so fine, so light. The decoration of the hilt was similar to Lucas's, with gold, copper and steel, but rather than an intricate pattern, it was inlaid with countless stars of all sizes, matching my belt and scabbard. I drew my finger to the blade and the tip stung as a bead of blood welled up. Ignoring the part of me that wanted to hide from even my own blood, I stepped back from the anvil and rotated the blade, then performed a series of ribbon cuts.

I shook my head. It was unlike anything I'd fought with—it was one of Wayland's swords. "I... I don't know what to say."

"You don't have to say anything at all." He beamed. "I hope it comes to good use."

"Lucas is the most duplicitous, nastiest piece of work in all Fae," Fickleturn squealed in a particularly piercing tone. I'd been filtering out his constant insults, but this one was way too loud.

"Excuse me for a moment," Lucas said. "It's past time I sorted out this little beast."

Wayland leant back against the wall next to me, watching with a glimmer of amusement in his eyes, his arms folded once again in what appeared to be his trademark power stance.

Lucas took a poker that leant against the forge and shoved it into the blaze. He wasn't going to use that, surely? He strode over to Fickleturn, knelt on him and slammed his fist into the creature's head. I flinched. Angry, much? It was a wonder Lucas didn't turn into a drac and eat him.

"You think you know what Fickleturn hates," Fickleturn croaked. "You think you know what I fear. But you'll never get me to talk—" This time, Lucas's fist met his jaw.

Fickleturn's head lolled to the side. "Not going to talk. Not going to talk," he sang, slurring his words.

Lucas had said to trust him about fae, but brutal violence against a small creature, no matter what he'd done, was too much. "Really, Lucas. Isn't there a better way? You're a doctor, for heaven's sake—and he's about three feet shorter than you."

He turned his head and glared at me. "He's a scumbag, Camille."

"And that makes it alright, does it?"

Wayland looked between us, amused. "You two are a fine pair!" he bellowed.

"Anyway," Lucas said, rising up, his eyes glinting. "I do have a better way." He strode to the hearth and grasped the poker.

He wasn't. He really couldn't.

Fickleturn's eyeballs bulged from their sockets. "Fire, fire, fire, pain, fire, heat," he gabbled. "Not fire, not heat. No. Never. Noooooo." He screamed and screamed and screamed.

Lucas inched toward him, brandishing the poker. Fickleturn strained frantically at his binds and the trouser magic that held him, only making himself shake uncontrollably, sweat beading on his forehead. "No. No. No. I'll talk. I'll talk. I'll talk."

"Good," Lucas said, and drew the poker back a little.

"It's the bounds," Fickleturn yammered. "They've been breached... something from the dark lands, one of the fettered fae."

"And?"

"That's... that's... that's all I know about it."

Lucas thrust the poker toward the creature again. "I think you know a lot more."

Fickleturn quaked and stammered, not managing to get his words out. Then he bulged, his skin turning from grey to blue.

Lucas shifted the poker so close that the air filled with singed goblin hair. I couldn't do it—I couldn't stand here and watch a creature being tortured, not to mention the thought of any more broken flesh. Lucas really was the lowest of the low. I strode over and kicked the poker from his hands. It bounced away. "Haven't you heard of the Geneva Convention?" I yelled.

Lucas's gaze followed the poker as it settled on the ground, his face frozen in disbelief, then he turned, fury blazing in his eyes. "The Geneva Convention doesn't count in fairyland," he shouted.

"Whatever," I said. "But I'm not going to sit by and watch you torture another creature, no matter how despicable he might be."

I honestly thought he was about to start growling again, but instead he rose slowly, his gazed fixed on me as though I was his prey, then he grabbed Fickleturn, tore off his binds, strode out to the entrance, and with an almighty roar, kicked him into the cornfield. Wayland howled with laughter.

"But... why did you...?" Okay, I'd objected to the red-hot poker, but kicking out our informer was a bit extreme.

"Because of the Geneva Convention!" he bellowed.

Wayland clapped me much too hard on the back, his laughter uncontrollable. "Perfect partners, indeed."

"We're not partners," I said, shooting Wayland a death stare, god or no.

"It's been centuries," Wayland said, holding his middle, "since I've seen anything quite that funny." He pointed at Lucas. "Not since that time you got on the wrong side of Baeserte and he rammed you halfway across the Pyrenees." He howled again.

Lucas raised his chin, his lips pressed tight, his tongue rolling around in his mouth as though he was attempting to restrain a laugh.

"I don't see what's so funny," I said.

Lucas was barely mastering himself. "Fickleturn fears fire more than anything, and despite what he says about not talking, he's the biggest blabbermouth going—I wouldn't have had to touch him with that poker for him to reveal his darkest secrets. But he turned blue—a sign he's been hindered. Something has control over him, so he couldn't say more if he wanted to." His grin broadened. "But we did get information. The borders have been breached by one of the fettered fae. Something nasty has entered the human realm, and it caused Henri's and Madame Bonnet's deaths. We have to secure the bounds right now—before it happens again."

CHAPTER 16

LUCAS'S HANDS FLEXED AROUND THE STEERING WHEEL as he navigated the moonlit Tarascon road. His fingers were fine, sinewy and strong, yet inside that skin lay desiccated, deadly talons. He was a mystery, just like everything I'd seen of Fae.

We'd taken a way directly back to Lucas's house, then jumped in the car. We needed some equipment from Tarascon for securing the bounds—and apparently we couldn't have gone direct via Fae, because we needed the transport.

On the return hike, I'd tried to make sense of all that had happened, but impressions spun through my head, the overwhelm leaving me defensive. I'd messed up with the tesson, then I hadn't been able to strike the rat, and to top it off, I'd misjudged Lucas with Fickleturn. Perhaps I should have kept quiet—after all, I knew nothing about Fae.

That aside, he really could have given me more information—about everything. "You know, through all of this, I've had no idea what's going on," I said. "Why don't you explain things properly?"

"Because I enjoy seeing you play catchup." A sparkle lit his eye.

Why? Why would he get any kind of pleasure from that? He was a cat toying with a mouse. At what point would he get bored and eat me? Although... Lucas the bog beast came to mind and my lips tugged into a broad smirk. He didn't always have everything under control.

"But seriously," he said, "I get that it must be overwhelming, and I didn't want to make that worse."

I studied him. He looked sincere. He also looked completely out of place in the car wearing his Keeper gear. A sort of timelessness surrounded him. According to Wayland, Baeserte had rammed Lucas across the Pyrenees centuries ago. How old was he?

"But ask away," he added. "What do you want to know?"

Best I begin with the most pressing matters. "For a start, what are fettered fae?" I shifted my bags and the scabbarded swords in the footwell to give my feet more room.

"There are various individuals and groups of fae that have committed the most atrocious deeds against fae or humanity. As punishment, they have been fettered to the dark lands for a thousand years."

I was intrigued. "But now some of them have escaped?"

"According to Fickleturn."

"And you don't know what type of fae."

"No idea."

I rubbed my eyes. It was the early hours, and I wasn't cut out for this. Lucas, on the other hand, looked bright as a button. "And why do the bounds need securing?"

Lucas took the roundabout and we turned onto the N20. "The two realms are repelling each other because of the lack of connection between humans and fae. Securing the bounds is a magical process that holds the realms together despite everything else going on."

"But how is that going to prevent fettered fae escaping?"

He fiddled with the car's touchscreen. "When the bounds draw apart just a fraction, a void forms that fettered fae can use to escape the dark lands."

"So when the bounds are secure, everyone is safe."

He tapped his finger on the wheel. "You've got it."

"You're a Keeper of the Bounds," I said. "Why—"

"*We're* Keepers of the Bounds."

"Why on earth do you think I'd take the job? So far I've almost been crushed by a rock troll and eaten by a giant rat." Anyway, he was distracting me. "Why aren't the bounds secure? Isn't it your job to keep them..." I couldn't think of the right word. "Tight?" I tried.

"No, Camille, it's not my job." His jaw clamped. We turned into the café car park. "Keepers make sure everything is in order in the borderlands. They don't generally perform the bounds magic itself."

"Well, who does?"

"Right at this moment, no one." Irritation laced his voice. "And if we don't rectify that, hell knows what will come across from Fae—what has come across already." He jumped out of the SUV and pulled on his scabbard.

I followed his lead, grabbing my bags. "I have to say, I'm feeling mildly ridiculous wearing this outfit in town, even though it's the middle of the night. The sword really tops it off—although I guess it looks like fancy dress."

"Don't worry." The corners of his mouth turned up as he gestured to his clothes. "To most humans, this looks like my work shirt and trousers. They can't even see my sword—it's glamoured." He headed to the café. "Come on."

I followed Lucas around the back, barely able to make him out in the darkness. He paused and I could just see him bending down, then with a grunt he hauled up a large bundle and slammed it against the wall.

"Ooooph," it grunted. "Trashirbruoszph... Whasss going on?"

Roux. It had to be Roux, drunk and sleeping rough as usual.

"I'll tell you what's going on." A dangerous edge sharpened Lucas's voice. "You've not been doing your job again. Because of it, fettered fae have crossed over." He shook the guy. "And if you don't get your act together, I'm going to feed you to them."

"Whasss... kreeorogtweesphd," came Roux's slur.

Lucas grunted in frustration and hauled Roux over his shoulder with considerably more effort than Fickleturn. The guy certainly had some muscle—Roux wasn't exactly slender. A brief flash of my fingers traversing well-developed pecs taunted me. I ignored it. But why was he hassling Roux?

"This idiot can't keep his hands off the scrapelather for five minutes to do his job properly." Lucas made his way toward the fae town. Roux mumbled incoherently as he swayed upside down, his long beard dangling.

"I didn't think Roux had a job." Once again, I had no idea what Lucas was going on about. "This is the bit where you explain, so I'm not left in the dark."

"This"—he gave Roux a jiggle—"is Tarascon's bounds mage. The responsibility for binding the two realms lies in his extremely competent and never inebriated hands. Aren't we lucky?"

As we strode along the main thoroughfare, passing the florist and the tavern, I tried to piece things together. The idea of Roux being a bounds mage wasn't completely out there. After all, he'd once turned up at the back door of the café wearing a Gandalf hat, which clearly qualified him for the role. And after the last couple of days, anything was possible.

"What's scrapelather?" I asked. A few lanterns illuminated vines that rambled everywhere, the place more like a wildflower garden than a town despite the tightly packed buildings. Apart from the murmur of drowsy conversation from the tavern, the place was silent and deserted.

"Scrapelather. Skuttleworm. The dubious comforter. Harbinger of the gutter. Hell's cherub. It's a highly addictive and slightly psychoactive herbal brew that this fool can't keep away from."

We headed further than I'd been before, passing more timber-framed buildings—a cobbler's, a tailor, some indistinct workplaces or possibly houses. When the thoroughfare split, Lucas turned left past what looked like an all-night boulangerie, its warm light extending onto the street. Inside, a goblin of Fickleturn's height served a lanky elf. Hell, I was hungry. Hungry and tired. My bed and the farm seemed a million miles away.

"Umm. Do you really need me for this?" I asked. "I'm worried about Grampi." And about the Men.

Lucas turned to me. "Yes, Camille," he said, a thread of something almost desperate in his voice. "We have to get this excuse for a human being sober, and quick. We need him to secure the bounds at dawn, meaning we have just over an hour to sort him out."

No rest for the wicked. I wasn't sure how I could help, but if we could prevent anyone else coming down with what Henri had, it would be worthwhile.

Lucas headed to a bright yellow building across the street and pushed his way inside. "The Keepers' post. Our base in town."

I wanted to take him up on the "our" business, but I'd made my position clear and I wasn't going to continue butting up against him.

As we entered, a number of wall lanterns lit of their own accord. "Neat trick."

The room appeared to be a meeting area of sorts, with a large table and chairs in the centre of a flagstone floor. The ceiling was low and beamed, and old, leather-bound volumes lined some of the walls. Weapons hung on others—swords, crossbows, daggers. A couple of doors led off to the sides.

Lucas flipped Roux over his shoulder and dropped him down much harder than was necessary. Once again, Roux was a bundle of rags on the floor. I stepped into the next room—a sort of laboratory. The place was lined with apothecary drawers. Lucas came in and rummaged in one.

A kitchen area with a range stood to the side. There was a sink too, the faucet dripping into an overflowing bucket. Boy, was I thirsty. I took a cup from the draining board and drank my fill. Noticing a door at the back, I headed over and pushed into a courtyard garden lit with lanterns. All kinds of plants bloomed in abundance. Paths skirted the edge and crossed in the centre, restraining the foliage a little. Even in the half-light of the lanterns, it was stunning.

Unintelligible protesting came from inside. I strode in. Lucas had Roux against the wall of the main room, those sinewy hands clamping the drunk's mouth open. Lucas pulled the cork from a vial with his teeth, spat it aside, then poured the contents down a screaming and choking Roux.

"Teach you how to administer drugs humanely at medical school, did they?" I said with more than a little vehemence. "Do you have to be quite so... physical?"

"He should've been sober and securing the bounds yesterday—no, a month yesterday."

"What's in that stuff?"

"It's just a little potion to clear his head."

He dropped Roux into a crumpled heap. Roux gabbled incoherently.

"Damn it!" Lucas yelled. "It's not working." He headed into the other room and hunted for something else.

I sank down at the table and laid my head in my arms, my eyes involuntarily closing. The thought of slumping on the floor next to Roux and taking a snooze appealed, all except for the being next to Roux bit—the vomit stain on his shirt wasn't drawing me.

Something thumped on the table. I looked up. Lucas had placed a vial there. "To wake you up. Like an energy drink, but it tastes better and doesn't leave you feeling as if your eyes are pinned open under duress."

I took the vial and twisted it between my fingers.

"You know, there are countless tales of how it really isn't a good idea to eat or drink anything fae. The consequences being forgetting the human realm exists and the like. Not to mention, I'm not keen after the verity."

Lucas manhandled Roux, propping his mouth open and administering another dose. Then he nodded to my vial. "It's completely safe. Made it myself. And that thing about fairy food—not true... generally."

That did nothing to reassure me. But what the hell. I'd already stepped so far out of the realms of normality. What was a little potion going to do?

I removed the cork and sipped it. The taste was pleasant —elderflower and maybe sage, with something I couldn't identify adding depth. I downed the rest in one and released a breath as it sank into my veins. The room, Lucas and every-thing around me appeared clearer, the world sharp, my brain honed and ready for anything.

I sat up straight. "Well, I do believe it worked."

Lucas waggled his eyebrows then poured one more vial into Roux, who was now green.

"Trouxlyesprjksveswyas," Roux managed, although his eyes remained closed.

"Can that stuff do any harm?" I asked.

"He's had four vials now. At six there's a good risk of total organ failure. I should have brought my work bag, then I could have given it intravenously. The scrapelather is damned potent. Its hooks get in deep."

"I'm kind of wondering if we should go quite so close to risking organ failure?" But he knew what he was doing, right?

"The bounds, Camille. We're running out of time."

"Isn't there anyone else who can help?"

"Not that I can get hold of quickly." He studied Roux for a moment, then sprang up and strode into the lab. "I'm going to try something else."

Feeling like a spare part, I glanced through the lead-lined window to the boulangerie across the street. Now I wasn't completely exhausted—or exhausted at all—I was ravenous. "I'm going to get some food," I called through. "Do you want anything?"

Lucas came in holding two more vials, a grimace on his face. "Nope, I'm fine." He placed the vials on the table and rummaged in his pouch, drawing out a small hessian bag pulled tight with twine. "Herbs," he said.

"What for?"

"Payment. They don't take Visa."

I hadn't even thought. I took the bag, made my way to the

boulangerie and attempted to purchase two filled demi baguettes.

The goblin glowered suspiciously at the new girl in town. "That will be two scruples," he said.

Not having a clue what he was talking about, I passed him the bag. He poured a small amount onto a scale then nodded.

When I returned, Roux was still slumped in the corner, and Lucas was pacing frantically back and forth. "That's it. He's had his six. Either he'll sober up or his organs will rupture."

I glared at him. "And then what will we do for a bounds mage?"

"Right now, I'm thinking good riddance." He gave Roux a kick. "His body is too used to the scrapelather—and too accustomed to repeated antidotes."

I tore into my baguette and froze as the taste of manure, burnt toast and rotten eggs met my tongue. I spat the mouthful into the paper bag. "What the hell?"

Lucas grinned. "Don't like fairy food?"

"If this is what it tastes like, then hard no."

"Only the most powerful fae can work with human ingredients and produce good results," he said without taking his eyes off Roux, although his amusement was all too clear. "Fae food is different—delicious in its own way, but different. I have no idea why that guy over there keeps attempting to work with human stuff, although he seems to have a few customers."

"You knew it would be disgusting."

He tittered to himself.

The total and utter git. Despite everything that was going on with the bounds, despite everything we'd been through tonight, he'd played a joke on me. I abandoned the baguette. I'd just have to be hungry.

Lucas rubbed his chin then headed into the lab. "Maybe if I give Roux one more dose..."

"Uh, I don't think so. You said it yourself, total organ failure."

He came out with another vial. "It'd be worth trying, though."

I really couldn't believe he meant it. But if we didn't secure the bounds, more people were going to suffer the same fate as Henri and Madame Bonnet. There had to be a solution. I scanned the room, searching for something that might help. My gaze caught on the sink as Lucas stepped over to Roux, the seventh vial in hand.

I met him and snatched the bottle, dropping it onto the draining board with a clatter. Then I hauled up the bucket of water, marched into the other room and threw the contents over Roux.

CHAPTER 17

Roux spluttered and choked, then opened his eyes and peered at us. "What in Abellion's sake did you have to do that for?"

Lucas stared for a moment, then he stepped over and grasped me by the shoulders, an ever so slightly manic grin on his face. "You did it, Camille. You damned well did it!"

"All she appears to have done," Roux said, clambering up and shaking out his bedraggled clothes, "is get me extremely wet. And anyway, what am I doing here?"

Lucas turned to him, his gaze darkening. He grabbed Roux by the throat and slammed him against the wall—obviously his preferred method of manhandling. "What happened to the rehab programme I put you on?" he hissed. "Drank it all away, did you?"

Roux spluttered. "I... You know how it is... Life's not always so great, and the scrapelather softens the blow..."

Lucas jerked Roux, cracking his skull on the stone, then he released him, dove into the other room and piled things frantically into a sack. "You've been neglecting the bounds," he called back.

"I do my job," Roux said defensively.

"I haven't got time to argue," Lucas growled, drawing the sack closed. "We need to sort this mess out, before it's too late."

———

The sky was lightening in the east, casting a grey glow all around as we strode up the stony and scrubby foothill to the place where the bounds would be secured, a few miles' drive past the turn to Lucas's house.

Lucas's potion had lifted me completely. Roux, on the other hand, was hauling himself upward with his staff as he mumbled about the incline, which wasn't that steep. The clothes he'd found in a cupboard in the Keepers' post—some kind of ankle-length robe—bloomed with sweat and looked almost as bad as his last lot.

He'd been updated about everything as we'd driven here, including the details of my involvement. Lucas had in no way hidden his wrath, and Roux had shrunk on hearing how his negligence had caused Henri's and Madame Bonnet's deaths.

Lucas took the lead, sack in hand, as though his long stride would hurry Roux up, but the mage only managed a snail's pace. Not that it mattered terribly. From what I could work out, we still had a while before dawn.

I took the rear so I could keep an eye on Roux as he teetered this way and that. His staff slipped and he stumbled, toppling precariously. I sprang forward and grabbed his arm.

"By Abellion's trousers," he muttered, then nodded to me. "That's kind of you."

I couldn't help chuckling at his mention of Abellion, sun god and ruler of the Pyrenean pantheon. What sort of trousers did *he* wear? Roux released a volley of coughs. The guy was not fit, but it wasn't surprising with the scrapelather and sleeping rough.

"You're out the back of the café a fair bit," I said. "Don't you have anywhere to bed down?"

He narrowed his eyes. "I have plenty of options. I just like a little fresh air... and Alice's coffee."

Fair enough. I scanned his face, taking in the lines, the touches of chestnut in his straggly beard and his mild, watery-blue irises. I guessed he was around sixty, but it was hard to tell.

"Keepers' post gets stuffy," he added.

"You've got a room there?"

"Which he's too plastered to find most of the time," Lucas called back.

Roux paused, leant on his staff and said to me, "You know, I keep my eye on the bounds. Not as often as he'd like. But there's a bit of natural uncoupling at times—and occasionally some overlap. Lucas is putting far too much weight on the bounds being separate." Roux was avoiding blame for

Henri and Madame Bonnet, and with minimal knowledge of everything, I hadn't a clue if it was justified. I was stuck between him and Lucas.

"Anyway, it will be super to have another new Keeper around." Roux hauled himself on up the rocky incline. "Been needed for a long time, so I'm glad you're here. The job's not a bad one. The pay is good."

Lucas snorted from ahead.

But pay? That hadn't been mentioned before, never mind *good* pay. The farm needed more money—the bills sponged it up every month so there was nothing left for repairs. I couldn't see myself ever working with Lucas, but I would have to find out about the pay... just out of curiosity.

As we rose further, Roux took a rest on a boulder and signalled for me not to wait. I headed onward and called to Lucas, "So how do we actually secure the bounds?"

"We perform a collude," he said without turning back. "What you might refer to as a magical ritual."

"I'm confused." I drew level with him. "I mean, fae are inherently magical, so why the extra magic?"

"Each fae has its own powers. Some types have a lot, some very little. The singular fae and the gods are the most powerful. The rest of us are pretty limited. Colludes and potions help us go further, but they're difficult, and many fae don't bother. Though glamours come more easily."

As we climbed, a massive boulder supported by three smaller rocks came into view a little way above. "The dolmen of Sem." I'd walked up here many times. "Legend has it the rock was left by Sampson, but it's a natural erratic, the stones deposited by glacial action."

Lucas raised an eyebrow. "Natural erratic is a good description of an irate ice god who wanted a nice dolmen on this spot to mark one of the key bounds. Not to mention, there's so much power in the area that the whole place is completely erratic—it's not possible to travel here reliably through Fae."

We rounded the brow of the hill. Mountains rose in jagged peaks all around, and the villages of Val de Sos and Auzat sprawled in the valley below. "Andos." Lucas nodded to the stone.

I followed suit, but as we neared, the far half of the dolmen appeared distorted and covered in a shadow that extended out along the mountain on either side. "What is it?"

"The umbra and the fissure it rises from are the start of the realms separating." Now he mentioned it, I could see the finger-width split running along the terrain beneath the shadow. Lucas shot Roux a glare. "A clear sign that Roux hasn't been doing his job. Considering the extent to which the umbra has grown, I'm surprised we've had nothing worse than two deaths."

Roux shrank back, his expression pained. Through breaths, he acknowledged the stone then turned to Lucas. "I'll repeat myself for the hundredth time, a slight umbra is not necessarily a bad thing. It usually takes more than that to release fettered fae."

Lucas scowled. "Doesn't look like it."

"I'll just get on with it, then, shall I?" Roux held out his hand.

Lucas pulled some linen bags from his sack and passed them to Roux. "How long since your last collude here?"

"Ummm, well..."

Lucas's scowl deepened. "If you don't get up here every morning, I'm going to eat you myself."

Roux muttered under his breath, his beard shaking.

Lucas followed the umbra along for a few steps, assessing it, then he paused and knelt down. "Damn it! Another patch."

Roux walked over and I joined him. Strange cracks radiated from the fissure where Lucas knelt. They were darker than the fissure itself—too dark—as though they were the absence of life. Just looking at them made me uneasy.

"The cracks appeared about two years ago at points here and there along the bounds," Roux said to me. "There's something wrong with the boundary."

"Something other than Roux not getting his scrawny ass up here to secure it." Lucas glowered at him.

"So the finer cracks aren't connected to the fissure or the umbra?" I asked.

Lucas shrugged. "When the bounds are secure, the fissure closes and the umbra disappears, but these cracks remain. I have no idea what they are, but I'm keeping my eye on them." He glanced up at the brightening sky. "We'd better make a start."

Roux and Lucas got to work scattering the contents of the small bags at points in the scrub around the dolmen. I leant back against the stone and watched, but unease crept through me at the proximity of the umbra, and I stepped away.

"We're using seven different herbs," Lucas called over. "Three with the earth element—blackberry, bryony and burdock—to represent the human realm. Three with the element of fire to signify fae—olive, rosemary and henbane. And for the binding, we use couteto, mother of the forest."

"Also known as honeysuckle." I'd learnt a bit of plant lore from local myths.

"A collude is a collaboration between a substance and a creature," he added. "The substance provides the power. The creature—fae or human—gives it direction. We use plants for the substance most of the time. Living plants or freshly cut work best, but dried will do. Minerals such as silver and gold help, but we shouldn't need that much oomph today."

"Herbs have value?" I asked. "Like in the boulangerie by the Keepers' post."

"Yep. Herbs and some minerals are the most valued things in Fae."

They finished emptying the bags, Roux rubbing his back and grumbling. Lucas beckoned me to a point just beyond the dolmen. I stepped across the fissured bound for the first time, passing through the umbra with a shudder. The air shimmered—I was in Fae. But like when we'd entered near Lucas's house, the surroundings remained the same.

"We've laid the herbs out in a seven-pointed star," Lucas said. "The points are marked by rocks. The geometry of the septagram lends power to the herbs, as do the location, the dolmen itself and the sunrise, although the sun itself won't appear above the ridge in the valley for a few minutes after we begin. Altogether, we have extremely potent conditions for a collude."

Lucas drew leaves from a larger bag and scattered them in a circle around us and the dolmen. "Most powerful of all the herbs, the alder leaf."

I gaped at him. "Never reveal the power of the alder leaf... It's an old saying. I thought no one knew what it meant."

A smile crept to his lips. "Now you know."

Roux came over, coughing. He was clearly exhausted from the activity, although I wondered how much of that had come from the scrapelather, and how much from whatever Lucas had forced down his throat. "Everything is in place." He glanced at the horizon, where orange and red streaked the sky. "It's time."

"Sure is," Lucas said.

Roux positioned himself on the opposite side of the dolmen, within the ring of alder leaves.

Lucas stepped behind me. "We'll do this together for the first time." He placed his hands on my shoulders, his touch solid. I jiggled, unsure if I was comfortable with it.

"Relax, Camille, it's just so I can show you the ropes."

I was damned curious about the collude. "I guess I can put up with your proximity for a minute."

He snorted. "So first of all, hold the geometry of the septagram in mind, then make a connection with each of the herbs at the seven points."

"I have absolutely no idea how." I'd studied magic, witch-craft and the likes within the remit of folklore, but I'd never even attempted a guided meditation.

"Sense the plants—link with them. Try the rosemary to the right of the dolmen."

I focussed in that direction, unsure what else to do.

"Good," he said. But I didn't feel anything. Was I supposed to? I shot a look at Roux. He was turning to each of the points, presumably doing something similar.

"Like this," Lucas said. Through his hands I could sense a tingle—maybe his life force—and it felt a little too intimate for comfort. It extended outward, meeting with the energy of the rosemary. "Let's try the olive in front of us."

I attempted to connect to the plant, but again, nothing happened until Lucas helped. We continued, creating links at the points of the septagram. Energy built until it thrummed around us, although I was pretty sure I wasn't any help at all.

Lucas squeezed my shoulders. "Finally, the alder leaves." Roux glanced at us and nodded. The two of them linked with the alder and the power quadrupled—most of it coming off whatever Roux was doing. Even though he shook and looked decidedly sick, I could see why he had the job. My jaw dropped as light rose from the circle and extended outward, delineating the septagram in shimmering gold.

"Now for the words," Lucas said. "Nothing fancy, just practical."

Roux raised his staff. "Fae and human realms, two halves

of the same inimitable sphere. One cannot exist without the other and so shall it always be."

"Alright," Lucas whispered in my ear, "Roux does tend to get a bit fancy, but it's really not necessary." I tried not to laugh.

"Superlative natures," Roux continued, "ethereal and material, diaphanous and structured, superlunary and corporeal... We bind—" He released another volley of coughs.

"Finish it," Lucas said to me. "Roux has already cast his intention—say something to complete the collude."

Through more coughing, Roux waved his hand in encouragement

"Really?" I asked.

"Give it a go."

"Uh..." I was completely not cut out for this, but hey, I could try. "We... bind... you...?"

The glow of the septagram expanded, mingling with the umbra, light and darkness vying for dominance. The light extended outward to envelope Fae to one side and the human realm to the other, a breathtaking aureole. I had the sense I hadn't done that—not in the least little bit—I'd just given the command from what Roux and Lucas had prepared.

But then the light dimmed and the umbra thickened. Inky silhouettes grew in its midst, expanding, darkening, solidifying. With unearthly screeching, a host of wraiths flew from the murk, tattered cloaks and hoods shrouding their forms—all apart from their bone hands, which extended out with long, curled claws.

Lucas released my shoulders. "That was not supposed to happen." He drew his blade.

I did the same, my heart thrashing. A wraith bore down on me from the side, its hood billowing. Underneath, its skull dripped with putrid flesh, eye sockets empty. Attempting to ignore the gagging in my throat, I swung my blade. But the edges of my vision grew dark, the mountain replaced by cold, rank, lifeless bodies. All I could see was death.

CHAPTER 18

Although I registered Lucas battling wraiths as I sank to my knees, I could see something else too... a pit... I was in a pit... surrounded by hideous corpses—rotting elves, broken goblins, torn sinagries. There were humans too, and other... things I didn't recognise. I scrambled, thrashing this way and that, but I couldn't stop myself sinking amidst the bodies. Blood and ichor smothered me as wraiths flew above. They shrieked as they circled, lit by an eerie light in the gloom. I slipped down further amidst the remains.

Fire ripped through my shoulder and the images vanished. Something had torn into me. I whipped around to a hideous, cackling wraith, its mouth open, its teeth rows of needles. I could only stare at its decaying flesh—decaying like the corpses in the pit.

Lucas dove to my side and sliced through the creature's neck, sending it convulsing to the dust in a spray of foul gore. I bent over and heaved. Lucas sprang around, protecting me.

Even though he was outnumbered and struggling, and Roux was flailing on the ground, I could only retch at the vestiges of the vision.

The wraith's screeching grew, the sound agonised rather than plain evil. I glanced up. A glimmer of light appeared to the side of a distant slope in the valley, casting a shard of brilliance across the dolmen. Radiance flooded the mountain as the sun rose, its rays effervescent—the golden glow of scintillating life. The wraiths writhed and struggled for the umbra, but their rotten flesh sizzled and crackled, and they disintegrated into nothing.

"Continue the ritual," Lucas yelled at Roux.

Roux stumbled up and repeated his invocation. This time, the light and force of the septagram joined with the sun. Power radiated out through the fae and human realms. The ground rumbled, and the umbra at the bounds disintegrated. The place felt different... whole. Even I could tell the bounds were secure.

Lucas rushed over and knelt down. "You okay?" He examined my ripped shoulder.

"Just about. It stings, nothing more." I noticed a heap on the other side of the dolmen. "But he's not."

Lucas hurried to Roux. I forced myself up and followed, attempting not to trip on tufts of grass and gorse as the remnants of nausea stole through me. The creatures had disintegrated, the dead ones included, but in my mind's eye, I was still in the pit.

"He's unconscious," Lucas said, checking Roux over. "He has flesh wounds, that's all. It's probably the scrapelather and the antidote combined with the exertion." He hauled him onto his shoulder once again.

I gathered Roux's staff and the sack, and followed Lucas across the bounds, the transition to the human realm now only notable by the slight change in atmosphere. As we headed down the mountainside, flickers of the pit strobed before me, and I couldn't stop shivering. What I'd seen—the bodies pressing in—it felt real... And the wraiths had been there too, circling above. "What were those... things?"

"Hantaumo," Lucas replied as he adjusted Roux.

"The fettered fae that Fickleturn mentioned?" After all, they'd come out of the umbra.

He nodded.

I winced as I adjusted the sack, pain streaking through my shoulder. "They looked like what Max saw—at least if the rumours are anything to go by."

"It all ties together," Lucas said. "The hantaumo escaped their fetters in dark Fae via the umbra. They can't survive in the human realm without life force, so they used Henri and Madame Bonnet..." We took a bend in the path. "Although that doesn't explain their initial vomiting and fever, it does make sense of the seizures and cardiac arrest."

"So how come we didn't see a hantaumo at Henri's?"

"It had finished feeding by then and had left him to die."

"And I guess Madame Dumas wouldn't have seen anything, being human... And Max being fae...?"

"Yep. Max must have caught sight of the one that killed Madame Bonnet, and he thought it would be fun to play with the story—creep everyone out."

"But what did the hantaumo do to get fettered?" I wasn't sure I wanted to know, but I couldn't bear not knowing.

"They went out of balance, that's what. Even though different types of fae butt heads on a regular basis, a general equilibrium is maintained. But when one race wants power and dominion over the rest, everything goes out of kilter. With the hantaumo's penchant for life force, most other fae were a tasty snack. They wiped out hundreds of thousands of fae, and humans were next on the list."

I shuddered. "But now the bounds are secure..."

He met my gaze. "Yes, we're good—well, fettered fae can't use the umbra to escape, at least. We can relax."

We walked on in silence, the events of the night swamping me. Henri's death had left me hollow, but I'd really not been able to handle the hantaumo attack, never mind the tesson and the rats. And the pit... what was that? It felt like a memory, but that was ridiculous.

I just hoped Lucas wouldn't ask about my flakiness because... because I didn't have an answer. One thing was for sure, like Wayland said—I needed to get a grip. I wasn't going to be forced on an emotional rollercoaster every time I saw a dead thing. And now that hell of a night was over, I needed to lighten things up. Either that or I'd crack.

I glanced at Lucas as I picked my way across some scree. "Is the job always like this?"

"I get the impression it usually involves snoozing at the Keepers' post," he replied, "but I've not managed to speak to the last Keeper about it."

"Well, you sure know how to show a girl a good time."

He grinned. "Yep. One hundred percent nonstop action."

I chuckled and my shoulder stung.

When we reached the parking area by the road, we laid Roux across the back seat of the SUV, then drove to Lucas's. After tucking Roux up in bed for what Lucas called "no-discussion cold turkey" and dosing him with something I hoped wasn't going to cause him any more distress, Lucas insisted on bathing and dressing my shoulder. For all his violence, his touch was tender.

I didn't have long to check on Grampi before work. Thanks to Lucas's potion I wasn't tired, which was a relief because I couldn't afford a day off. Lucas drove me back to the farm. The journey was silent, although I caught him glancing at me twice, his gaze assessing.

"I'll pop in and check on your grandfather," he said as we pulled up.

"I'd appreciate that." I made to get out of the car.

Lucas placed his hand on my arm. "Camille, what happened back there?"

"What? Back where?" But I knew he meant at the dolmen. In the corner of my eye, one of the goats strode across the yard, and the real world descended after hours of the unthinkable. "Oh, no!" I'd been so wrapped up in the night's events.

"What?" Lucas asked.

"The morning milking, that's what. I completely forgot about it. I've barely got time to do Grampi's breakfast, never mind the goats, and I can't be late for work." Alice was short-staffed today, and I didn't want to drop her in it, especially when I'd not made it in a couple of weeks ago after a party. I grabbed my blade and bag, climbed out and headed into the yard, mentally kicking myself for forgetting.

Lucas jumped out and followed. The goats were wandering slowly back to the mountain path. I'd expected them to be queuing around the barn door, waiting for the feed they gobbled during milking. Daisy stood nearby. I stepped over and rubbed behind her ears, glancing at her udder. It was flat, as though she'd been milked. "How—?"

"Almost done, ma'am." Slaughter popped up from nowhere with a salute. "We figured as you were out late doing Keeper business, you'd want the milking done." A few Men of Bédeilhac were scratching Daisy's, Lavender's and Hyacinth's backs, the goats' eyes half closed in contentment.

I stared at him then rushed to the barn, visions of my loft the other night flashing before me. Inside, the place was normal. The last goat, Marigold, was finishing her feed on the milking stand. Two Men of Bédeilhac tugged gently at her udder, a stream of milk flowing into the bucket.

Lucas peered in after me. "Good job, Men."

"Also, breakfast is done," Slaughter added. "The old guy was getting peckish."

"You fed him...?" I was unable to believe my ears.

"Yep. We kept out of sight." Slaughter adjusted his jerkin proudly. "Izak just thinks it all appeared out of thin air."

And that wasn't going to worry him? I rushed into the farmhouse and dropped my blade onto the kitchen counter. Nothing had been destroyed. I ran into the bedroom. Grampi was propped up in bed, looking perfectly calm and happy, and possibly a little better than last night.

I hugged him. "How are you doing?" The curse rot seemed to be at the same stage as when we'd left. That was something.

"The feed buckets need cleaning," he replied contentedly.

Lucas opened his bag and began checking Grampi's vitals. I stepped back, wrapping my necklace around my fingers. The remains of a croissant lay abandoned on a plate to Grampi's side, along with the dregs of a hot chocolate. I had to admit, I was impressed with the Men. Perhaps they weren't only a force of destruction, although I had no idea how Grampi hadn't been startled by his breakfast materialising from nowhere.

"Has he had his medication?" Lucas said quietly.

Slaughter emerged from under the bed, keeping out of Grampi's eyeline. "Of course, boss," he replied, then disappeared again.

"Rose has been in the brambles," Grampi said. "Thorns all over her."

"He's doing well." Lucas zipped up his bag. "Vitals are all good, and the other problem appears stable."

"That's good to hear." Carefully, I picked up Grampi's mouldy hand and rubbed it. "I'm late for work. I've got to go, but..."

Grampi looked me up and down, focussing on me properly for the first time since we arrived. His eyes grew wide. Had he noticed the outfit? But it was glamoured.

"The small water trough needs cleaning out." There was a hardness to his voice that hadn't been there before. "But it's not in the water trough." He shook his head vehemently, his eyes narrowed, almost pleading, then he sat up straight, the covers falling to his lap.

I studied him, trying to find meaning in his frustrated expression.

"It's not the water trough," he insisted. "You can't use that, or the broken feed bin." He got out of bed and grabbed my top, shaking me. "Don't touch it!" he yelled, jostling me harder and harder. "Leave it alone. The goats will be fine."

My breath stuck in my throat. It wasn't the shaking—I could handle that—it was the fervour behind it. Grampi was never like this. I tried to pull away, but he continued to shake me.

Lucas dove in and placed his palm firmly on Grampi's chest. "I think it would be a good idea if you rest for today, Monsieur Amiel. Get your strength up a bit."

Grampi shook me harder with surprising vigour, sweat beading on his brow. "Clean the feed bowls." He strained at his words, as though he was trying to alter them.

"It's alright." I kept my voice soothing, not knowing what else to do as the shaking undulated the room. "Everything's alright."

"Not the water trough, or Delphine won't like it," Grampi roared, his face red.

Lucas tried to pry his fingers off me. "What's going on?" he asked.

"I think he's trying to say something."

Lucas's prying worked and Grampi released me. I straightened my top and drew a breath. Grampi hobbled to the window and roared at the top of his lungs, over and over again, his body trembling, his eyes bulging. I swallowed.

"Camille, I think a sedative might be an idea."

Grampi's yelling continued. I nodded.

Lucas rummaged in his bag, pulled out a syringe and a potion vial and drew a measure. Before Grampi knew what was happening, Lucas grasped his arm and pressed the needle in. "I'm sorry, Monsieur Amiel," he said through the relentless bellowing as he withdrew the syringe. "But this might help."

Grampi's shouts diminished to a mutter. He lurched at Lucas, trying to grab him, then he slowed, the potion taking effect. As he stumbled forward, Lucas caught his arm. I took the other, and we guided him to the bed, then helped him lie down. By the time I'd tucked him up, he was at peace, staring into nothing.

We headed into the kitchen, and I met Lucas's gaze. "Was that the curse?"

"I don't think so. Those weren't typical symptoms."

"I'm sure he was trying to tell me something." And I hadn't a clue what.

Lucas peered at me for a moment then glanced at his watch. "I have patients to see very soon. I've only got a few minutes... and I know this isn't a good time, but, Camille, I need to know what happened earlier?"

I attempted to extract my thoughts from Grampi.

"The hantaumo," he added. "You froze when they

attacked. But it was more than that, wasn't it? You didn't just freeze, you zoned out. And the rat earlier, you did the same."

"I..." Blast it. He wasn't going to let this go. Yes, I had a problem, and in no way did I want to admit it to him. But what else could I do? I didn't want him thinking I had his back when that wasn't the case. It was time for the truth.

"I don't like death," I said stiffly. "Flesh, dead things, blood. I don't like seeing them and the thought of driving my blade..." Nope, I couldn't think about it.

He wiped his hands over his face. "So, let's get this straight. I have a partner who is apparently a superb swordswoman, who has one of Wayland's finest blades, but can't actually kill anything?"

"I'm sorting it out." I glared at him. "And what the hell does it matter? Because I'm not your damned partner."

Chapter 19

Releasing a lengthy breath, I straightened my top then adjusted my hair in the truck's rear-view mirror. I'd made it to work with a couple of minutes to spare, and I'd not had time to change, never mind shower. Wayland's clothes were extremely comfortable, though, and the glamour would conceal them.

I took a whiff of an armpit. Argh, not good. Tessons, rabid rats and hantaumo hadn't exactly left me smelling like roses. I'd grab a minute to freshen up. But what with Grampi's outburst, that was the least of my worries. We'd not found anything to help him last night. I'd intended to ask Roux about it after securing the bounds, but with him passing out, it hadn't been possible.

On top of all that, I needed to keep my job. I didn't want to put a strain on my friendship with Alice by being a bad employee, and the money was essential for the farm. Truth be told, I loved it at the café. It was by far the nicest environment I'd worked in since leaving school. It definitely beat the cashier job at Super U, although my colleagues had been lovely. And the cleaning job at Parc de la Préhistoire had been exhausting, especially in the summer. Not to mention that my argument with one of the guides about evidence for a prehistoric bear cult hadn't gone down well—he really needed to get his facts right.

Well, at least I had the Men of Bédeilhac to keep an eye on Grampi whilst I worked. Rummaging through my bag, I checked I had everything I'd need for the day, then paused. I had a troop of small prehistoric men who were invisible to the rest of the world looking after my grandfather, plus I'd spent the night in fairyland. It was taking some getting used to.

I jumped out of the truck, slinging my bag and my scabbarded blade over my good shoulder. The sword had to be priceless—I wasn't leaving it behind. And anyway, it was glamoured too.

Tiredness and burning hunger swamped me as I pushed open the café door—Lucas's potion was starting to wear off. Customers were tucking into their breakfast or nursing coffees. They glanced my way as I walked through to the counter, eyebrows raised and lips quirking, some of them gaping. I glared back. Yeah, I looked a mess, but they didn't have to stare.

Alice bustled out of the office and stopped short. "Have you heard about Henri?" Her face was ashen.

What could I say? That I'd witnessed his death just before I'd headed into Fae? Even being out with Lucas would take some explaining. "Yeah, I heard. He was such a great guy."

"I can't believe it. And everyone is talking about the possibility of a contagious disease causing his death—and Madame Bonnet's." She shuddered.

I wanted to say that the risk was over, but I couldn't.

"Sweetie." She peered at me. "What are you wearing? Fancy dress party?" She tugged at my top. "But damn, that outfit is well made. It's like the Chanel of warrior cosplay And those trousers... Girl, you look hot." She stepped to my side and peered at the hilt of the blade. "And that sword. It looks real."

Lucas, the sod. He'd tricked me. How was I going to explain this?

She nodded to the wadding covering my torn shoulder. The wound felt a lot better now due to one of Lucas's potions. "Obviously a wild night."

"Uh, something like that. Tell me you've got a change of clothing."

"As always. Help yourself." She headed over to take an order.

I went into the office to stash my things. As I closed the door, she called, "Next time, invite me."

I pulled out my phone, tapped on Lucas and texted, *You asshole. Where's the glamour on this getup?* He came back a second later with three rolling-on-the-side-laughing emojis, and then, *I never said your clothes were glamoured. Mine are, though.* Another laughing emoji, and a moment later, *Got you back for the tesson.* Tongue-sticking-out emoji.

How old did Wayland imply he was? Five? And the town trusted him with their lives. It really didn't bear thinking about. I put the phone face down on the desk. I wasn't going to encourage him by responding. Even so, the corners of my mouth tugged upward.

After freshening up in the bathroom, I went back to the office for the clothes. Alice was at the desk. "Don't go in the kitchen right now." She flicked through a pile of invoices.

"What's up?" I pulled jeans and a T-shirt out of the cupboard and stripped off the fae gear.

"Maman is interviewing. Apparently this guy is a really experienced viennoiserie chef." She looked up. "I seriously hope she hires him. She's been in so much pain lately."

"If he's experienced, he'll be expensive." I tugged on the jeans.

"I know," she said almost in a whisper. "I don't know what to do with her. One thing's for sure, she can't go on like this. I'm not going to watch her crying with pain at the end of every day."

"Oh, Alice." I hauled on the T-shirt, stepped over and hugged her. I hated to see her suffering because of Inès's high standards. I appreciated that Inès was an amazing chef, and that she wanted the same from her employees, but she couldn't maintain her current pace. "We'll sort something." I drew back. "I'm keeping my ears constantly open for someone suitable."

She forced a smile. "Time for a change of subject. Last night I had dinner with Raphaël." The sparkle returned to her face.

This was news. "Tell me everything."

"He's an estate agent…"

I couldn't help chuckling as I put on an apron and tied the bow. "I'm thinking he might not be your usual rebel with a cause."

"Don't laugh. He's very committed to his job. Oh, and he loves snowboarding, and he's so enthusiastic about everything—"

Inès came in. "He's gone," she said. "The interview is finished."

I could see by her frown that the news wasn't good. Alice could see it too, and her face fell.

Inès shuffled her feet. "The pain aux raisins were ever so slightly soggy in the middle, and the brioche didn't have that *je ne sais quoi.*"

———

What with my worries about Grampi, Alice's dark mood due to Inès's rejection of the latest viennoiserie candidate, and the whole café mourning for Henri, it wasn't the best of days. Not to mention that during quieter moments the images of the bodies in the pit forced their way into my head. At least I managed to get some food. I took an early break and wolfed down some of the viennoiserie that hadn't lived up to Inès's standards.

As the hours passed, thick exhaustion swamped me. I struggled to remember which buttons to press on the till as a smiling brunette waited patiently. Max joined her in the queue. Great.

"Don't take too long, Camille," he said as I put the order through for the second time. "A man needs a snack when he needs a snack. And a little waitress like you needs to be ready to give him one."

The brunette rolled her eyes.

Surely Max had heard about Henri's passing. But what did I expect, that the death of a friend would cause him a rare moment of introspection? Never.

I checked the amount. "That will be thirteen euros fifty cents." When I glanced back up, Max had shifted closer to the brunette and was peering sideways down her top. Despicable, odious creep. And... he was a troll. Was cross-species partnering even a thing? I thought of my night with Lucas and groaned to myself. The woman scanned her card, thanked me, then gathered her bags and left.

I glared at Max as I did his order. "Don't you think women deserve a little more respect?" It was a stupid question as the answer was all too clear, but I had to say something.

He paid, then narrowed his eyes and studied me as if I was the most ignorant thing that had ever been born. "Frankly, Camille, I'm surprised at you, questioning the actions of a man. This better not be troll prejudice again. It's a disgusting and biased practice." He stomped away, shaking his head.

Hmmm, the troll thing was obviously his sore spot. "I'm not questioning the actions of a man," I called after him. "I'm questioning the actions of a troll."

He turned and stared at me as though he wanted to say something, then he stormed out.

"Winding Max up?" Guy said as he steamed the milk.

"Yep." He held up his fist and we bumped.

I caught a glance from Félix in the D&D nook. The guys were looking hungry. There were no customers at the till for the moment, so I went over for their order. The girls were stationed in their usual place, mean giggles ringing out.

"Quest going alright?" I asked, shooting a glare at Nora and the gaggle, who hushed immediately.

"We're currently battling a hoard of evil girls," Gabe said. "Their hit power being the utter annihilation of confidence of anyone standing in their way. They're actually our most challenging foe yet."

I didn't quite get it. "You mean in real life or in the game?"

"Both," he replied. "Félix wrote them into the quest. They've already done untold damage to Hugo's thief with their Glare of Scorn."

I laughed.

"Yeah, but the guys are fighting back with a potent spell of Pretending They Don't Exist," Félix said, his leadership qualities coming to the fore.

"Way to go." And it really was. They were processing this hellish adolescent torment in their own way, and doing a damned fine job of it. "So, what can I get you?"

"The usual, please," Félix said. The guys all nodded.

I headed to the kitchen, skirting customers in the late-afternoon busy spell, then barely dodging Alice with a tray full of patisserie.

As I prepared the order, my limbs were hefty with weariness, my eyelids lead weights. With nothing else to distract me, my concerns about Grampi surged to the fore once again. I couldn't sit back and watch him deteriorate. I grabbed the chocolate sticks and wrapped them in brioche. It had only been yesterday that I'd caught the osencame with his hands on Gabe's order. So much had happened—not only my trip to Fae, but the massive paradigm shift I'd had to make.

But... the osencame—Mushum, wasn't it?—it had said it would give information in exchange for patisserie, and I needed information. Perhaps I could lure it back.

I opened the storage fridge, took out a pistachio macaron and broke a piece off, then I opened the window and placed the piece on the sill, leaving the rest on the worktop. That would do it. Now I just had to wait. The orders needed finishing, anyway.

I hauled the bowl of strawberries from the fridge, and when I turned back to the brioche, the little goblin was sitting in the window munching the piece of macaron, its eyes rolling with delight. "Thank you," it said, its bulbous eyes sincere, the wisps of hair on its head quivering slightly.

I eyed it... him... warily. After last night, this thing could be lethal, but it was worth the risk. "You said you could give me information."

"Ooooh, yes," he squealed. "Mushum knows lots and lots

of information and is happy to tell you whatever you want to know." He stepped in cautiously.

"Alright." I picked up the rest of the macaron. "I have questions, and if you give me answers, you can have the rest of this."

"Anything." Mushum goggled at the patisserie. "Ask anything."

"My grandfather, Izak Amiel, has a fae curse, and it's getting worse. I want to know what the cure is, or any other information you can give me about it."

Mushum grinned. "Just one moment." He vanished out the window, leaving me staring at the fae town, wondering what to do next. In a flash he was back. "Mushum knows everything he can find."

"Are you sure? I mean, you weren't gone that long."

"Mushum is very quick."

I thought of Slaughter's ability to appear in an instant. I had to go with this. "Alright. What do you have?"

"Mushum couldn't find out what will make the curse better or anything else like that, but Mushum knows there is a circle of maleficence around Izak Amiel, a maleficence so great it makes Mushum shudder... and it's growing."

Fae talked in riddles, right? "Can you be a little more specific?"

"Mushum is being very specific." His hands rose and circled in broad motions. "It's a big circle of maleficence. Don't you understand?"

"Circle of maleficence. Got it." This wasn't going any

further. I slid over the macaron. Mushum jumped with glee then guzzled it with very sharp teeth.

"Thank you," Mushum said. "My friend."

That was sweet.

"Come to Fae," he added through his mouthful, "and Mushum will help you find the source of the curse, if Mushum can."

Chapter 20

Back home, I hauled myself from the truck and shuffled to the farmhouse kitchen. It was a job to put one foot in front of the other, I was so tired. I had no idea how Grampi would be, and I needed to muster reserves to cook him something half decent for dinner.

The door was open, a delicious smell wafting out. I peered hesitantly inside.

"Good evening, ma'am." Slaughter popped up from behind a pile of boots. "Hope you don't mind, but we took the liberty of cooking Izak and yourself a little dinner. Blather, here"—another Man appeared wearing an apron over his prehistoric skins, his dark hair tied back—"is an ace chef. We thought after last night you might be tired. And the Men are all set to do the milking. It's still a bit early, but we'll be on to it as soon as the goats are ready."

I stepped into the kitchen, glancing around, the Men following. No mess. In the scullery, the washing-up was done. I guess I'd just caught the Men of Bédeilhac at their worst when they'd trashed my loft. They'd been directed by Lucas, of course. No doubt that explained it.

"We've plated the food up," Blather said. "You only need to take it in. His medicine is mixed with water in the glass."

"Uh, thanks," was all I could manage. I couldn't quite believe someone had cooked dinner for me. I picked up the tray that held a delicious-looking cassoulet and carried it in to Grampi. He was sitting up in bed watching Netflix. "It's the right foreleg," he muttered peacefully. "Very lame." He was back to the Grampi I was used to, and apart from the green on his arms, he looked normal. I placed the tray on his lap. "How's your day been? You feeling any better?" His eyes sparkled, a positive sign.

I took the glass from the tray and handed it to him. "Drink up. Doctor's orders."

He downed it in one and nodded. "But she had the best horns, that one."

Yep. He was good. I breathed a sigh of relief. This morning had completely unnerved me. "If you're okay, I have to go to bed. I didn't sleep at all last night, and now I can barely stand."

"A change of feed. That's what Daisy needs." My interpretation, "Get into bed before you fall down, girl."

I kissed him on the cheek. As I drew away he pulled me to him and kissed me back. A smile tugged at my lips. "Love you, Grampi," I said, and headed out.

The kitchen was empty, and actually it was spotlessly tidy—even cleaner than Grampi's usual standards. "Slaughter," I said. He sprang out from behind the central unit, accompanied by Blather. "Where do you go when you're not —" I raised my hand. "No, don't tell me, not right now. I'm too tired."

"Right-oh, ma'am," Slaughter replied. "We'll keep an eye on Izak overnight, and don't you worry about the morning milking or breakfast. The Men are on it. Oh, and your dinner is plated up."

I was sure the tray hadn't been there a moment before. More delicious cassoulet. I gazed at it, a surge of gratitude bubbling from deep within. Although Grampi wasn't much trouble, he'd been constantly on my mind for years. This was the first time anyone had given me more than a brief hand. A couple of neighbours helped out occasionally, like last night, but my parents certainly weren't bothered. Their opinion—if I wanted to live with a crazy old man, then I could handle the situation myself.

I crouched down. "Thank you, Slaughter. This means a lot to me—the cooking, the goats and keeping an eye on Grampi. And you too, Blather."

Blather went red and ducked under the counter. I bent down and kissed Slaughter, catching his forehead rather than his cheek as he was so low.

Slaughter blushed. "Uhhmm, well..." A huge grin extended from one side of his face to the other. "Never got one of them from Lucas."

I laughed. "Alright. I'm heading to bed." I picked up my tray and walked out, shutting the door. As I crossed the yard, I cast an eye over the goats that were ambling across the yard to the barn, ready for milking. They all looked healthy and happy.

A small pile of items sat outside my door—my cushions, my saucepan and some other bits the Men had broken the day before yesterday. On top of it all was *The Great Encyclopedia of Faeries*. They'd returned everything in mint condition. The little guys were Men of their word.

Upstairs in the loft, having hauled all my returned goods inside, I took a bite of cassoulet. It was utterly delicious. I'd thought I'd have to eat the chouquettes I'd brought home from the café for dinner—the choux pastry and the cream wasn't the healthiest of evening meals, but it sure beat cooking when I was this zonked.

After a couple of mouthfuls of cassoulet, I couldn't muster the strength to eat. I put it and the tub of chouquettes in the fridge and flopped onto the bed, Mushum's words ringing in my ears. "There is a circle of maleficence around Izak Amiel, a maleficence so great it makes Mushum shudder… and it's growing."

———

Something bounced on my stomach. I was in too much of a deep sleep to care. It bounced again. A rational part of my mind insisted that if something was bouncing on me, I ought to at least wake up and check it wasn't dangerous. I managed to open an eye. The room was dark, but even so I could make out the small, skin-clad form of old Wrench springing up and down on my abdomen.

He landed. "Glad you're awake, ma'am. Slaughter sent me. There's something wrong with Izak."

I sprang up, still dressed from the night before. We headed downstairs and over to the house. The Men had left lamps on here and there. I rushed through the kitchen and into the bedroom.

Grampi lay there sleeping softly. Slaughter stood on the bedside table. "It's worse, ma'am. Just happened a few minutes ago, right there as he slept."

The tips of his fingers were turning black, and tendrils of curse rot extended out the neck of his pyjamas. Without disturbing him, I pulled the covers down and unbuttoned his pyjama top. The curse rot crossed his chest in curls and spirals. I felt his forehead. He was burning up, and his breath rasped. "I don't like the look of it," I said as I buttoned Grampi back up.

"That's what I was thinking," Slaughter said.

I took out my phone, noting the early hour of the morning, and dialled Lucas.

He picked up after one ring. Did that man—drac—sleep? "Camille. Found something else to wear?"

"It's Grampi." The urgency was clear in my voice.

"What's wrong?"

"The curse rot has spread, the tendrils are covering his trunk, his fingertips are black and he's feverish."

He was silent for a moment, then, "That's the usual progression, but it's happening so quickly. Is he comfortable?"

"He's sleeping peacefully but his breath is a little laboured."

"Alright. The potion I started last night is getting there. It needs another two hours. I have to finish it, but I'll bring it over as soon as it's ready. There's nothing else we can do in the meantime." There was a clatter on the other end of the line. Lucas was obviously busy, but there was something I wanted to ask him.

"I spoke to an osencame at the café today. He said a circle of maleficence is surrounding Grampi."

He chuckled. "Give it a mille-feuille, did you?"

"Macaron, actually."

"Look, Camille, they're tricksters, and they'll do anything for cake. I wouldn't take what he said too seriously."

My stomach sank. Had Mushum made it all up?

"The other thing is," he continued, "fae minds don't work like humans'. Their perception isn't the same. A circle of maleficence might mean a hundred different things with vague, metaphoric relationships to reality. You won't get much out of him."

"Well, after everything we went through last night, we didn't get anything about the curse, and now Grampi's worse." I couldn't keep the shrill edge from my voice.

"Look, just wait for me. I'll be over soon, then we'll discuss our next move. I've got to go. I need to alter the heat on the potion."

I tucked the phone into my pocket and paced about the room. I hated being so impotent. Eventually, not knowing what else to do, I kicked off my shoes, slipped into the other side of the bed and curled up against Grampi, just as I'd done when I was little. I nestled into his furnace body, breathing in that comforting smell as I twisted my necklace between my fingers—the necklace he'd given me on my thirteenth birthday. He'd said, "No matter what happens, no matter what the future holds, I'll always love you, chérie. Be certain of that." His words had felt weighty. I remembered wondering at them all those years ago. Then he'd gone away for a while—something connected to his past military service—and when he came back, he had the goat-speak. Despite my best efforts, the lack of conversation formed a fathomless void between us. The necklace reminded me of who he'd been—of who I knew still existed inside. But maybe I had to admit to myself that Grampi was old. He was an octogenarian and he wouldn't live forever. My chest hollowed at the thought.

But the longer I lay there, the more restless I became. I could see Mushum's sincere face, his bulging eyes. He'd been so proud of himself, bringing me information and receiving his macaron reward. He'd said to visit him in Fae, and he'd help find the source of the curse. Perhaps he was a trickster—although Lucas appeared to be ten times the trickster than that little goblin—but what if Mushum wasn't playing games?

I turned over the idea for a while, Grampi's burning heat making me way too hot and bothered. Nope, I couldn't lie next to him when there was a chance I might be able to help. And I had an idea.

Ever so gently, I slipped out of bed. "Will you keep an eye on him?" I asked, certain Slaughter was somewhere near.

"Of course." His voice came from under the bed. "We'll be right here the whole night long."

CHAPTER 21

I HEADED UP THE TRACK BEHIND THE FARM DRESSED IN my Keeper gear, my blade on my back, the tub of chouquettes in my pouch. My mobile lit the path, dark trees looming on either side. The undergrowth rustled—no doubt a badger or a fox. Wolves and bears were rare, but they came to mind anyway, the hair on my arms standing up.

The light caught on long curling horns and an upright goat's body before the creature disappeared into the bushes. Only Aherbelste again, goat god and Christian personification of the devil and all evil. Nothing to worry about at all. Walk in the park.

Up I went, until the flank of Picou de Bompas sloped steeply and the path narrowed to not much more than a goat track. I broke through the tree-line to sparse higher ground.

I'd noted a change in the air up here numerous times over the years when I'd been out running or checking the goats. I even remembered sensing it as a child, but I'd always put it down to the weather or a trick of the eyes. It was the same change I'd observed at the dolmen and above Lucas's house. Lucas said the bounds could be found on most mountains and remote places in the Pyrenees, which meant I'd crossed into Fae so many times before without knowing.

Of course, yesterday's craziness had shown me that Fae was not a safe place, and I'd be a fool to wander in alone with so little knowledge. Plus, there were countless stories of folk getting lost there forever. But there was a way I could enter and stay completely safe.

A few steps further, and there it was, that slight shift in atmosphere, the air shimmering a little. I'd entered Fae.

My phone light went out and I cursed. I hadn't thought about my mobile not working, but the moon shone bright above, almost full, illuminating the mountainside with a mysterious tinge. I could see well enough, and anyway, I wasn't planning on going far. Mushum had said to come to Fae and he would help. Well, I was in Fae—not very far inside, but inside nonetheless. I'd keep a firm eye on the path back down the mountain. I wasn't going to take stupid risks, but this small venture would be worth it if I could find out anything that might help Grampi.

I undid my pouch, tucked away my mobile and pulled out the tub. As I snapped off the lid, the faint scent of choux pastry and sugar wafted out. "Mushum," I called, my voice much too loud in the night. I searched the mountainside for him, scanning the trees further down and the open, rocky slopes above. Nothing. Just mountainside.

A movement disturbed the bushes below, near the path. I

peered through the gloom. A dark shape slunk from the trees, its form wolflike but bigger, much bigger. Over the curve of the summit, four shapes appeared, bodies canine, heads low, hackles raised.

I drew my blade, my chest tightening. This had been a stupid idea. But, come on, I'd been up here loads of times, even at night, without beasts around. Although perhaps I hadn't been able to see them. Even so, nothing had happened to me then—which would mean these critters were harmless.

They prowled closer, moonlight glinting on black fur, lips curled against shining teeth, large goops of saliva dripping from their maws. They were sinagries, spectral hounds and omens of death. Great.

Assessing my possibilities, I turned around. Three more approached along the flank of the foothill, and five from behind. My path back down was blocked, and if I ran, they would pursue.

They circled in close, eyes gleaming, growls rumbling from powerful chests. I cut my blade through the air as a warning. If they attacked, I would have to defend myself. An image of their spilled guts flashed before me, and I attempted to ignore the nausea in the pit of my stomach.

"Mushum," I tried again. I couldn't see how a small goblin could help against this lot, but I didn't have many options. Sweat beaded on my brow as I searched about. There was no sign of him, and I was all out of ideas. It just didn't make sense that it was so dangerous here now, when it had been perfectly fine before.

A sinagrie on higher ground snuck forward. I lunged at it,

not wanting to strike and feel my blade slice its flesh. It shuffled back, as did the one next to it. I spun around to check my back. The sinagries held their circle.

The beast to my side crept toward me. "Get back, you mangy, flea-bitten bag of dogwood." I lunged again, the chouquettes jiggling in my other hand. I needed to stow them in my pouch—they were my chance at finding Mushum and helping Grampi—but I couldn't risk the distraction.

Another sinagrie stole closer. I slashed my blade, stepping forward, and it sprang away. The beasts shifted to maintain a perfect ring of teeth and claws around me. Strange. I'd expected them to close in and attack.

Taking an experimental step, I thrust my blade at the nearest set of pearly whites. It snarled and reversed, as did the rest of them, holding formation. "Ah, so poor Fido doesn't want his nose scratched?" I took another step and then another. They shifted together again. Their formation was rattling me, but perhaps I could use it to my advantage. If they held position until I was out of Fae, they might not follow me over the bounds.

I edged toward the sinagrie that stood in the path. It sidled back and the circle shifted with it. That worked. I took one more step—the sinagries moved again. Cautiously, I walked along the path. The mutt circle held, ringing me as I descended. I had no idea why they weren't attacking.

The atmosphere changed as I entered the human realm, but the beasts continued to surround me. Panic gripped my chest. I knew I shouldn't run, but this wasn't exactly an everyday hike-in-the-Pyrenees situation—they were omens of death. One dove forward, snapping. It was all the incentive I needed. I charged down the hillside, patisserie rolling around in the tub. It was completely the wrong thing to do, but to hell with it—I needed to get out of there.

The sinagries broke array, unable to fence me in at speed on the narrow path. Instead, they drew into a tight knot and followed in a lope that was the hellhound version of a little jog, their growls morphing to snarls. Why hadn't they taken me down? Were they biding their time, watching and tracking like wolves? The thought did nothing to slow my thrashing heart. But even if they were playing with me, they didn't know where I lived. If I could just make it back to the farm, I could get to safety. I had to try.

Another shot forward and gnashed. I screamed and surged onward, faster than I'd ever run. That was until something small and leathery hurtled into me. I bowled over and over, tumbling down the slope before settling into a bruised heap, dirt filling my mouth. I'd managed to hold on to my blade, but the patisserie was long gone.

Wary that I was vulnerable on the ground, I lifted my head and peeked about. It was darker amidst the trees, but I could make out the lump that had tripped me sitting in the grass nearby. Mushum's eyes were closed in ecstasy as he chewed a chouquette. Further back on the moonlit path, the sinagries were scuffling in the earth around the abandoned tub, gobbling the patisserie. One of them, not finding any more, swayed contentedly then rolled onto its back, its legs in the air, its tongue lolling out. Another nuzzled it, then sprang to the side in a play pounce. Realising my dirt-filled mouth was open, I spat out the earth and whatever else had ended up in there.

Mushum shook with laughter. "Mushum never saw anything quite so funny as Camille running down the mountain with a tub of chouquettes, a pack of sinagries following." He fell onto his side, he was laughing so hard.

I eyed the sinagries cautiously, but having eaten their fill, they appeared content, some of them slinking back into the bushes. "I fail to see what's funny in being chased by a load of death omens," I growled.

He managed to gain control of himself and sat up, tittering. "What does Camille expect if she goes into Fae and wafts cream cakes around?"

My jaw sank. Cream... Fae couldn't get enough of the stuff. It was common folklore—most kids knew it from fairy tales. I flopped back into the grass. How could I have been so stupid? The sinagries hadn't wanted me—if they had, I wouldn't have stood a chance—they'd wanted the damned chouquettes.

"What was Camille doing in Fae with patisserie anyway?" He giggled again.

"You," I said. "I went there to find you. To bring you the chouquettes."

His giggles ceased. "Camille brought cake especially for Mushum?" Tears beaded at the corners of his eyes. I shifted. The chouquettes hadn't exactly been a gift. "I... uh... You said if I came to Fae you could help me find information on my grandfather's curse. I thought the cake might bring you to me—"

"Camille brought cake for Mushum!" he cried. "Mushum would've found Camille anyway, but Camille thought Mushum would like some nice chouquettes." Well, if he put it like that... An almost pitiful gratitude filled his gaze. He really was a sweet thing.

I brushed off the mud and dust that covered me, then adjusted my scabbard into position and sheathed my sword. "So you'll help?"

He sprang up. "Of course Mushum will help. Mushum will always help." His tiny hand clasped mine and he attempted to pull me. I clambered up and followed him back toward Fae.

CHAPTER 22

"I DON'T WANT TO GO ANYWHERE DANGEROUS," I SAID AS Mushum led me into Fae, the atmosphere changing. "No murderous creatures with big teeth, no getting lost, nothing like that." After the sinagries on top of everything else, the idea of going into Fae was even less appealing. I wasn't yet certain how hazardous the place was, but I had so little practical knowledge, I was liable to make another stupid blunder, although there was no way I could refuse Mushum's invitation.

"Of course," Mushum replied. "Mushum knows someone who can help Camille with her grandfather, and Mushum will show the way so Camille can return home easily."

He led me over the apex of the foothill, past a small menhir that looked pretty similar to the other stones scattered about. "Andos," he squeaked.

I followed his example, and as we headed onward, our

surroundings changed. It was day, and snow swirled across the shallow valley before us, drifts thick on the ground. Mushum tugged at my trouser leg. "Come on. Camille will get cold if we hang around in this."

My boots and trousers were already soaked and glacial. He ran ahead down a track that descended into the valley. I jogged to keep up. At the bottom, by a frozen, winding river, stood a stone cottage, its roof and windowsills iced like a cake, smoke rising from the chimney.

"Here we are," Mushum said. "Hurry, hurry." He ran into the garden. I turned back to trace the track so I could find my way home. Even with the snow, I could still make out the path up the hill. Satisfied, I followed Mushum to the door.

It opened at our approach and an elderly woman beamed out. "Hurry in, dears. Come and get warm." She met my gaze and smiled, and that smile was radiant, welcoming, like a cosy fire in winter or a warm duvet on a comfy bed. All of her was round and homely, her white hair whirled into a bun, her blue eyes sparkling and keen. She wore an ankle-length dress with an apron, a knitted shawl over her shoulders.

"Blanche!" Mushum squealed, and wrapped his scrawny arms around her legs. She picked him up and nestled him in the crook of her arm. "Dear Mushum. Good to see you. No doubt back for a little more brioche? I managed to get some of that superb flour from the mill outside Tarascon, and this batch really is quite toothsome."

He snuggled into her like the happiest goblin in the world. I followed them into a large, cosy kitchen, an old iron range burning at one end, the heat radiating through the place. Above, brilliant white sheets hung in the rafters. I breathed in the aroma of freshly laundered washing, Marseille soap verte, a touch of wood smoke and something heavenly baking in the oven. All in all, it smelt of home. A small feather drifted in the air.

"Camille Amile," she said, "lovely to meet you. Mushum has told me all about you."

I smiled, hoping he'd communicated the part where I'd fed him patisserie rather than the part where I'd grabbed him and chucked him out the café. "Blanche, pleased to meet you too." And then I realised what I'd said—Blanche. With snow tumbling at the window and washing hanging above... could it be? "Dame Blanche?" I ventured.

She beamed at me. "The one and the same."

Dame Blanche, Mother Holle, Mother Hulda, Mother Frost, a form of the mother goddess herself. I didn't know whether to get down on my knees or to... well, I had no idea what to do.

Her lips pursed at my hesitation. "Come. You must need refreshment. Have a seat." She carried Mushum to the table, placed him on a chair and pulled one out for me. Trying not to stare, and not succeeding very well, I sat down. She did the same.

I still couldn't believe it. *The* Dame Blanche. I was fangirling harder than I had for Wayland. Hell, I was in the presence of the personification of the earth itself—at least one of its aspects—and the cat well and truly had my tongue.

Tea things stood on the table, a loaf of brioche in the

centre. Dame Blanche poured tea into old china cups and passed them out, then sliced into the brioche.

"With Blanche," Mushum whispered to me, "Camille must ask the right questions." He slurped his tea. What questions? I couldn't even think what to say.

"Drink up, my dear. You look weary," Blanche said.

I studied the amber liquid in my cup. I did feel weary. Not just from the past few days, but from before, from the years of being there for Grampi, for the years of trying and trying again to make something of my folklore research. All I wanted to do was curl up in the corner of this cosy cottage and fall asleep, forgetting it all. But I couldn't do that, so I gathered myself and added a squeeze of lemon to my tea. Lucas had said it was safe to have fae food and drink most of the time. I had no idea what "most" meant, but this was Dame Blanche. How could I refuse?

I clasped the china in my hands and took a hesitant sip. Warmth flooded through my body, not only the warmth of the tea itself, but a safe, snuggly feeling, as though Dame Blanche had wrapped her arms around me. Contentment eased through my limbs, my inhibitions falling away. I sighed and met her gaze. "Thank you. It's delicious."

She nodded. "Well, Camille, it's good to have you here. I believe you're our new Keeper." She plated up slices of brioche and handed them around.

"Yes... I mean no..." I took a breath. "There have been a lot of new experiences and I've not decided yet." And although I'd been glad to help Lucas sort out the bounds—not that I'd been of much use—all I wanted to do now was help Grampi.

"The human and fae realms are necessary parts of each other. Keeper of the Bounds is an honourable and indispensable role. There are those who would wish the realms to separate for their own dark purposes, but that would only lead to destruction." She adjusted her shawl. "You have the full support of myself and others. The folklore research you've compiled makes you perfect for the task."

I was getting used to deities knowing everything about me. "Actually, I'm beginning to think my research is a waste of time," I said. "Compiling snippets of folklore from here and there seems pretty redundant in the face of all this." I gazed about the cottage and through the window to the snowy garden. The whole of Fae lay beyond.

She shook her head. "Not so, Camille. The stories you collect are more important than you know. Tales of fae help humanity remember the other parts of themselves—help them remember us."

I certainly hadn't thought of it like that. "But it's just that the fae realm is so much more than tales like *Jean de l'Ours* and *The Belle de Balandraou.*"

"Every little helps." Her soft smile grew, a dimple forming in her cheek. "And if those stories are all humanity can accept at this time, well, that's everything."

I made to bite into the brioche, then paused. That baguette yesterday hadn't been good, and like the goblin boulanger, Dame Blanche had said she'd used human ingredients. I took a nibble. The buttery crumb was light as a feather. It tasted of oranges and vanilla... of gatherings with friends... of old traditions that held deep meaning. It was something else, and in truth, it was the best brioche I'd ever tasted—even better than Inès's. I took another mouthful.

She inclined her head. "It's acceptable?"

"Utterly delicious," I mumbled through chews.

"Good." She sat back, her hands on her lap. "Now, my dears, do tell me what brings you to my hearth."

"It's Camille's grandfather," Mushum said before I had time to swallow. "Got a curse."

I nodded. "Do you have any information on it at all? He's going downhill—"

"That's not the right question," Mushum whispered.

I had no idea what he meant.

"I may be able to help you," she replied. "I believe the solution lies in what troubles you most." She took a bite of her brioche.

Mushum chuckled. "See. Ask the wrong questions, get unhelpful answers."

Definitely unhelpful. "I don't mean any disrespect, but could you be a little clearer? Only Wayland said the same thing, and I can't see how it's linked to Grampi."

Her lips quirked. "I understand, Camille. But all Wayland and our kind can do is assist in revealing what you already know."

I frowned. That was so like the fae riddles of old. "I could be wrong, and I've been wrong many times concerning fae, but I'm guessing you and Wayland, as deities, know pretty much all there is to know. So couldn't you just tell me what's going on?"

A feather drifted down between us. "We have vast realms of knowledge," she said, "but where to begin and where to end? When to help and when to remain silent? If humans, or most fae for that matter, could know anything they wanted, or have a deific boon whenever they desired, they would destroy themselves with greed and lust for power." She sipped her tea. "We limit ourselves in that regard for the benefit of all, but we can always assist in the revelation of what an individual already knows."

That made sense, so then... "What's troubling me is my overreaction to blood and dead things. I suppose on some level, a part of me must know what caused it."

Her eyes sparkled. "Now you're getting the idea."

"Then..." And here it was, the burning question. "Can you help me find the cause of my reactions?"

"She asked it right! She asked it right!" Mushum cried, springing about.

Dame Blanche placed her cup down. "Now, *that* I can help you with. But, Camille, take a moment to consider, are you prepared to confront such a thing?"

Dead rats, slain hantaumo and rotting corpses flickered through my head. I shuddered. But if the cure to Grampi's curse was connected, I had no choice. I fixed her in the eye. "I'm ready."

CHAPTER 23

DAME BLANCHE ROSE AND CARRIED HER CHAIR TO THE hearth. A couple of eiderdowns hung above. She climbed up, sprightly despite her apparent age, and pulled one down. Grasping the end firmly in both hands, she shook it. Pure white down filled the air, spiralling like snow, twisting and turning, spinning and whirling...

I sat in the grass on the edge of the farmyard. The trees, the buildings, everything loomed above me as though I'd shrunk. I peered at my pudgy hands, a dandelion clasped in my fingers. I hadn't shrunk, I was young. I don't know how young, but I had the sense I didn't have many words. I also had the feeling that Maman was somewhere close by. Perhaps she'd popped back into the farmhouse for a moment.

My toes curled amidst the grass, the blades tickling my feet. I followed a shiny brown beetle climbing a stalk until a dark shadow fell across the ground. Hands seized me around the middle—sharp, pointy hands—and I rose into the sky. My stomach dropped away with the motion, and something flooded through me that I'd not experienced before—a dark and deathly fear. Instinctively, I knew I was in terrible danger.

Then it was later. Everything looked different, the trees dead, a pale, eerie glow all about, but I was still clutched by the same claws and the same fear. I forced myself to look up at the thing that carried me. A cloak hid its body, a hood concealed its face. Then its head shifted, revealing a skull hung with rotting flesh. It opened its mouth and screeched, displaying hundreds of needle teeth, its breath the stench of a decomposing fox I'd once found under the trees. I cried out, but the creature gripped me tighter, its claws piercing my skin. I couldn't think, couldn't see, couldn't listen—the thing that held me was too hideous, the sense of malice over-whelming.

The claws released me. I plummeted and hit the ground, breath rushing from my chest. All I could do was gasp, not only from the fall, but from desperate panic. Eventually, I looked up. There were more creatures swarming in the air above, but they'd been distracted by something—a woman with dark curly hair stood at the other end of the clearing, a sword in her hand. They attacked and she cut a couple down, driving the rest into a frenzy. There was a man there too, fighting, his back to me so I couldn't see his face. Somehow, I knew them, and I wanted them to take me away from the horror—I wanted Maman, and I wanted this nightmare to end. But my whole existence was slashing and gore and death as swords tore flesh and unearthly shrieking rent the air.

One of the creatures snatched me up. We flew away, further and further from the man and the woman. I fell again and landed with a thump on something soft and sticky, the stench like that fox. I bent my head. All around me were bodies, faces, limbs. They were different to people—similar, but not exactly the same—some with pointed ears, some with eyes that were too round or arms that were too scrawny, but all of them torn and rotting, lifeless and stinking, eyeballs split open, skulls maggot-ridden. I screamed and screamed and screamed.

All the time the hideous creatures flew over me, their tattered cloaks flapping. But then something else rose up, hovering above, something so dark, so terrifying that I couldn't acknowledge it. The adult part of me tried to see, but the child wouldn't allow it—I wouldn't allow myself. All I could do was tremble, my eyes screwed tight against the horror.

When I opened them, snowy down twisted this way and that. I lay on a warm bed, bright, hazy light all about. Dame Blanche perched beside me, smiling.

I sat up. The terror of the pit clamped my throat and I fought not to vomit.

"Well done, Camille," she said, her voice mellow, easing away the nausea. She took my clammy hand and pressed something into my palm, closing my fist around it. When she drew back, I opened my fingers to reveal a golden alder leaf. It was stunning—exquisitely crafted and detailed down to the smallest veins and grooves. Worth a fortune, no doubt. I looked up in askance, unsure why she'd given it to me.

"A gift." Her brow rose in encouragement.

It would help pay the bills, for sure. I tried to express my thanks, but after what I'd seen, words wouldn't come. She raised a finger to her lips, indicating that speech wasn't necessary. I tucked the leaf safely into the bottom of my pouch, then everything went black.

———

To and fro. To and fro.

Strong arms supported me as I rocked, secure arms that wouldn't let me go. My cheek lay against a sturdy chest. The scent... rosemary and cedar, dark and fickle yet welcoming... warm. I breathed it in, knowing I was completely safe, knowing I had nothing to worry about with this... this...

I forced my eyes open and made out a broad, straight mouth. Above, a shrewd gaze studied me with concern—a goat-eating, hideous, duplicitous, shrewd gaze. I twisted and struggled.

"You've been unconscious," Lucas said, attempting to hold on to me. "Give yourself time to adjust."

"I don't need to adjust anywhere near you." I struggled some more.

"Alright, alright." He placed me down. My knees buckled and I fell to the ground. "Yep. Thought so," he said.

The world spun as I pushed myself up to sitting. "What

happened?" We were on the path near the farm, the sky above Picou de Bompas streaked with early-morning orange.

He dropped into a crouch, level with me. "What happened was you didn't have the sense to ask me to go into Fae with you." His voice grated with anger.

The hillside had almost stopped revolving. I peered at Lucas. Irritation lined his face, and something more. Worry, perhaps. "Since when do I have to ask you before doing anything? And anyway, I was trying to help Grampi."

"So how come I found you unconscious in a heap just over the bounds?"

I couldn't answer that. "I went into Fae for Mushum's help. And Dame Blanche..." I tried to piece it all together, but it swirled about like feathers.

"Dame Blanche—how the hell did you get there? And didn't you worry about getting back?" His voice rose.

"I had it all under control."

"Come on, Camille. You've seen how dangerous Fae is. You can't go running in without assistance. What the fuck were you thinking?" He rose and scraped his hands through his hair. "You're vulnerable... you've had no training. It's my damned fault—it's my duty to show you the ropes, but with everything kicking off, there's not been time—"

"I'm not your charge, Lucas," I snapped, wishing he'd be quiet so I could grasp what had happened after Dame Blanche had shaken the eiderdown. He was right, of course. I'd almost gotten myself eaten by sinagries. But... "You gave me the verity, and now I can access Fae. It's your problem if you don't like what I do with it."

He was silent, his gaze lit with fury. Then he appeared to remember something. "I have to get back. Right now. Either you walk or I carry you." He wasn't going to carry me, that was for sure. I rose and the ground swayed. Lucas offered an arm. I ignored it and we set off down the path.

With every step I grew steadier, returning to myself. Glimmers of corpses appeared in my mind's eye. I was sure I'd seen the pit again at Dame Blanche's. But there was something else playing on my mind. "Did you see Grampi?" I asked.

"Yep. I've given him the new potion. The curse rot is stable, and when I left, he was dozing contentedly."

I barely heard his words as the pit, the bodies, the smell, everything I'd experienced flooded back. My breath grew shallow as the gory details unravelled. What I'd seen *had* been a memory. I'd been to Fae before, and it had been bad— so bad. It wasn't difficult to see where my revulsion of blood and death had come from, but the revulsion was just the surface. Underneath lay the terror of my young mind confronted with more than most adults could handle in a lifetime. But what was it I hadn't allowed myself to see? I had the unnerving feeling that it was the most horrific thing of all.

"Camille?" Lucas's brow knitted. "What's going on?"

I'd zoned out. "Hantaumo," was all I could think to say.

"What?"

I needed to explain properly "I was in Fae."

"I'm well aware of that."

"No. Not now. Years ago, when I was small. The hantaumo kidnapped me. My reaction to death started then, which according to Wayland and Dame Blanche is related to Grampi, so maybe the curse and the hantaumo are connected in some way."

He studied me, anger replaced by curiosity. The sun rose to the side of the foothill, the luminous glow bathing the slope. "Alright, perhaps it's a lead. But, Camille, in the past few hours I've had five calls from town residents saying they have the early stages of what killed Henri and Madame Bonnet. I've adjusted the original potion to take into account the hantaumo involvement. It won't be ready until later today, though I'm hoping it will slow things once I can get it to the sick."

My lips parted. "What? But the bounds are secure."

"Yes... no..." For the first time he looked tired, his eyes shadowed in the dawn light. "The bounds are secure, and I was wrong. The hantaumo didn't escape through the umbra. Which means they must have help from someone in the human realm."

"Who?" Stupid question. If he knew, no doubt he would've torn them to pieces already. But how many humans even knew the hantaumo existed, never mind had the where-withal to help them? The culprit had to be fae.

He dragged a palm over his chin. "At this point, I'm at a complete loss. I don't know the town—I've lived here for a total of three weeks—and I've run out of leads."

Not to mention, I wasn't of much use with my academic knowledge of fae. But there was someone who knew the ropes better than either of us. "Roux," I said. "Perhaps he can help."

CHAPTER 24

"Curious, curious," Roux said as we finished updating him. He adjusted his not-too-moth-eaten cloak and smoothed his beard. With the support of Lucas's rehab potion, he seemed to be doing alright—well, he was sober at least, and his hands only trembled a little. He'd even fortified the bounds at dawn before making his way to the Keepers' post. "It wasn't the umbra allowing the hantaumo through," he muttered, clearly relieved not to have Henri's and Madame Bonnet's deaths on his hands.

"Although they were definitely taking advantage of it," Lucas replied. "Otherwise we wouldn't have been attacked yesterday. But people are getting ill, so I have to admit, it's likely they're using another method to breach their fetters."

"They want to manifest in the human realm." Roux poured coffee from the jug into three earthenware mugs and passed them around. "That's why they used Henri and

Madame Bonnet—they couldn't survive here without life force. And if they didn't use the umbra, then someone in the human realm is helping them."

"My thoughts exactly." Lucas dug his thumbnail into the table. "But how? It's not exactly easy to release fettered fae from their bonds."

I pulled my mobile from the pocket in my Keeper trousers and glanced at the time. I had a couple of hours until work, although that was inconsequential compared to the safety of the townsfolk. Roux sat up straight, sloshing the coffee, then dove through one of the side doors with surprising speed, revealing a book-lined room.

He came back with a tome and slammed it onto the table, clattering the coffee things. "One of the Keepers' journals." He flicked through the pages and settled on one. "1793, there was a case of a hantaumo being evoked in a ritual by a group of unsuspecting teen girls. That night, a hantaumo took possession of one and drained her life force. She died a few hours later. If I remember rightly, there have been a few similar cases recorded over the years."

"So perhaps someone is playing with magic," Lucas said. "It must have been the ritual that created the initial link between the girl and the hantaumo. But I can't imagine Henri or Madame Bonnet were up to anything like that. And although the hantaumo involvement explains their seizures and cardiac arrest, it doesn't explain the early stages of the sickness—the vomiting and fever hours before."

"Well, what does explain the early symptoms?" I asked.

He shrugged. "A potion, maybe. A potion is basically a portable collude... a ritual in a bottle. It would be hellishly difficult to make, but prepared in the right way, it could link victims with the hantaumo, and it would account for the symptoms."

"And me being kidnapped by the hantaumo as a child?" I said, looking between them. "Could that be linked?"

"First I've heard of it," Roux replied. "I have absolutely no idea."

Lucas's phone chimed, the ringtone out of place in the medieval surroundings. "Hello, Monsieur—" He spelled out instructions that by the sound of it were becoming automatic —keep the patient cool, ensure fluid intake, he would be along as soon as possible. Roux sucked his cheek and shook his head. I took a long swig of coffee.

Lucas hung up and tapped on his phone. "That makes eight. All in Tarascon."

"No prizes for guessing where the hantaumo want to party," I said.

He scrolled down the screen. "I've collected details of who the sick have been in contact with, although the list is far from complete. No particular individual stands out. René Thierry has been out and about doing mayoral canvassing to raise public opinion of... himself. He's been in contact with a few of them, which is suspicious, but then I get the impression he tends to knock on doors rather a lot."

"Completely typical for him." He couldn't help himself.

"Then there are a few other people," he continued. "A

nurse has been around to two of the elderly. One of those plus a middle-aged woman took a taxi with Max. All eight have been into town for shopping or other reasons, and there's no one place they all visited. I can't see a connection."

"I have questions," I said.

Lucas placed his phone on the table. "Shoot."

"Firstly I'm guessing going into the dark lands to fight the hantaumo or re-fetter them is out of the question."

Roux almost fell off his stool. He straightened up and tittered to himself.

"Combat in the dark lands would be certain death." Lucas's lip twitched. "And their fetters are extremely powerful colludes that for the most part are still in place, or believe me, the whole of Fae would know about it. The problem is, no collude is completely infallible—loopholes are possible. The umbra, for example, disrupts some colludes."

"But isn't there anyone else who can help?" I asked. "I mean, the human realm has its police and armies. What does Fae have?"

Lucas and Roux looked at each other.

"Fae is pretty self-governing," Lucas said, "the way one season follows another or the weather stays in balance. It can be a bit tooth and claw, and races occasionally come up against one another—which is one reason ability with a weapon is a necessity for a Keeper—but it usually sorts itself out. So basically, there's nothing."

That wasn't possible. "What do you mean, nothing? Come on... Who fettered the hantaumo?"

Lucas sat back in his chair. "The assembly."

"Well, why can't they help?"

"The assembly is made up of representatives from each of the fae races. If they do agree on something, they have to return to their kind to garner support for the decision. It's not a quick process."

"Definitely not quick," Roux murmured into his cup.

I leant forward, my elbows on the table. "Just to be clear, who's going to sort this mess out?"

Lucas grinned then took a mouthful of coffee. "We are, as Keepers. It's happening on our turf and it's our responsibility. If things blow up, the assembly or a deity might get involved, but not at this level."

I had a feeling he was going to say that. "But what I don't get is why the hantaumo want to manifest in this realm—what are they going to do here?"

Lucas met my eyes. "That's the billion-euro question."

"It won't be good, I can tell you that much," Roux added.

"Well, it's not going to get that far." Lucas placed his mug on the table and drew a long breath. "We need to be ready for whatever they get up to. What do we know about the hantaumo—strengths, weaknesses, intel? Let's go over everything, even the most obvious details."

"Their main advantage is flight," Roux said. "Apart from that, their presence engenders a pale glow, and they are strong, tearing victims to shreds with teeth and long talons." He was beginning to sound like a natural history presenter. "Their screech is pretty agonising too. And to feed, they position their jaws around the jugular, then pierce it with several needle-like teeth to suck blood and life force remarkably gently, as though using a delicate straw. They take their time, savouring their food."

Oh, joy.

"They somehow pass the life force of their victims between the group," Lucas added, "so the feeding of one will fuel the others. The more life force they can get their hands on, the more hantaumo will be able to manifest and the stronger they'll be. The potion I have on the brew should make it more difficult for them to feed, although I don't know how effective it will be. Oh, and they love negative emotions —the icing on the cake."

The more I heard, the more I wondered if I could go hide under my duvet.

Roux turned his mug in his hands. "Not to mention, they're led by a queen, the largest and most vicious hantaumo, who is the epitome of evil."

"But they're as susceptible to the blade as any other creature," Lucas said. "They've got that going for them."

"And they didn't like sunlight the other day," I volunteered.

Roux nodded. "Major weakness. Though they have a degree of weather magic and might be able to do something about direct sunlight. But it's most likely they will use the cover of night."

Lucas shifted, creaking his chair. "Anything else we can make use of?"

"There's gods, of course." Roux's nose twitched.

I raised an eyebrow.

"Deities can overpower most fae," he clarified.

"But that's not much use," Lucas added. "Gods rarely get involved in human or fae affairs—only if it directly inconveniences them in some way." Was that a hint of sarcasm in his voice? Dame Blanche implied that all hell would break loose if deities helped everyone who wanted it, but surely some situations were more eligible than others.

I remembered something about the hantaumo from folklore. "Bells?" I ventured.

They both turned to me. "Bells?" Roux said in a strangulated voice.

"Yeah. It's recorded in folklore that hantaumo don't like bells of any kind."

Lucas unsuccessfully restrained a smirk. "I guess bells might give them a mild case of constipation."

"Only trying to help." I glared at him through his laughter. "Not bells, then."

"What about our defences?" Lucas asked, gathering himself.

"Herbs for ward colludes," Roux said, "and some minerals—gold if we need it. We have the usual range of basic weaponry"—he inclined his head to a door at the side—"plus the Men of Bédeilhac are a massive force. They'll support Lucas in anything he does."

"But can't you do something with colludes other than wards and bounds?" I asked. "Maybe give us mega strength, or a way to blast fire from our hands?"

"This isn't a super-hero comic," Lucas said dryly.

"No, no, no," Roux muttered. "Those kinds of colludes

take lengthy preparation by mages skilled in those areas. They are extremely challenging. My own talent lies in bounds magic, wards and evocations, plus a few other minor things. Lucas's skills are healing and potions. We must work with what we have."

"But what about guns?" I asked. They stared at me blankly. "I mean, if necessary, couldn't the hantaumo be taken down with machine guns or something?"

"Fae don't use guns," Lucas said with a hint of disdain.

"Well, humans do," I replied.

Lucas shook his head. "If you have a hit squad with M16s on speed dial—one that's taken verity—then by all means, call them."

I flashed him another glare. "You have a point."

"Anyway, fae have much more effective weapons," he added. "Although with such short notice, we don't have access to them. The Men are lethal and unnaturally quick, they'll have to do." He tapped his fingers on the table. "Then our options are to kill the hantaumo or force them over the bounds where their fetters will re-bind them. But if we could figure out who might be aiding them, we could put a stop to this right away. No life force means no hantaumo."

"We're back to searching for some kind of connection," Roux said, "possibly involving a collude or a potion. Remind us who the sick are, apart from Henri and Madame Bonnet."

"There's Victor Badeaux at Les Coumamines," Lucas read off his phone. "August Gouin at Bompas…"

I gazed out the window, recognising a couple of the names as Lucas continued, the others going over my head.

How was Grampi doing? I guessed the Men would report if
there were any changes. Lucas and Roux went on with their
discussion, throwing out ideas, none of any use. With more
people getting ill, Grampi's curse was understandably not
their most pressing concern, but I was worried, especially
with him getting worse last night. Mushum had said there
was a circle of maleficence around him, and Mushum had
been pretty reliable. Dame Blanche certainly had been a
good call.

I slumped back and saw the locations of the victims in my
mind as Lucas and Roux discussed them. Henri in Gourbit...
Victor Badeaux at Les Coumamines... Madame Bonnet at
Prairies de Flourac... Strange. They were all spaced out
pretty evenly around the town and surrounding villages,
rather than being scattered or clustered in one particular
locale. Lucas repeated the details for the third time. There
were a couple on the other side of Picou de Bompas, and they
were definitely evenly spaced. That was weird—random
attacks shouldn't be so uniform. But perhaps they weren't so
random. I pulled myself upright. "I need a map and something to write with."

"What is it?" Lucas asked. Roux jumped up and
rummaged in a drawer, then placed a pencil on the table
along with a map that was at least fifty years old, but it
would do.

I grabbed the pencil and drew an X for each of the deaths
and sicknesses I could remember. "Remind me of the other
names and locations."

Lucas read out the rest and I plotted them, my heart

thudding in my throat as a pattern became clear. The crosses formed an unnervingly regular circle that edged the town and intersected some of the surrounding villages—a perfect circle around Picou de Bompas. And right at the centre stood our farm.

Grampi.

CHAPTER 25

"A circle of maleficence around Grampi," I said, my entire body thudding with my heart. "That's no coincidence. Why him?"

Lucas shifted in his seat and avoided my gaze. I had the distinct feeling he knew much more than he was letting on.

"Well, it's not rocket science, is it?" Roux blustered. "On account of him being a Keeper and all. It's not unusual to make a few enemies in Fae, and he, well, he was particularly effective at his job."

"Alright, please go slowly for me, Roux. You lost me at the bit where you said 'on account of him being a Keeper'."

Lucas met my eyes and swallowed.

Roux turned to him. "You didn't tell her? Why on earth..."

Lucas rose and paced about then turned to Roux, an arrogant tilt to his chin. "I was going to, but a lot has happened.

It's only been a day and a half since Camille accepted the existence of fae."

I wasn't listening. Pieces were coming together—it all made sense. The swordsmanship, of course, although I'd thought it was an eccentricity from his military days. His frequent walks over the foothills—he hadn't been taking leisurely strolls, he'd been going into Fae. His attempt to talk to me yesterday—he'd seen my Keeper clothes. Had he been trying to tell me about all of this? And of course there was the curse. I hadn't even considered it, but why should a regular guy have a fae curse? Not to mention the goat-speak thing was something straight out of a fairy tale.

I rose slowly, my fingers twisting around the scabbard on the back of my chair. Quick as a flash, I drew my blade and lunged at Lucas, stilling the point precisely on his Adam's apple. It bobbed and his hands rose in surrender. This time my blade was very, very sharp. Roux stepped cautiously to the other side of the room.

"A busy few days," I said slowly, my voice low and lethal. "Are you telling me that in the last couple of days there wasn't one moment for you to mention this little, inconsequential, completely insignificant matter? A matter which may mean life and death to my grandfather."

"You were having doubts about being a Keeper." His voice was crisp with arrogance, his eyes assessing. "I didn't think revealing that your grandfather had been cursed on the job would make your invitation any more appealing. And I didn't think he had anything to do with the hantaumo, or of course I would have said."

Roux laughed from his relatively safe position by the kitchen door, no doubt ready to dart out back if necessary. "Come on, Lucas. Everyone knows Izak Amiel's partner was Mathilde Laurent, the hantaumo queen's daughter."

My mouth fell open, as did Lucas's. I lowered my blade, gaping at Roux in disbelief.

"Mathilde was one of the good ones," he added. "A reformed hantaumo who escaped their clutches early. When she rejected them, she lost their powers and the ghastly appearance. She became a Keeper—and a damned fine one at that. But the queen blamed Izak, even though it initially had nothing to do with him. As well as committing all kinds of terrible atrocities, the hantaumo came after Mathilde. Izak and some others restrained them and petitioned the gods to have them fettered. But before it could be done, the queen killed her daughter out of spite. She tried to kill Izak too, but didn't succeed, although she managed the curse years later."

I tried to absorb the revelation and failed miserably, only managing to stare at Roux's apologetic face, my eyes wide, my mouth still agape.

Lucas got a grip. "And you only thought to tell us this now!" he roared. Clearly the Mathilde Laurent connection was news to him too.

"I... I thought you knew," he spluttered. "Everyone knows!"

"I just moved here," Lucas said. "What the hell, Roux?"

"Uh... well..."

"I'll tell you what happened," Lucas bellowed. "You were

too strung out on scrapelather to have the wherewithal to think straight." He spun around, his fists clenched, his neck red, his gaze seeking something other than Roux to pummel.

Roux's words repeated over and over in my head. That pretty woman who had defended me when I'd been taken by the hantaumo, and the man whose face I'd been unable to see —they must have been Mathilde and Grampi.

Then, as if all of this was as normal as milking a goat, a cold clarity came over me. Despite whatever reason the hantaumo had me in the first place, Grampi had saved me, and now I had to do the same for him. Arguing wasn't going to help.

"The hantaumo queen wanted to kill Grampi," I said softly, logic clarifying it all. "But she didn't manage it. Now the hantaumo are creating a circle around him, a circle of life force from which they will draw power and manifest. Is it too much of a leap to guess that the queen wants to try again?"

Lucas eyed my calmness warily then nodded.

"But she'd cursed him anyway," I said. "Why go to the effort when he's already sick?"

"I'd imagine she found an opportunity to break her fetters," Lucas said. "And Izak was coping pretty well with the curse. I'm sure she had worse in mind for him than rambling on about goats."

I studied his dark eyes, as though the answers lay there. "And the curse got worse when the hantaumo started to be active."

"From what I know now"—he glared at Roux—"I'd take a

good guess that Izak has cast potent wards around the farm to protect himself and you from the hantaumo, but I've heard of cases where curses get worse due to the proximity of the caster. And I doubt Izak accounted for that possibility as the hantaumo were fettered—if he even knew about it.

"Then we move him," I said. "We move him away from their circle of maleficence."

Roux shook his head. "With the hantaumo already drawing life force from the sick, they have power. It may only be Izak's wards around the farm that are keeping him alive. Move him and he's dead."

"What do we do, then?" Urgency tightened my voice. I sheathed my blade. Not that I'd forgiven Lucas for this or anything else, but there were more important matters to focus on.

"Number one." Lucas sat back down and clasped his coffee. "We need to find out who's aiding the hantaumo locally. That's the most important thing. It will mean we won't have to fight and risk loss of life. Ideas for that?"

"It's full moon in ten hours," Roux said. "Naïs will be there at dusk."

Lucas rolled his eyes.

"Naïs?" I asked.

"A water nymph," Roux replied. "At full moon sunset she is at La Bessède spring, where she has potent divinatory powers. She might be able to see who's behind this."

"Great," Lucas said through gritted teeth. "I knew her in Athens, and one thing is for certain, she's not going to help me."

Roux raised his chin. "Well, there's no chance she'll do anything for me either after the incident with the badger and the washing mangle. But there's no reason she wouldn't help Camille."

"Happy to give it a try." Although, what was I getting myself into? Not that I cared if it helped.

"You'll need an offering," Roux said. "Take some of the roman gold coin. Its rarity might appeal to her."

Lucas nodded. "Apart from Naïs, the full moon isn't a good sign. Fae draw power from it. What with that and the sudden increase in cases, it wouldn't surprise me if the hantaumo strike tonight."

"It wouldn't surprise me either." Roux's mouth twitched, his beard quivering.

That was reassuring. "Other than waiting to see Naïs, me doing my shift at the café today is probably sensible. The amount of gossip that's passed around there, I might hear something."

"Good idea," Lucas said. "And I'll send the Men out to scout in town, keeping a large contingency at the farm with instructions to warn us if there's the slightest hint of trouble there, or if Izak goes downhill. And I'll cancel all non-urgent patients, then get the hantaumo potion sorted and take it out to the sick."

"We need to be prepared for an attack." Roux leant on the doorframe, possibly to ensure he continued to stand upright. "We need to keep weapons and equipment with us at all times, and pouches fully stocked. And we'll have to ensure Izak's wards stay strong. I'll pop up to the farm and perform a strengthening collude. If it comes to a fight..." He ruffled his beard and looked away.

"If it comes to a fight"—Lucas glared at him—"we have the Men of Bédeilhac. A lethal defence force."

Roux raised his brow. "Better than nothing. I'll go into Fae and request help from the most amenable deities, but I don't expect any response if I'm honest."

"We'll keep in touch," Lucas said to me. "If there are no earlier developments, I'll pick you up after work and we'll compare notes. You too, Roux, if you're back."

Roux bustled into the lab, rummaging in cupboards, pulling out jars, filling the little herb bags. Occasionally, he drew a hoarse breath. I wondered how up to this he was. He glanced at me. "Make sure your pouch is full."

Roux placed piles of herb bags on the table for me and Lucas, then went back to the lab and continued bustling around.

"Tell me," I said to Lucas as I tucked one of the bags into my pouch, "did I get the job of Keeper because of Grampi?" It kind of irked. I liked that I'd been chosen because of my knowledge of folklore—because of my own qualities—even if there hadn't been many candidates to choose from. A stupid thing to be thinking of at a time like this, but I wanted to know.

He smiled softly. "Nope. Doesn't work that way. Of course, the fact that Izak taught you to wield a blade was a bonus, but otherwise it's down to your inherent talents, particularly your knowledge of lore and openness to the idea of fae."

I tried to stop the corners of my mouth from tugging upward.

"Plus your pig-headed personality," he added.

He had to spoil it. Not that I was going to take the job—I mean, I couldn't even strike a killer rat, not to mention that I'd never work with Lucas. I glanced away and watched an ogre pass by outside. What use was I going to be in the face of the hantaumo?

Lucas's warm fingers drew my chin back until my gaze met his. "It's going to be fine. Just a load of psychopathic, murderous, witchy wraiths. What's not to love?"

There was no point dwelling on it. I released a breath and finished stuffing my pouch.

Lucas pulled his watch from his pouch and strapped it on. "I have to get going."

"Oh no you don't." I pointed at my chest.

He looked me up and down more slowly than was polite, a wicked grin developing. "I wish I had time, Camille. But you'll have to wait until the hantaumo are sorted."

I glared at him. "Glamour it, skunk bucket. I'm not wait-ressing looking like this." I had a change of clothes in my truck. But it would be ideal if I could be ready for action... and I was more than a little curious to see how a glamour worked.

I picked up my scabbard and looped it over my shoulder to include the blade in the collude. He drew out a bag from his pouch and tipped some dried herb onto his palm. "You could do it yourself if we had time. What do you want others to see?"

"Jeans and a T-shirt will do."

A small smile pulled at his lips. He concentrated on the herb and it glowed soft amber. The glow grew and surrounded me, a gentle tingling warming me all over. Once again, a collude with Lucas felt a little too intimate.

Chapter 26

All through the breakfast rush, Roux's revelations coursed through my head. I was edgy, knowing the hantaumo were out there planning their revenge. I wanted to call Slaughter to check on Grampi, but the place was too busy.

The usual crowd came in, the D&D guys for breakfast takeouts, followed closely by Nora and her posse. Had they taken to tailing the poor lads? Max came in too and nursed a coffee for a while. Then he started lecturing an Algerian couple sitting next to him, bestowing his thoughts about why they had no right to live in his town. The couple gave as good as they got, and Max left looking rather disgruntled.

I hung around the tables, clearing away any stray cups in the hope of hearing something that might help. The usuals came and went, but all I picked up was concern about the mysterious illness spreading through the town. It seemed that Lucas had played it down, though. The general impression was that if symptoms were reported early, there would be no complications. That had been a sensible approach—better than mass panic.

"What's so fascinating about the tables today?" Alice asked as I carried over the one cup I'd gleaned. "I've never seen you so ready to clear away a plate." The breakfast rush was finished and I couldn't continue lurking if I wanted to keep my job.

I set the cup on the counter. "I... uh... I'm just being an attentive waitress."

"First time for everything. Oh, and Maman is sleeping in the office again. She was up super early to finish baking before the gas engineer gets here, and she's completely done herself in." For a moment Alice's face darkened, the tension with Inès clear. Then she buried it, tugged at the leather of my Keeper top that was doing a great job of pretending to be a T-shirt, and grinned mischievously.

I had an idea what was behind the look. "Things going well with Raphaël?" I fished.

"Last night..." She bit her lip.

"Alright, give me all the details." I was glad of the distraction, though a flash of guilt streaked through my body. I hadn't confided about Lucas, and I'd not wanted to tell her how worried I was about Grampi. Usually we shared everything.

"All I can say is," she whispered as she took a payment, "he's athletic... and imaginative. You know how he's massively enthusiastic about everything?"

"From what you've told me." But I hadn't had a conversation with the guy.

"Well," she continued, "imagine that enthusiasm in bed."

I tried to picture it as I filled a box with demi-gateaux for the next customer, Alice ringing up payment on the till. "So, I'm guessing he's keen to try new things, or maybe quite... umm... vigorous...?"

She nodded slowly, her lips pursed. "Yes and yes. Damned keen—" A customer waved from along the counter. Alice waggled her eyebrows and went to help.

The place had quietened down considerably. I headed to the kitchen, the room empty in preparation for the engineer. "Slaughter," I whispered.

He popped up from under the worktop, a massive-for-him basket of wrapped cheeses on his head. "Yes, ma'am." He saluted.

I eyed the cheese with curiosity. "What's this?"

"With all the milk in the fridge at the farm, the lads thought we should do something with it before it went to waste."

Gratitude bubbled up once again for the little guys. "Thanks, Slaughter." Inès was asking about the next delivery for the filled baguettes, and we needed the cash. "This will do nicely. How's Grampi doing?" I placed the cheese in the fridge and passed him the basket.

"The new potion is holding everything at bay. He's sleeping peacefully after a restful morning." My shoulders dropped. He was still alright, for now at least. "Well," he continued, "all apart from when Blather spilled..." He cleared his throat, thinking better of what he'd been going to say.

Talk about suspicious. "What spilled?"

"Ummm... it was only a plate of scrambled eggs. Blather dropped it and Izak caught sight of him. Not to worry, though. He just laughed."

"You don't have to hide. Apparently Grampi was a Keeper, so I guess he's seen fae like yourselves in his time." Then a few more pieces of the puzzle clicked together. "But, Slaughter, you're a Man of Bédeilhac, which means you originate from the cave of Bédeilhac, just up the road. Didn't you know Grampi was a Keeper?"

"Of course we did, ma'am. It's common knowledge. And a good and honourable Keeper he's been, too. He helped us folk out on a couple of occasions."

"But why didn't you say anything? I mean, didn't you think it was strange that you were hiding from someone you knew?"

He shrugged. "Just following the governor's orders."

I released a sigh.

"Also, the gov said we should keep you abreast of everything that's going on."

"Let's hear it then."

His chest inflated. "A contingent of Men have been scouting the town for information. We haven't come up with anything of use so far... only that Leonard Vaux stole four cigars from the tabac, Estelle Houde and Veronique Janiver are having an affair, and Adrien Garnier's cat has mange. Also, Roux has been up to the farm to strengthen the wards, but he's gone into Fae now. If that's all, ma'am, I need to be getting back to the Men."

I was truly impressed with their information gathering. He'd certainly found out more than I had. "Sure. Thanks, Slaughter." He disappeared behind a box.

I leant against the counter and pulled at my too tight apron. The café hadn't ended up being such a good source of info and I wanted to do something to help Grampi—anything other than waiting tables. Maybe Mushum could help again.

I opened the fridge and grabbed the nearest cake, a Paris-Brest. I placed a piece on the windowsill, and by the time I'd wiped my hands, Mushum was grinning in rapture as he wolfed down the patisserie.

"Mushum said he would help Camille, and he helped. Didn't he?" He looked so pleased with himself, the grin almost wider than his face.

"You did." I gestured for him to have the rest of the Paris-Brest. "I'm really grateful you took me to Dame Blanche, and you were right about the circle of maleficence."

"Camille and Mushum friends," he managed through a mouthful of cream.

"Mushum, I really am grateful for what you've done, and I value your friendship, but all hell is breaking loose and I need more information."

"Not a problem. Mushum likes to help Camille."

"Alright, well... the maleficent circle around Grampi is the hantaumo." Mushum paused in his guzzling and shivered. "We think someone from the human realm is helping them escape their fetters. If you could give me information on who is helping them and how—"

Mushum vanished. Then he reappeared.

"Always speedy," I said.

"Mushum very quick, and Mushum knows something useful. There is an elf helping the hantaumo, but that was all Mushum could find out."

An elf. Curious. I hadn't met any elves yet, although Gabe sprang to mind. Just to make sure... "Do you mean a real elf, or someone dressed up as one?"

"A real elf, of course." He went back to wolfing down the Paris-Brest.

"That's what I thought." I needed to let Lucas know. "But I have to ask, where are you getting this information from? I mean, can I question your source to see if there's anything else to find out?"

Mushum shook his head. "Mushum listens to the voice of the wind. Sometimes the wind tells Mushum useful things. Mostly there's just rushing and swishing and roaring. It's Mushum's talent—listening—that and eating cake."

Listening to the wind was definitely beyond my skillset. "You seem to get information easily enough. Didn't the wind say anything else?"

The corners of his barely existent eyebrows raised in frustration. "The wind and Mushum are friends, but the wind is a free thing... wild. It doesn't just tell Mushum *everything*."

I heard footsteps in the corridor and glanced over. Alice and the gas man were coming this way.

"You have to go." I grabbed Mushum, deposited him on the windowsill with the last of the Paris-Brest, then closed the window. His face squashed against the glass, the patisserie smearing across the pane.

"Just putting out another dragonfly," I called, turning to them as they entered. She stared at the window, frowning. I followed her gaze to see a dollop of cream sliding down the glass.

"There she is," the man said, noticing the oven. "I shouldn't be too long. Couple of hours maybe."

"Let me know if you need anything," Alice replied, still following the cream. Perhaps she thought it was bird mess, but that was a stretch. Boy, I hated the subterfuge.

"It's a matter of mayoral importance," came a haughty voice from the shopfront, clear even from in here. We glanced at each other and headed in.

"I must speak with Inès," René said to Guy as we entered. René's chest was inflated even more than usual, his canvassing bag strapped across his torso like the string on a puffy parcel. An officious man stood at his side.

Alice raised her eyebrows at me, then she turned to the mayor. "René, how can I help you today... again... so soon?"

"I'd like to speak to Inès."

Inès appeared from the office, her gait stiff, her bag over her shoulder. She stopped short. "Oh, it's you."

René looked down his nose. "I'm here on official business. I believe you're having the necessary updates to your gas system. The building regulations compliance officer would like to check that everything is being done to his standard."

"I bet he would," Inès mumbled.

"But that's ridiculous," I said. "René can't just do spot checks. It's a matter for the planning department anyway, not the mayor."

Inès glared at him. "You'll have to speak to the manager." She kissed Alice on the cheek. "I'm not feeling up to any more today. I'm going home."

"Good," Alice replied. "Put your feet up. We'll be absolutely fine."

Inès shot her a smile before leaving.

Alice gestured to the compliance officer. "Go through. But, René, you can wait outside."

As René left the café, grumbling with indignance, a figure pushed in through the doors. Alice released an excited scream, bounced over and wrapped her arms around the neck of a large goblin wearing a suit.

All I could do was stare as she kissed that wrinkled, bristly mouth, taking her time about it. Please, please, please... let that not be Raphaël.

She released his neck and tugged him to the counter. "Camille, meet Raphaël."

I gawked at his leathery grey skin, his bulbous eyes, the wisps of hair standing up on his head. He was a tall and scrawny version of Mushum with a pouched belly.

Alice frowned. "Aren't you going to say something?"

"I... uh..." I closed my mouth with a snap and met his bulging eyes. "Hello, Raphaël. Uh... nice to meet you."

He grinned, revealing a row of very sharp teeth. "Nice to meet you too, Camille. I've heard so much about you."

"Cute, isn't he?" she said in a whisper. Cute if he'd been the size of Mushum. And only then in the way that a toy gremlin is cute—because you're glad it's a small toy that is in no way real and about to bite your finger off. And goblins did not look good in suits. But he was glamoured to Alice. The rat was a faker, pretending he was an everyday, normal, typical human being.

Alice nudged me with her elbow, glaring because I hadn't said anything. I was gaping again. "Sorry, Alice, I'm not feeling great. I just need a mo." I bolted for the office, closed the door and drew out my phone, tapping on Lucas.

"Camille—"

"Why is my best friend dating a goblin?"

"Not 'have you found a cure for Izak?'" he drawled. "Or 'have you managed to uncover the mystery of the evil wraiths from hell about to take over the world?' You have your priorities in perfect order."

He was completely right. As much as I wanted to suss Raphaël's game, there were more important problems. "Update me," I said.

"Four more cases have come in. I've been to see all the victims, and they're okay for the moment, with only the initial symptoms. I'm just hoping they'll stay that way until I can get the potion done and out to them. I'm twiddling my fingers waiting for it to finish. And the Men of Bédeilhac haven't found anything, apart from some scandalous town gossip—"

"Slaughter told me. And apparently Grampi is fine. But I've been chatting to my osencame friend again."

"Oh?"

"He thinks an elf is helping the hantaumo."

Lucas was silent for a second. "Alright... I guess he might be of some use after all. I'll get the Men to check on the elves in the vicinity. I don't think there are many."

"So, we're up to date?" I asked.

"Yep."

"Then, if you have a moment, please tell me why Alice's boyfriend is a giant, gangly goblin." It wasn't world-shattering, except to me, but I had no idea what to do about it.

He chuckled. "What's the matter, Camille? You have a problem with interracial dating?"

"I don't have a problem with the goblin part," I said, wondering if that was true. "I have a problem that Alice doesn't know he's a goblin. He's lying to her."

"Prejudiced against anything with sharp teeth, that's what I think."

I ignored his tease, trying not to see Lucas as he'd been in the cave. "She doesn't even know what he is. And he's masquerading as an estate agent, for heaven's sake."

"There are plenty of fae that have never come into contact with humans—Fae is as big as the human realm. When they do finally meet one, they can be fascinated. Some find you lot so engrossing, they take on human roles for that really authentic experience."

"But still... it's not right to be deceptive."

"Perhaps now you can appreciate my openness," he said.

My fingers curled tight, my teeth grinding. "Before you slept with me, Lucas. That's the point." I ended the call.

But it wasn't only Raphaël's dishonesty—although that was bad enough. I'd always been completely open with Alice, and now I couldn't be. I couldn't tell her about Lucas, or fae, or Grampi, and I definitely couldn't tell her that her boyfriend was a goblin. Not to mention, each time I spoke to Raphaël, I'd have to pretend he was human. I'd be lying to Alice constantly, and it was so wrong.

I tried to rub away the tension in my forehead. The events of the past few days had become a huge gulf in our friendship—one that Alice didn't even realise existed.

CHAPTER 27

During the last few hours of work, I'd grown increasingly restless wanting to do something other than serve brioche, but I'd had to wait it out. Lucas's SUV drew up to the café the moment my shift ended. I grabbed my things, including my blade from its hidey-hole in the office, and headed out. Alice had noticed the doctor's car and gaped as I jumped inside. I rolled down the window and waved as we pulled away. Hell, I was in for it tomorrow for not telling her what was going on.

We briefly checked Grampi, who was content and not particularly worse for wear, then as a load more reports had come in, we spent the next few hours distributing potion. With each visit we tried to find out who the sick had been in contact with, but we found nothing conclusive. What with that and the Men of Bédeilhac drawing a blank on the local elves, we were completely in the dark as to who was helping the hantaumo. Roux was still petitioning deities in Fae—unsuccessfully, I guessed, by the time he was taking.

As Lucas's phone kept ringing with more cases, I took over driving from patient to patient, leaving him free to handle calls. Eventually, he had so many, he made a voicemail advising that the sickness should be reported via text. As evening drew in, the sky grew dim, at first from the ominous billowing cloud that built above the town, and then from the dusk.

"Reports are coming in from beyond the circle of maleficence," Lucas said as we climbed back into the SUV after the most recent visit. "My best guess is that the potion is reducing the hantaumo's ability to drain life force, so they're using more victims wherever they can get them from."

"Well, we can't continue delivering at this rate." I clicked my seatbelt then rubbed my eyes, feeling my very early start. "Anyway, it's time to see Naïs."

Lucas rummaged in his bag and handed me a vial. "Wake-up potion."

I nodded my thanks and knocked it back. The world came into focus, my head clearing. I turned the ignition.

"Head for Cantegril by Tour Saint-Michel," Lucas said, tapping at his phone in response to another text. "The Men can take over deliveries. They can leave the potion on doorsteps."

"Good idea."

"Slaughter," Lucas called.

I expected to see an axe popping up from the backseat. "Doesn't he do cars?"

"He does most places. Slaughter," he tried again. Nothing. Lucas's face grew dark. "Something is blocking our connection."

"Hantaumo?"

"Could be, although I have no idea how."

"Landline, then." I pulled out into traffic and asked my phone to dial the farm on speaker. There came a terrible crackling. "Slaughter?"

"All is good here, ma'am," I made out before the crackling increased. I caught the words "fine" and "goat" and then there was too much interference. The line disconnected.

"That's normal," Lucas said. "At least for the Men. Certain kinds of fae and electronics don't mix. But at least we know all is okay up there." That was something, but I felt weirdly bereft knowing the little guys weren't on call.

Lucas responded to another text. "We need to find a way to get the potion out," he murmured, his thoughts half on the phone.

We drove past the cinema, the crowd filing out the door and trailing across the concrete forecourt. Félix and the D&D guys were amidst the throng.

"I have an idea." I drew to a stop and wound down the window. Lucas raised an eyebrow.

Félix and the two I didn't know so well headed over, Gabe's cloak absent. "Hey, guys," I called. "Where's Gabe?"

"He's got stomach-ache or something," Félix said. "What's up?"

"You've got bikes, right?"

"Uh, yeah."

Lucas glanced at me, catching on, a sparkle in his eye. "You know the sickness going around?" he said.

The gang's heads bobbed.

"It's spreading and I can't keep up with it. I need you to deliver medicine. Are you up for that?"

"Totally," Félix said. All of them looked pleased to be asked.

"I'll text you through the addresses. All you need to do is drop medicine on doorsteps. I've got more cases coming in, so this might keep you busy for a while."

They nodded keenly. Lucas jumped out, exchanged numbers with Félix, then hauled the potion box from the boot. "No contact with the families, in case it's contagious." More like in case the hantaumo were about. "But whatever you do, get the medicine out there. There's a load more in my consulting room if you need it." He handed them a key.

"No mission is too dangerous for our skilled warriors, no dungeon too dark." A caramel curl fell over Félix's forehead. "You can rely on us."

Lucas climbed in and forwarded the addresses as I pulled out. I sped to Chemin de Cantegril. Once I'd parked on the grass at the bottom, Lucas took a small pouch from the glove compartment and handed it to me. "The offering."

I unknotted the string. Inside were stunningly wrought gold coins. I couldn't imagine how far they'd go toward the farm's bills. And if Keepers had this kind of wealth to give away, it indicated that the pay might be significant. Roux had said as much. I sealed the bag in my pouch.

We jumped out and strode along the lane, then Lucas led

the way up through the woods. I could just about make out the footpath in the fading light. From the unnatural lack of snarky quips or any other conversation coming from Lucas, I guessed he was distracted. "So how come Naïs won't help you?" I asked.

"What?" He looked over his shoulder and frowned. "It was years ago..."

It didn't sound like he was going to volunteer any more information, but I was curious. "What was years ago?"

He paused and turned to meet my gaze, a scowl marring his too-good features. "I had a fling with her daughter and it ended badly."

"Oh?" I grinned just a little. "How badly?" As we rose, the breeze stirred the trees and wafted around, almost as though it was tugging at my clothing.

"I broke her heart and her mother was quite... physical about it. But her anger should have worn off by now. I haven't seen either for years. Satisfied?" He turned around and we continued our ascent.

"Satisfied," I said. I was finding out all about what kind of a person he was.

The wind rose a little more. I glanced up. The trees above swayed, although the cloud cover remained still and heavy. Something yanked at the back of my top. I swung around, and a faint giggling died out in the trees. My wrist was pulled, then my waist, my hair. I was tugged in all directions, Lucas too, his arms outstretched. The breeze was playing with us, flowing, dancing, swirling. Elfin eyes and gossamer forms shimmered within its gusts. Sylphs—elemental spirits of the air.

"They're servants of Naïs," Lucas said through gritted teeth. "It's just a friendly little greeting." He struggled on amidst yanks and pulls. I watched, fascinated, as we strode upward, smiling as I was jostled this way and that.

The path opened out into a small clearing, the flank of the foothill rising at the back. Water gushed from the slope into a pool surrounded by limestone boulders, and an alder tree arched over the rippling water. Despite the gathering darkness and the cloud cover, moonlight somehow glinted off the surface, casting glimmers against the branches.

A spring was a water nymph's eye on the world, from where she could see and know everything. Yet a water nymph was also a succubus with the ability to lure a victims until they drowned. As we stepped closer, I tingled with an unnerving sense of presence and beauty, and then something else... wrath, rage, fury...

In the centre of the clearing, the breeze whirled, forming a furious, spinning mass. It blasted out, hurling Lucas against an oak, pinning him to the trunk way above the ground. Part of the gust held him and part recoiled. It condensed, then slammed into his head, knocking him first one way then the other. I drew my blade, unsure what good I could do against the wind. At least there wouldn't be any blood.

"No," Lucas managed. "I'm okay. Just get the information."

The pool bubbled and gushed. Water rose in a spout,

then took on more and more form—the curve of a breast, the sweep of a back, the slender line of a thigh—until a woman stood there. Her hair cascaded to her buttocks, a glinting waterfall of silk. Her curved eyes, delicate nose and tender mouth held welcome and promise. Yet amidst all of this, I sensed pounding monsoons, raging seas and rushing torrents. I couldn't take my eyes off her.

"Lucas Rouseau," she purred, glancing to the oak. "What brings you to me this moon? Nothing good, I am quite sure. Perhaps you would like to break another heart?"

"It was a long time ago, Naïs," Lucas growled. "Think you might be able to move on?" A gust slammed his head against the tree. Lucas gasped, a trickle of blood running from his nose.

"It seems I have a long memory," she replied.

"Well, you know me, Naïs... I wouldn't risk being here if it wasn't of utmost importance."

She appeared to consider this, then turned to me. "Camille Amiel, how lovely to meet you. Your grandfather and I sometimes crossed paths. How may I help you?"

"Uh..." I sheathed my sword and stepped before her. How to explain everything to this force. "Andos... I'm... honoured to meet you," I managed, feeling as though I was addressing the oceans of the world. "My grandfather and the townsfolk are under attack from the hantaumo. We think someone is working for them in the human realm, and we'd like to know who it is."

She contemplated me for a moment, her gaze cool

droplets on my skin. "And what do you have to offer the spring?"

I drew the bag from my pouch and gave it to her. She loosened the ties and peered inside. "This is not yours, my dear. It is not something you've had to work for, nor a sacrifice. It is not worthy of gazing into the eye."

I gaped at her. But we needed the information. A bag of priceless treasure had to be enough.

"Come on, Naïs..." Lucas called. "It's coin from Julius Caesar. Extremely rare."

"Julius Caesar the adulterer who ruined so many women's lives? I remember... I was there. As an offering, it is completely unacceptable." She cast the bag into the trees, the coins scattering.

Way to go, Lucas. But we had to do something. I stared into the dirt and twisted my necklace. If we didn't find out who was aiding the hantaumo... it didn't bear thinking about. The townsfolk aside, I couldn't bear to lose Grampi. I tugged at the chain—there had to be something I could do, some way out of this. What did I have of value that Naïs might find acceptable?

My fingers stilled around silver, and my stomach sank. The chain was the only jewellery I wore, and it wasn't worth anything—except it was priceless to me. It reminded me of Grampi's strength, of how he'd been before the curse, and of who he was inside. It would crush me to part from it.

I lifted my head and met Naïs's gaze, then drew my hands behind my neck and fumbled with the clasp. Silver pooled in my hand. I closed my fingers around the necklace one last time, then with a shaky grip, I held it out to Naïs.

She nodded, looping it reverently over her fingers. "This is a priceless offering indeed. I accept." She extended her other hand. "Those who wish to gaze into the eye must see for themselves." I clasped her palm, and she drew me up over the boulders, engulfing me in her torrent.

Endless water surrounded me. I couldn't make out a light source, and yet I could see. I wanted to breathe, but of course, I couldn't. Instinct took hold and I paddled upward. There had to be a surface, a way out.

"To see through the eye, you must enter the realm of the dead," came Naïs's voice from all around, a part of the water itself. "And the realm of the dead does not lie above…"

Instinct screamed that I needed to rise, to escape this watery grave, but I knew what I had to do. I angled downward and propelled myself into inky blackness, my chest burning. Down I went… down until my lungs were bursting. I couldn't continue like this—I had to breathe. I gasped. Water poured into me and consciousness trickled away.

I opened my eyes. I floated above Tarascon. The five mountains that bordered the town lay below, the place sprawled out like a map. But the sky wasn't the impenetrable blue of night, or the azure of day—it was red and scorched, a storm billowing above us in angry grey and scarlet. To my side, on the slopes of Picou de Bompas, lay the farm. It shone in warm gold, even in the overcast red, a haven amidst the tempest.

And there, around the town, around Picou de Bompas

and the neighbouring villages, were points of a pale and unnerving glow. As I stared at them, my vision telescoped in. The glow engulfed houses here and there. I peered further, seeing through the walls of one dwelling, then another and another. Inside, men, women and children lay in their beds, wraithlike figures hovering above, tattered robes caressing bodies. Claws dug into flesh—a leg pinned down, a hand skewered. The faces of the victims were gaunt, hollow, parched—agonised by the teeth piercing their necks.

Something sparkled in the victims' torsos—the life force that animated them. Yet as I watched, it grew dim, siphoned off by the wraiths, leers of gluttonous pleasure warping their rotting features.

My vision drew back, and I was above the town again. The eerie light that engulfed each dwelling expanded, melding into an immense ring surrounding the town. "A circle of maleficence indeed," Naïs whispered in my ear.

"Is... is this happening?" I said. The glow, the redness, the way I'd zoomed in, it was so phantasmagorical. "It's not real."

"Oh, it's real," came Naïs's voice. "You're seeing another side of reality. You're seeing death."

I shook my head. "No, it's too much." I knew the hantaumo were a dangerous threat, but to see them like this, using people, gorging themselves... If these creatures managed to spread, to victimise countless people... I couldn't even consider it.

I lowered my gaze, wanting to see anything but the agony that consumed the place. My eyes caught on a thick murk covering one of the streets above the town centre to the east of the river. I tried to peer within, just as I had for the houses, but I was met by an impenetrable screen. "I can't see inside."

"No, you can't," Naïs replied from all around and nowhere. "There's a ward over that place guarding against the sight—against *my* eye on the world. I believe that is where you will find the heart of your problem."

CHAPTER 28

I BROKE THROUGH THE SURFACE OF THE POOL, GASPING for breath, my chest blazing, my arms outstretched, balancing me in the water. Lucas fell to the ground below the oak, released from his bindings. The air was motionless. The pool, apart from my ripples, lay still. The clearing, other than the two of us, was empty. I kicked to the side, climbed out and ran over to Lucas.

"I'm fine, I'm fine," he mumbled. He turned onto his hands and knees and pushed himself up, then delicately touched several areas of his face and head. One cheek was already swollen, his lip split.

"Looks like you're not forgiven." I tried to prevent the corners of my mouth flicking up as I adjusted my soaked gear.

He spat blood into the dirt. "Did you get the information?"

"I got something. We need to move. Are you up to it?"

He glared at me. "It'll take more than Naïs to put me out of action."

I led the way down the hill at a run, springing over brambles and dodging branches, just about managing to see in the darkness, although the reality of what I'd seen with Naïs was all too clear. What the hantaumo were doing to the people of the town—my friends—was worse than anything I could have imagined. But now we knew where to look, we could do something about it.

"What did you get?" Lucas called from behind.

"A location in the town centre, the southern end of Avenue Victor Pilhes—there was a ward, I couldn't see inside."

As we continued on, Lucas's phone pinged again and again. "Shit," he muttered. No doubt something about Naïs had disrupted the signal, and now all the messages were coming in.

We sprang into the SUV. I pulled out and put my foot down.

Lucas tapped madly at his phone. "Too many sick. There's no point me relaying messages like this. I'm going to change my voicemail, telling people to text Félix."

It took minutes to get to the town centre. I reined in my speed and followed the avenue at a dawdle to where I'd seen the ward. Nerves taut, I reached for the familiarity of my necklace, but it was gone.

The street lay empty. Most folk had turned in for the night. I gazed up, expecting to see the murky-grey ward that had blocked my view in the vision, but it was too dark above the streetlights.

"Pull over," Lucas said. "We'll have more chance of finding something on foot." I drove the SUV half onto the pavement. We jumped out and headed down the empty street, the faint outline of the Castella Tower rising on the promontory at the end. In the distance a dog barked, a car started and traffic rumbled on the N20. The sense of heaviness grew. It was damned hot under the building weather front, my clothes almost dry apart from perspiration.

We strode along, searching the street. Most house windows were shuttered, the post office and the shops deserted. My stomach lurched with unease and my skin tingled uncomfortably. I glanced at Lucas.

"It's a ward," he said. "It's let us through, meaning it's not defensive. It could be some kind of glamour or a warning system. It's impossible to be certain."

"So we're here." Whatever here meant. I turned around, scanning the street. The town hall stood opposite, the architecture a modern interpretation of local styles mixed with bureaucratic blockiness. The lilac paintwork, almost red in the streetlight, was an effort to add jollity to the place. On the other side was René's boulangerie, forlorn as it waited for the early-morning baking session. Next to it lay a side street, then a few homes. Nothing indicated... Well, I didn't know what we were looking for.

Lucas gazed through the boulangerie window. I strode to the entrance of the town hall. The tingling got a little worse.

"Lucas," I whispered.

He came over. "Yep. This is the direction."

I peered through the glass doors. Nothing. Lucas tried the handles. "Locked." He inclined his head. "Let's try around the back."

We trod along the front of the building, gazing through windows as we passed. The tingling grew, but nothing else stood out. At the corner, we took the side alley. Another entrance was located close to the dead end, and we headed toward it. A few strides from the door, scuffling came from behind. We turned.

The margins of the alley swarmed with hundreds of rats —the big kind with very sharp teeth that had attacked us in Fae. They cut off access to the door. We drew our blades.

"Slaughter?" Lucas called, but nothing happened. "It's likely we can't reach him because of the ward. And as its effects extend to the cinema, it's powerful."

"Fickleturn?" I asked, my heart drumming in my throat. He'd instigated the last rat attack.

"I don't know. But I do know the rats are protecting whatever is behind that entrance."

More rats poured in, their eyes glinting red, their fangs bared. They surged around, edging closer but remaining out of reach of a blade swipe. We were circled.

"We'll have to cut them down," Lucas said. "Don't think about it, just plough into them, and we'll edge to the door."

I nodded, but inside I was in shreds. I'd flaked when Fickleturn's rats had attacked us, and I couldn't see myself doing any better now. Alright, I knew where my revulsion came from, but that didn't mean I was any more prepared. I'd give it a try, though. Otherwise, we weren't getting out of here alive.

The rats shifted, their ears pricking as if listening to some invisible command, then as one, they leapt forward. Lucas swept around in a circle, faster than humanly possible, cutting into the hairy front line. He darted this way and that, taking out the fiercest vermin. "Come on, Camille," he growled. "I could do with a little assistance."

I took a deep breath—I could do this, they weren't hantaumo, at least. But already blood splattered the ground— entrails in pools, eyes dull, mouths open never to close.

"Think of Izak," Lucas yelled. "And the town."

I ignored the ringing in my ears and the urge to hurl as I tried to bring my blade down, but I could see the pit again, the lifeless gazes all about. And something more niggled at the edge of my mind—the horror of whatever it was I hadn't allowed myself to see floating above me. I shoved the memory to the side and willed myself to strike with every fibre of my being. I couldn't, and I had no idea why. But I was being ridiculous. If I didn't do something, it would be us gazing up from the ground.

Lucas cut into one rat after another. Some flew against the walls. Some fell under foot. I dodged severed limbs and open cavities. But regardless of how many vermin he cut down, more poured in from the street.

"Come on, Camille, come on," Lucas cried, desperation edging his voice.

The rats were bigger now, I was sure of it—teeth longer, eyes brighter.

Lucas darted around, twisting and slashing, but there were too many. A rat sprang for his throat. As he drove his blade into it, one caught him on the back of his thigh, gripping on with its fangs. Then another sank its teeth into his wrist. And no matter how hard I tried, I couldn't use my blade. What the hell was wrong with me? I braced myself, knowing I'd be next, but the rats ignored me. More and more dove for Lucas, until he teemed with vermin.

"Camille," he choked out as he dropped to the ground.

All I could do was stare, terror rooting me to the spot.

"Enough!" cried a voice.

CHAPTER 29

THE RATS PAUSED AND DREW BACK TO THEIR RING formation.

I turned to the cry. A cloaked man strode into the alley, his face shrouded by a hood. He extended his hands and my sword tugged from my grasp and flew into his, then Lucas's blade did the same, dragging out of his still hand. The cloak put the weapons under his arm then reached out again. Our pouches and our phones followed, and he tucked them away.

Lucas's eyes were closed, his body still and torn, blood pooling around him—whether it was his or the rat's, I couldn't tell. Watching the vermin warily, I dropped down to check his pulse. As I touched his wrist, his eyelids flickered. He was alive, thank heavens. But knives of guilt pierced every part of me, my core sickened—I hadn't helped him. I wanted to step out of myself, step away from the person who'd let this happen. But that wasn't going to help anyone. I ran my gaze over his body. He'd been slashed by their teeth countless times, although I couldn't see one particular wound that had taken him down. Damned hell, he needed a hospital.

Something pushed me gently back. I glanced around for the source, but there wasn't anything. The cloak twisted his fingers. The air around Lucas shimmered, and he rose a foot off the ground, maintaining his prostrated slump. Then he drifted toward the door as though suspended on an invisible stretcher, carried by a magic more powerful than he or Roux possessed. The door sprang open. Holding formation, the rats shifted to the dark entrance, forcing me to move with them.

The doorway was a black hole, but as I shuffled forward, concrete steps leading downward became clear. Lucas floated down the stairway, and thanks to the furballs, I had no choice but to follow.

We descended into a basement lit by a couple of candles and dull streetlight coming from a small window near the ceiling. In the gloom, all I could make out was a table holding what might be chemistry equipment, and the white lines of a large pentacle painted across the ground. I may have been new to all this, but schooled by eighties movies, I knew a pentacle drawn on a dark basement floor meant trouble.

The cloak trod down the steps after us. Lucas floated to the far side of the basement, then thudded to the ground by the wall. I was directed by my hairy entourage to follow. The rats allowed me to join Lucas, then they retreated back up the steps and out of sight. The cloak raised his hand, and my wrists and ankles were bound by invisible threads. Lucas groaned in agony.

"Slaughter," I tried under my breath. Nothing.

I could just make out the cloak doing something with the chemistry equipment. "Umm, excuse me," I called, annoyance prickling that I had to be polite to someone who'd attacked us, but I wasn't going to risk more rats. "He needs medical attention." No response. "If we can just get him to a hospital..." But what was the chance of that? If the guy was of a considerate frame of mind, he wouldn't have mauled us—Lucas—with giant rats.

Lucas groaned again. I levered his head into my lap with my bound wrists, guilt hollowing me out at his torn and bloody face. I couldn't believe what I'd done—not done. I shifted a little, repositioning Lucas more comfortably. The candlelight guttered and I thought I caught his eyes flicker.

"Something I didn't tell you," he slurred. He was talking. That had to be a good sign. He moaned almost contentedly for a moment. "Hmmm, lying in your lap is paradise..."

Unbelievable. He'd been mauled by rats, yet this. "Don't get used to it," I whispered, not wanting to attract the attention of the cloak.

He let out an almost-chuckle that turned into a groan, then added, "Those rats..."

"What about the rats?"

"Poisonous teeth. Inject deadly venom from their canines. Didn't want to worry you earlier." He was quiet for a second, then... "Do rats have canines?"

I was still absorbing the first thing he'd mentioned. Poison. "How deadly?"

"Couple hours' survival, tops."

"Shit." I had to get him out of here. "Who... What can help? I mean, I guess not a normal hospital... Herbs or something?"

"Something..." he managed. "Maybe Roux..." Silence. I wanted to shake him, to wake him so I could be sure he was still with me, but what good would that do? Better I find a way out of this mess.

I glanced about, not knowing what to do. Out of the window, the lower part of René's boulangerie was just visible. Perhaps I could shout, and someone on the street might hear me. Or I could beg to be freed. But I had visions of being kicked in the mouth then gagged, or worse. Then, what else could I do?

Lucas shifted in my lap. I stroked his head and opened my mouth to whisper something comforting, but light blossomed in the gloom. The cloak had lit a taper. He touched it to a candle, the glow revealing a little more of the room. He lit other candles all around, illuminating the individual flasks and tubes of the chemistry equipment and a pile of junk shoved to the end of the room.

"We're not dead," Lucas murmured. Then his words became incoherent.

A canvassing bag caught my eye on the floor next to the chemistry table. I'd seen a similar one on René yesterday when he'd come into the café with the compliance officer. And next to it sat a basket stacked with croissants. Oh, no— René. It couldn't be. But it all made sense—the town hall, the leaflets. He'd been canvassing, offering free croissants as he usually did—anything to get people to listen to him. He'd doused the croissants in potion he'd brewed right here—potion that linked victims to the hantaumo.

But René, really? He was many things, but I wouldn't have taken him for a dabbler in the occult, and he certainly wasn't an elf, although Mushum could have been wrong about that. I studied our captor... It couldn't be René. The form under the cloak was too slight.

Something shifted in the shadows to my side. Someone had been strung up by the wrists to pipes—a woman in jeans. The cloak carried a candle across the room and adjusted something on the edge of the pentacle close to the captive. I caught sight of her face. Pretty—even prettier than normal with her eyes closed and her mouth not spouting insults. It was Nora. And there was only one person who wanted to string up Nora. Well, actually, there might have been quite a lot of people—but one person in particular who'd been the butt of her snide remarks at the café.

As if sensing I'd worked it out, the cloak turned to me and drew back his hood.

Gabe.

CHAPTER 30

But Gabe wasn't an elf. I'd seen his ear tips fall off on countless occasions, though they appeared secure today. And anyway, Gabe might have wanted to get his own back on Nora, but I'd never peg him for a homicidal maniac bent on the destruction of his town. I couldn't deny it, though. Here he was.

"We're... not... dead," Lucas murmured.

I followed Gabe as he continued his tour of the pentacle, examining something at the points—possibly herbs. In the candlelight he seemed to shake, as if he was straining at himself. His face warped grotesquely for a split second, and I'd seen those awful features before. Hantaumo. Gabe was being controlled.

"Not dead..." Lucas slurred again.

No, we weren't, but with that thing controlling Gabe, it wouldn't be long. Although why hadn't it killed us already...?

I peered at Gabe. He... it... they—whatever was inside

that cloak—really should have ended us. That's what Lucas had been trying to tell me. Lucas with his potion was the only one with the means to bring the hantaumo down, so why hadn't they taken him out? Granted, he had been mauled by poisonous rats, but they could have easily polished him off. And me... they'd not touched the granddaughter of the man who helped fetter the hantaumo because... the D&D guys liked me... Gabe liked me. A hantaumo controlled Gabe, but by the strain on his face, he was fighting it.

I had to help him somehow. What did the D&D gang call me...? Perhaps I could appeal to whatever urged them to give me my crazy title. And I could do it in D&D style. "The High Warrior of the Borders," I pronounced, "Protector and Holder of the Knowledge of Free Men and Fae, orders you, Gabe, to cast off your hantaumo tormentor and free us."

"High Warrior." Lucas sniggered from my lap. "I can die happy now." I resisted the urge to nudge him with my thigh.

I thought I caught a glimmer in Gabe's eye, a moistening. He took a step forward, sweat beading on his brow, then he turned away and laughed—a bitter and twisted cackle. "Nice try, Camille." He returned to the chemistry equipment and lit a flame under a flask.

I had to think of something to get him on my side. "Looks as though you're doing your own bit of D&D here... and you're obviously doing a great job, summoning demons and the like."

He turned slowly, his gaze filled with hate and destruction, but also with honesty and nerdiness. "I... I've seen it all," he stammered. "They're real, the demons, they're inside me, taunting me, commanding me... They're outside too, creatures... goblins... trolls, in the streets, in the café. Don't tell me I'm mad. I know what I've seen. I've seen it all my life."

Oh hell. The poor kid. "I know about it, Gabe. The fae, the goblins, the trolls, all of it. I've only just found out, and it was a shock for me too. I can't imagine what you've been through."

He stared at me. "You know? You *are* the High Warrior."

Lucas snorted.

"Look," I said, "I can help you. I know about the hantaumo—what they're doing to the town. I know one is controlling you, but you can fight it, and we can get through this. I know you wouldn't have administered the potion without hantaumo influence."

A sneer warped Gabe's lips and he laughed. "You do, do you? You know how I played with potions, how I bonded with the first hantaumo, how it instructed me to refine the process, so that drawing its sisters to the human realm was as easy as eating a croissant." His face contorted again—a flash of needle teeth and fury. "The hantaumo listened. They cared. They knew that the creatures I saw were real."

They'd done a first-rate job at grooming him, but probably best not to state the facts too harshly. "I get that—really, I do. But people are dying out there, Gabe. And it doesn't have to be this way. Magic is possible without death, and there's a whole fae realm for you to explore. Plenty of people are aware of it... Lucas, the doctor here, is a drac. We just have to help him—"

Gabe's mouth dropped open. "The doctor is a flesh-eating incubus?"

"Uh... yes." In hindsight, it hadn't been the best thing to mention.

"That's supposed to reassure me?" He returned to the table, filled a vial and adjusted tubes. "It doesn't matter now, anyway. None of it does. Most of the town has consumed the potion. The hantaumo are feeding and soon they'll be strong enough to attack."

Shit. Shit. Shit. We were too late. Now our only option was defence, and Lucas and Roux hadn't exactly been excited at our chances. I glanced down at Lucas, the full force of my guilt descending again. How were we going to get out of here, let alone fight? I could only hope that Roux and the Men would manage to defend Grampi.

Thunder rumbled faintly.

"Happy..." Lucas muttered. "Happy... thoughts." I surveyed him, his eyes closed, his body twitching occasionally. He was trying to think of nice things. Anything was better than this hell hole. "Happy... Gabe..." Or did he mean something else? But Gabe wasn't happy... Perhaps Gabe needed to be happy. Lucas had said back at the Keepers' post that the hantaumo feed on negative emotions. If I could get Gabe to focus on positive things, the hantaumo's influence might weaken.

But I didn't know much about Gabe. His mother had been lovely, though. And years ago, before her death, René hadn't been such an arse. "Your mum, Coralie, I remember her. She was so warm. Worked at the hydroelectric plant, didn't she?"

Gabe paused, his hands resting on a vial.

"She loved the town," I continued. "She would want you to help us... help me keep everyone alive and safe."

Gabe's trembling grew to violent shudders. "It doesn't matter what she would've thought," he growled. "She's dead."

"But she wouldn't have wanted this. Gabe, I can sort the whole mess out. But first we have to stop the hantaumo before anyone else dies. I know you can do that. I know you have the strength to fight them."

Gabe spun around, his eyes blazing with inhuman light. "No," he said softly, and turned back to the potion. Damn it. I needed to find something that would really speak to him.

Nora moaned, wriggling in her binds, blinking as she came to. She searched the room, taking it all in. Her gaze settled on Gabe and her eyes widened with terror. How had she been caught up in this? She really needed to be away from poisonous rats and hantaumo. If I could get her out of here, it would be a start. "At least release Nora," I said. "Let her go. We don't need to drag her into this."

"Nora is evil spawn." His roar had an edge that wasn't humanly possible. He strode over, pulled a knife from his cloak and drew it to her throat. Another bad call.

"No... no... no..." she stammered, her body twisting as she tried to jerk away from the blade.

"All those comments... all that giggling," Gabe growled. "Do you know how much torment you and your friends put people through, Nora? Do you know how mean you are?" His words dripped with malice.

"I'm... sorry," she muttered as he pressed the knife into her skin. A trickle of blood ran down her neck. Shit. I had to do something... Happy thoughts... Happy thoughts...

"Your dad," I called. René was a dick, but there had to be some love there behind closed doors... "Think of your dad. He's a... nice guy." Try to sound genuine, Camille. But how could I when he was such a knob?

Gabe opened his hand. The knife dropped to the ground with a clatter. He twisted to face the window and glared at René's boulangerie, his hands balled into fists at his sides. He hauled in a massive breath and released it with an ear-splitting cry. "Aaaahhhhhgggg."

The boulangerie exploded, the fireball illuminating the hell-pit basement, the boom shaking the foundations. Okay, message loud and clear... not the dad—don't mention the dad.

On the street, little pieces of burning rubble tinkled down. How much power did Gabe have? He gaped at the blaze, a single tear trickling down his cheek. He was in there, I just needed to find a way to make contact. Happy thoughts... damned happy thoughts...

Gabe turned back to the table and measured herbs into a beaker, his hands trembling. Nora resorted to sobbing quietly. Happy thoughts... What made him happy? But of course, D&D and the guys—his friends.

"Uh... you're a high elf, right?" I tried. He paused. "In the game," I continued. "Defender of all that's good, holder of the light. I think I heard Félix saying that once."

He turned around, the strain clear.

"You wouldn't go to the dark side, then." I sounded a lot more confident than I felt. "You would fight with everything you had... you and the guys..."

At the mention of the guys, his eyes opened wider.

"Together, you'd fight. Even alone you'd fight if it meant saving the gang's lives. They would fight for you, and you would fight for them. You wouldn't even think twice."

He took a step toward me, his face shifting, one moment pleading, almost hopeful, the next malicious. "Saving throw," he murmured, straining. With an agonising struggle, he forced his hand into his cape and drew out something. Opening his fist, he revealed an amethyst twenty-faceted D&D die. It glittered in the boulangerie's blaze. "One to ten," he mumbled, "the hantaumo claim the high elf, snaring him for eternity in the darkest of hells. Eleven to twenty, the high elf has the strength to defeat the most terrible foe of his life."

I goggled at the die. The throw had a fifty-fifty chance. Couldn't the high elf just eliminate the hantaumo then and there? But in the game, as in life, there was always the element of chance—or was it fate?

Fighting himself with everything he had, Gabe threw the die onto the concrete. It bounced toward me, rolled, then came to a stop by my foot.

A nine. No, no, no, no.

Tentatively, I glanced up at Gabe.

He was staring at me, hauling breaths deep and fast, then he clutched his head and roared—this time the high, broken roar of an adolescent, though it was just as brutal. He hacked at his face with his nails, pulling, clawing, tearing... his roaring ceaseless—a battle-cry.

Nora screamed and screamed. I wanted to look away, to look anywhere but at Gabe tearing himself apart, but I couldn't. Lucas shifted feverishly in my lap.

On Gabe clawed, blood running down his face, then his hands stilled on his cheeks. Slowly, his fingers and thumbs drew together, and he pulled. There was something in his grasp, not his skin—not him—but something that glowed cold and lifeless. With herculean effort, Gabe hauled it from his face, the mass slurping out, forming a hideous head, all teeth and bone and evil.

Sweat poured down Gabe's brow as he pried it out further, trembling with strain. The creature fought to re-enter Gabe's body, gnashing at his hands, but on Gabe heaved. Its arms and torso popped out, claws slashing. Gabe released another cry and levered his foot up against the creature's chest, prying its body from him. As thunder cracked and lightning lit the place, the creature fell to the floor, a single thread of luminescent connection remaining, joining the two navel to navel. The hantaumo rasped and choked, weakened from its removal. Gabe had done it. He'd gotten this far on the roll of a nine.

He eyed the thread warily, then raised his hands above his head. Light shimmered between his fingers with the same unnerving glow as the hantaumo that lay beneath him. I could sense the focus of power building from here. The wraith rose up, rallying itself, regaining its strength as though it was feeding off whatever Gabe was doing. It sprang at

Gabe, piercing his neck with its teeth. Hands raised, encumbered with the mass of raw energy, Gabe was only able to writhe. He released a primal bellow, and force surged from his hands. Nora fell to the ground, the atmosphere lightened, and my wrists and ankles were freed. At a guess, he'd removed the wards. And if there were no wards... "Slaughter," I cried.

"Yes, ma'am." That wild head popped up, then balked at the state of Lucas. I stared at the little Man, mind blown that he was here. Gabe and the hantaumo were struggling, claws against much too soft skin, Gabe was almost submerged in the black shrouds of the creature as he edged over to where Nora slumped on the ground.

"Slaughter," I said, "save Gabe."

Just as a hundred Men of Bédeilhac charged, Gabe dropped to his knees, grabbed the dagger and thrust it into the hantaumo. It fell back, yanking Gabe by the cord, then it rose, glaring with the malice of hell at the boy, before springing at him. With the subtlest of movements, Gabe slipped the blade through the cord, breaking their connection. The creature thudded to the ground mid-leap, fury on its face. Then it was submerged under a throng of Men.

I shifted, wanting to help Gabe, but Lucas groaned in agony, his face so pale he could have been made of china.

CHAPTER 31

THE HANTAUMO STILLED. THE MEN STEPPED BACK, leaving a lifeless mass. A siren wailed in the distance.

"Slaughter," I called as I eased out from under Lucas and gently lowered his head to the ground.

He zoomed over. "Yes, ma'am?"

"We have to help Lucas. Can you do healing?"

"Not us, ma'am."

"Then Gabe. The amount of power he wielded—"

"It's gone. It was from the victims, channelled through the hantaumo. He doesn't have anything now the cord has been cut."

"Then Roux, of course... Lucas said Roux. I need my phone." I strode to the table and searched around. A short Man with curly hair popped up with my phone resting on his head. "Great," I said. "And our pouches and swords, while you're at it." He grinned and zoomed away.

I dialled Roux and waited for him to answer, noticing

Nora shaking in the corner. She'd huddled up with her arms over her face, trying to block out the sight of the wild-looking Man attempting to be nice to her. Gabe sat by the hantau-mo's body, eyeing a group of Men as they bathed his lacerations. They'd managed to manifest a bowl of water and first aid equipment. Out on the street, fire engines arrived.

Roux picked up. "You're back," I said with relief.

"Just returned to the post, no help from any of those pompous, self-important—"

"Lucas is sick," I said. "Badly. Can you do anything?"

"What caused it?"

"Rats. Big ones with glowing red eyes."

"Sharp teeth?"

"Goes without saying, doesn't it?"

"That's very, very bad. How long?"

"I don't know." My sense of time was shot. "Maybe an hour. But he's gone very white."

"He doesn't have long. Where are you?"

"In the basement of the town hall."

"Be there in five." He ended the call.

Our equipment had been placed on the table. I sheathed my blade, Nora studying me with disbelief. If she could see the Men, she could see my Keeper gear. I buckled on my pouch and tucked our phones inside, willing Roux to hurry with every fibre of my being.

Lucas was still moaning faintly now and again. That was something. I went over and crouched down. "Roux is coming. He'll be here in a moment." No reply.

A small purple jewel sparkled on the floor. The D&D die

still displaying nine. I picked it up and stepped over to Gabe, who was already looking a little less bloody thanks to the Men. I sank to his level. "The hantaumo... What happened?"

"I didn't mean to," he blurted, lowering his head. "I was experimenting with the occult, went on to potions and managed to make some potent brews. One of them drew the hantaumo. They controlled me..." His lips trembled. Yep. He'd been played.

"And her?" I inclined my head to Nora.

"She... she was pissing me off, and I had all this hantaumo power, so I made her see the world just like me, then brought her here..."

"Kidnapping girls. Not cool."

"I know, I know. I... didn't hurt her—apart from the knife." He swallowed. "And I didn't give her the potion." He buried his head in his hands. Where had his actions begun and the hantaumo's ended? But the poor kid had been victimised himself.

"Hey," I said. "How did you defeat the hantaumo on a nine?"

He looked up, eyes shining, and tapped his chest. "Fifth-level wizard. My proficiency bonus is three."

It was still way too close, but if he'd thrown low, maybe he would've gotten around it somehow. After all, that's what D&D was about. "High elf," I said gently.

"Always have been." He tugged hard at the top of his ear. The tip didn't shift. "And always will be." I stared at the point and it all made sense. Those times Gabe's ear tips had fallen off to reveal the curved normality of a human ear underneath, they'd been before I'd had the verity. He truly was an elf, and he wore ear tips to ensure his true nature was seen. "How long have you known?"

"All my life. Mum was like this too. But it was our secret, and we didn't talk about it between us. After she died... my dad, well... no one wanted to know."

Did that make Gabe half elf, half human? But all that could wait. "You must have seen so much. And no one else knew?"

"Nope."

I wiped my hands over my face. "But not any longer. We've got your back, okay?" That was if we ever got past this evening. He nodded. I passed him the die.

A moan came from the corner. I walked over to a shivering Nora and knelt down. "You alright?" Thunder bellowed, and a stark flash of lightning cast the basement in too much clarity. Rain lashed down on the street, whipped up by the gale.

Nora looked up. "Please tell me that apart from a possessed maniac dressed as an elf, there aren't a load of small, prehistoric men running around in here. Otherwise there's something seriously wrong with me."

"I can confirm there are plenty of pint-sized prehistoric men in the room." She burst out crying. Didn't Lucas say that sometimes humans needed their memories of fae wiped, or they'd go mad? This might be one of those times. But there were more important things to deal with first.

"Ma'am." Slaughter tugged at my leg, his brow furrowed. "I've just had a report—the hantaumo have begun their attack on the farm. The wards are holding for the moment, but the Men need assistance—"

Roux ran down the stairs, staff in hand, cape swirling about. He paused and took in the basement then Gabe. "My, my. Someone has been busy in here."

"Leave a few Men to watch Nora and Gabe," I said to Slaughter. "Take the rest with you. We'll be there as soon as we can." I hoped I could hold to my word. He saluted and vanished under an old chair.

"Roux," I called as I strode to Lucas. Roux ran over—well, for him it was more of a stiff trot, but he was doing his best.

He bent down and examined Lucas, tutting. "This is bad... bad indeed. Lucas is the expert on healing. I know very little—"

"Whatever you know"—urgency sharpened my voice—"do it right now."

He rose, teetered a little, then fumbled under his cloak, producing some of the small herb bags. "It will have to be a collude. There weren't any potions at the post to treat this kind of poison." He glanced at Gabe and gestured to the pentacle as he stepped within. "This yours?"

Gabe gaped at Roux. He'd probably only ever seen the bounds mage curled up in various doorways around town.

Roux scattered herbs at the points of the pentacle. "You play D&D, right?" he said as he continued.

Gabe nodded, speechless.

"It all starts with D&D. Then it's a little too much whisky and a scantily clad sylph. The next thing you know, your party has abandoned you because the thing from the abyss has taken up residence in the microwave and is eating yesterday's pizza." He shook his head. "It all starts with D&D."

How long was he going to take? As well as the general whiteness, Lucas now appeared to be stiffening. "Roux, can you please start the ritual?"

He continued scattering. "Bring him into the centre of the pentacle."

The crowd of Men that had been left with Nora and Gabe shot over. In unison, they picked Lucas up and carried him into position. I knelt down by him. His arrogant features were much too still. A lip should have been twitching. Even a little conceit would have been welcome right now. "Hold on," I whispered. "Roux has things under control." And I hoped to high heaven he really did.

Roux scattered alder leaves around Lucas, then raised his staff. "Essence of herbs, I entreat you. Join for healing and recuperation. May your curative powers imbue the one who lies here. St John's wort, celandine and milk thistle for poison. Marigold for binding, daisy for bruising and fortifica-tion..." The pentacle lit up in a flash of gold, which joined with Roux and then Lucas. "Bestow your essences unto restoration." The alder leaves flared and the light around Lucas intensified. He lurched and cried out. As he fell back, I caught his head. Then he turned onto his side and threw up. His pallor was returning to normal... It was working, although his rat-teeth slashes remained. Gabe and Nora gawked at the spectacle.

The light flickered and dimmed. Lucas groaned.

"By Abellion's boots," Roux muttered, "this is not my area of expertise. I've run out of steam."

"Ma'am." Slaughter appeared from nowhere. "The wards are starting to crack, and me and the Men are no good at colludes and the like to sort them out—but of course if the hantaumo get through and it comes to a battle, we'll die defending all the boss stands for."

Lucas sat up and swayed. "I'm ready," he just about managed. "Let's go."

Chapter 32

"The collude isn't finished." Roux ruffled his beard in frustration. "I've only addressed the poison, nothing else."

Lucas rose, then tottered. I caught his arm. "We don't have time," he said, getting his balance. And apart from appearing stiff and completely rat-mangled, he did look sort of okay. Relief eased through me, although a tight knot in my middle remained. I'd almost let him die because of my own stupid problems.

I gathered his blade and passed him his things, then glanced at Gabe and Nora. "We can't leave them here."

"Take them to my consulting room," Lucas said. "We'll deal with them later." He shot me a grin and headed to the steps. "Race you to the farm."

More glad than I ever thought I'd be to see that devilish smile, I followed him out, Roux trailing behind. We attempted to appear innocuous as we ran through the storm past the glowing remains of the boulangerie, dipping under cordons to get past. Two police cars, an ambulance, three fire trucks and countless firemen packed the street. A couple of policemen swayed, looking decidedly sick. We were the least of anyone's concern.

We made it to Lucas's SUV. I jumped into the driver's seat, Lucas into the passenger side, Roux in the back. Lucas was clearly in a lot of pain, though attempting to hide it. I made a U-turn and sped down the road, the thunder deafening, wind-lashed rain strobing with relentless lightning.

Lucas rang Félix. Despite the storm, the gang was managing to deliver the potion, but it was slow going. None of them were sick—Gabe wouldn't have given them the potion—and they'd managed to enlist some other guys to help.

A little further on, the flank of Picou de Bompas sparked as countless spears of lightning struck something up on the hill—the wards around the farm. My phone rang. I would've ignored it, but it was Alice's ringtone. I chucked it on the dash and requested speakerphone.

"Camille, you okay?" Alice cried above the thunder and driving rain.

"I'm good," I yelled.

"We're ill... this thing that's going around." Not her. Please, not her. "I don't know what's happening in the town," she added pitifully. "The storm... everyone's ill."

"Call this number for treatment," Lucas said. He gave Félix's details then some brief self-care instructions. I sent a silent prayer that Félix and the guys would get there.

"You're still with the doctor," she managed when he'd finished. Even now I could tell she was curious.

"Helping out." I raised my brow at Lucas. Some help.

"Damn good help," he said in a low voice. I wasn't sure where that had come from. "Not with the rats," I mumbled back, then I said to Alice, "Rest up. Look after yourselves and we'll be there as soon as possible. I've got to go... love you." I hated disconnecting, but needs must.

I pulled up the hill into a torrent of water gushing down the lane. Too much water. I forced the SUV on.

The road curved then levelled for a short way. The headlights caught a mudslide plummeting down the mountain to our side. It pummelled into the SUV, sending the back end skidding into the trees.

"Dear gods," Roux cried.

"Keep going," Lucas shouted as he fiddled with the touchscreen to alter the drive. I thrust the car into a low gear and bumped and jolted over the debris, almost losing control as a rock hurtled into us.

As we approached the farm, silver met arcs of gold as lightning struck the wards. We were almost there. Slaloming around boulders and fallen branches, I headed for the turning.

Crunch. Something slammed into the roof, then the side. With a crash, the windows shattered. All I could make out as the storm lashed in were shrouds of black. I swerved precariously, unable to see. We were smashed into again and again, the SUV buffeting around. A long, bony hand dove in through where the windscreen should have been. It groped around. We dodged its claws.

"Just keep going," Lucas yelled.

"Right now, scrapelather would be preferable to reality," Roux cried. Yep—I'd agree.

Bones and shrouds obscured my vision. I angled the SUV toward what I hoped was the farm gate and put my foot down. We shot forward and then... silence. We were inside the wards, the hantaumo gone.

I thrust my foot on the brake and we skidded to a halt before the loft wall. The battered SUV doors not working, Lucas kicked his open and we all clambered out.

In the valley below, the gale-lashed lights of Tarascon were just visible. The ward flashed warm gold each time it was struck by hantaumo, revealing its protective dome and the criss-crossing fractures. The wards were holding off the weather as well as the wraiths. The timing of the storm wasn't inconsequential. Roux had said the hantaumo possessed weather magic.

"I'm surprised the wards have lasted this long," Lucas said. "Izak's originals must have been potent." With hundreds of wraiths pounding the arc, I shuddered to think what they were doing with the townsfolk... my friends... Alice.

I glanced around the yard. Countless mini prehistoric warriors were stationed about the place—in the yard, in trees, on walls, on goats, on the roofs of the farmhouse, the loft and the barn. The goats were milling about the yard, distressed by the commotion, releasing the occasional bleat. Rose paced from one to another, nudging her muzzle into their necks—the goat equivalent of "Buck up, girls—keep calm and carry on".

"Men, report," Lucas called.

Slaughter emerged from behind Hyacinth, who chewed at his tunic. "All is fine on the farm. Izak is stable. We're awaiting your instructions."

"We need to strengthen the wards," Lucas said. "Where's the central point?"

Roux pointed to the milking barn. "From the shape of the dome, it appears to be over there." Yep, that was right where Grampi would have placed it. The goats were the centre of his world.

"Let's get Izak," Lucas said to me. "We'll garrison in the barn. Roux, prepare the ward collude as fast as you can."

Lucas and I sprinted into the farmhouse. Grampi lay in bed, surrounded by a sturdy guard of Men. His fingertips were as rotten as when I'd last seen him, but not worse, and for some reason he was grinning.

"How are you doing?" I cried as I wrapped myself around him. Part of me had wondered if I'd see him again.

He pulled me into a bear hug, patting the blade on my back. "Grab them by the horns," he roared. And for once, he made sense.

"Monsieur Amiel," Lucas said, "I'm going to carry you to the barn. We'll settle in there for a bit." I stepped back. Lucas hauled Grampi carefully over his shoulder, wincing as the weight pressed into his wounds. Flanked by Men, we ran through the herd of antsy goats as the wards flashed above.

"Almost ready," Roux called as we entered the barn. He continued scattering herbs.

Lucas lowered Grampi onto a pile of straw in the middle. I knelt down beside him and a battalion of Men drew into formation around us.

"The last few components..." Roux scattered the alder leaves.

A terrible splintering echoed from above. I glanced out of the window to see the wards striated by twice as many cracks.

Roux opened another bag and pulled out broken pieces of greyish rock, specks of yellow visible here and there. He noticed my gaze. "Gold ore. Ritual rocket fuel."

The wards creaked and groaned louder than the thunder.

"Let's start," Lucas said.

Roux grabbed his staff from its resting place on the goat stand and positioned himself at the front of the ring of alder leaves. Lucas stood at the back, me and Grampi between.

Raising his staff, Roux began. "Unknowable power that spans darkness and light, that animates breath, that nurtures root and stem and blossom. We link with your essence..." A glow arose as Roux and Lucas connected with the herbs. It shot from point to point, forming a shining septagram. "That which shapes rock, which carves earth, which sculpts hollows. That which creates a sublime, resplendent, unending geometry. That which carries sunlight and moon-light and starlight. That which bonds and fuses and coalesces, and is unfathomable in length, breadth and width. That which—"

"Roux!" Lucas yelled, the creaking growing.

"Strengthen the wards about this place," Roux jabbered. The light from the botanical star rushed inward, illuminating the alder leaves and flaring as it linked with the gold. It expanded outward beyond the walls of the barn and joined with the existing dome, saturating it in light. One by one, the cracks fused and vanished.

Roux lowered his arms and nodded. "That should hold—"

Boom. The tremor flung us to the ground. Grampi groaned. I raised my head from the straw and peered through the window. The wards were cracked like the safety glass in a car, scored with countless fissures, so many more. If I hadn't known what it meant, the myriad of glinting edges would have been beautiful. But the implication... The collude hadn't been enough. Lucas, Roux and I exchanged looks, Lucas's eyes wide, Roux's jaw open. The Men sprang up bearing battle-ready grimaces.

Boom. Rubble crashed down. I threw myself over Grampi and covered my head with my hands as air blasted through the barn. Debris stung me, and rain lashed my skin, soaking me instantly. Except it couldn't—we were indoors. I glanced up. The roof and the front of the barn were gone— blasted away.

A few hessian sacks lay in the straw. I threw them over Grampi, hoping they might hold off some of the downpour. I peered out through the deluge. Everything was black. As my eyes adjusted, a glow grew outside, pale and unearthly. It delineated the streaking rain, its starkness reminding me of Gabe's magic.

In the cold light, the farmyard lay before us. A part of the loft and the near wall of the farmhouse had also crumbled. I gazed about, unable to comprehend that the farm—everything I'd worked for over the years—had been wrecked in the blink of an eye.

My ears rang, possibly a result of the blast, but my neck prickled and the sound became shrill—rising and falling and rising again, until it formed a hellish wailing.

And with it came the hantaumo.

CHAPTER 33

We sprang up. Lucas and I drew our blades. Fat lot of good mine would do me. Roux brandished his staff. Rain dripped off us and our weapons.

"Remember, the hantaumo are here for Izak," Lucas shouted above the storm. "Protect him at all costs. The potion will be taking effect on more and more victims. If we can reduce the wraiths' numbers, we'll have a chance." There was way too much chance in that for me. "And it's not only Izak and the townsfolk," he added. "There's no telling what the hantaumo might do beyond Tarascon."

We positioned ourselves next to Grampi. A number of Men circled us, just far enough away so we could swing a blade without risking them. The rest of the little guys thronged about. There had been hundreds before, but now there were thousands. They filled the yard, lined the remaining roofs and crowded the steep slope to the back of the farm, their weapons a range of axes and spears with spear throwers, although some had slingshots and bows. And right at Grampi's side stood Slaughter. He gave me a black-toothed grin. Perhaps our chances were better than I'd thought. The goats milled about amidst the Men. They were defenceless bystanders. I couldn't understand why they didn't have the sense to run off up the mountain.

The wailing rose and the storm whistled as it bore countless black shrouds. The hantaumo swept over the trees and closed in, the unnatural glow growing as they approached. They were met by a barrage of spears, the Men reloading their throwers again and again at preternatural speed with an inexhaustible supply of ammunition from who knew where.

Despite the hantaumo's aerial acrobatics as they dodged this way and that, the wraiths were struck through the eye, in the neck and all along whatever was under those shrouds. They crashed down to be swarmed by Men, axes chopping into rotting flesh, goats springing away to cower in corners.

My stomach pitched at the violence. I wanted to hide in a corner and vomit, but it wasn't only the battle, it was the almost tangible malice that filled the place. It was beyond unnerving, and it reminded me of the pit. Horror rippled through my veins just as it had back when that terrifying presence had risen above me.

The hantaumo changed tactics. They pelted in and dove for the legions of Men on the ground, ploughing them into mud and groundwater as they swept along. Men pounced on their backs mid-flight, hacking into bones and putrid flesh. The wraiths retaliated, tearing warriors to shreds with teeth and claws. But their low flying was a kamikaze tactic, and they were soon overwhelmed. That didn't stop them coming, the onslaught disrupting the Men's first line of defence. One of the hantaumo thudded into Daisy, ripping into her with its teeth for no good reason. I couldn't watch as she fell. And through it all, Lucas, Roux, Slaughter and I stood there, rain drenching us as we waited for the first hantaumo to make it past the outer defences.

Above the kamikaze wraiths, more hantaumo flew in, this time in a tight formation, their wailing deafening. "Be ready, everyone!" Lucas cried.

The outermost wraiths fell to the ground, speared or arrowed. Those in the centre remained unharmed. They plunged toward us, the sense of malice doubling with their proximity. Lucas sprang forward, grunting as he thrust and slashed, bony heads falling. Roux just about managed to defend himself, cudgelling a hantaumo with his staff. Slaughter bristled, not having the opportunity to fight due to his height. All I could fight was the roiling in my stomach and the gagging in my throat. There was too much blood. I sank into the soaked straw at Grampi's side, trying not to hurl. A hantaumo shot toward me. I had to kill it. My fingers trembled around the wet hilt of my blade. It was kill or die. Kill or die... Die like those bodies in the pit.

"Camille, strike!" Lucas roared. "At least defend yourself!"

With a deafening screech, the wraith's claws pierced my back, searing through my skin. Lucas dove over and severed its head. It released me and I clutched the wound, clamping my teeth to stifle a cry that wasn't just at the pain—it was at my impotence as countless Men lost their lives.

Slaughter finished a wraith that had fallen close by. Roux batted one as though he was playing baseball, until it yanked the staff from his hands. He fished inside his cloak, and two swords and a dagger fell out. He grabbed a sword and attempted to slash the hantaumo. It swerved and landed on Lucas's point.

Another wraith converged from the back, aiming straight for Grampi. I followed its descent, unable to do anything, my sword hand shaking. Grampi rolled over on his bed of straw and grabbed one of Roux's daggers. As the wraith reached him, he pierced it through the nose hole, gore splattering us both. "Damned fine wattles," he yelled.

A host of hantaumo nose-dived for us, razor teeth bared, claws outstretched. "Inner circle Men," Slaughter shouted. "Defend."

The closest Men spun around and launched spears, but the wraiths had closed in too quickly. Lucas sprang over. With his legs either side of Grampi, he cut down the first, the second, the third. The Men had adapted their defence and were taking down higher hantaumo as they plummeted through the downpour at our weakest point. Roux was managing to dodge attacks with surprising speed as he flailed his blade.

But more and more came, swamping the Men's defences. Lucas and the others couldn't keep up, and I just sat there.

"There's too many," Roux called.

A wraith dove into Lucas, taking a chunk out of his neck.

It spiralled upside down to avoid his blade, then lacerated his thigh.

"I should perform a collude," Roux yelled as he swiped. "Petition a deity. It might be our only hope."

"What's the point of that?" Lucas shouted. "You've been trying all day."

"They might respond now we're under attack."

Lucas barked a laugh. "Fat chance."

A movement other than fighting caught my attention. On the rising ground behind the broken barn walls, one of the goats was strutting confidently toward the battle, long brown hair tussled in the storm, curved horns resplendent. The hantaumo were thankfully ignoring it and most of the other goats, presumably because they weren't a threat, meaning that this goat could descend unhindered. There was something about her. A certain presence... a bearing. She trotted through the commotion into the yard, bleating—calling to her herd. Rose came first, leaping slain hantaumo and Men. Then the surviving goats joined her side, obedient to their true queen.

"Delphine," I muttered, unable to believe it. "She's back."

"Damned fine milker. Best queen ever," Grampi said.

Lucas managed to raise his brow as he drove his sword into shrouds and sinews. "Told you I didn't eat her."

I don't know how I'd been mistaken, but he really hadn't.

The herd mustered, Delphine lowered her head, her huge horns curling over her, her foot scraping the ground. Her yard was a mess, and she was not happy. She charged, the herd following suit. The goats stormed in and skewered hantaumo left, right and centre.

Then, through death cries, screams, the raging storm and the constant shrieking of the hantaumo, came a low-pitched rumbling that grew until it reverberated in my chest. From the edge of the trees stalked countless black shapes. The dark forms were almost indiscernible in the eerie glow, although the bared muzzles dripping with saliva were clear. The reverberation was the unearthly growl of sinagries.

They pounced in, leaping to catch airborne wraiths, snapping necks and crunching bone. I guessed they'd liked the chouquettes. What with the sinagries, the goats butting and trampling and the Men soldiering on bravely, few hantaumo made it through their onslaught.

Lucas and the others stilled, poised and at the ready, their chests heaving. The wraiths' numbers diminished rapidly, the shrieking and battle-cries lowering. In the pause, the carnage was clear, bodies of Men and hantaumo scattered about. It grew quieter, then the storm abated to deathly stillness. We... They'd done it. The few remaining wraiths formed a black cloud that retreated back over the town.

But slowly the cloud expanded until it teamed with a mass of shrouds. It built and built, burgeoning closer, until, with an unearthly keening, in swept thousands of hantaumo.

"Okay, Roux," Lucas said. "I'm not averse to trying an invocation." Because it was all too clear, even with the help of the sinagries and the goats, we were as good as dead.

CHAPTER 34

LUCAS, THE MEN, THE GOATS AND THE SINAGRIES rallied as the hantaumo came in from all sides. Roux dropped his sword, drew a bundle of herb bags from his cloak and handed me some. "Faster work with two."

Fighting nausea and the urge to curl up by Grampi, I sheathed my sword and took the bags from him. I couldn't fight, but at least I could do this.

"Scatter them in a circle at the Men's perimeter," he said. "We're never going to make a complex geometric form in this chaos."

"Men, cover them," Lucas called as he speared a hantaumo through its screeching jaws.

I sprinkled the herbs as I'd done at the dolmen, although with a lot more haste. All the time, Lucas, Slaughter and the Men had our backs. Goats and sinagries were falling, and the Men were thinning. My vision tunnelled from the carnage. It was better if I didn't look.

"Today might be nice," Lucas yelled.

We sprinkled the rest at double speed.

"Get in the centre," Roux shouted.

Standing either side of Grampi, Roux scattered alder leaves and gold around us. As Lucas fought one hantaumo, another dove into his chest, hurtling him to the ground. A knot of wraiths headed in from the back. Lucas rolled across the circle and lanced two. Slaughter sprang on a wraith, then climbed its back and tomahawked its skull.

Roux raised his arms. "O unknowable omniscient light that illuminates fae and human realms," he chanted in a tone that really did seem a little slow considering our impending doom. "O Abellion, god of light, ruler of the mighty Pyrenean host, resplendent majesty of deities, we entreat you most humbly in our time of need..." The circle of herbs glowed, but so many more hantaumo were coming in. Lucas and the Men were a blur of movement as they gave and received blows. "We call you here for your protection!" Roux cried. The glow built as it joined with the alder leaves, then it pulsed outward, shining brighter than the wraiths' cold light. It illuminated the vast host of hantaumo poised above, ready to attack. Roux and I waited as the battle raged.

"Should something be happening?" I called. The light dimmed.

"It should... but Abellion, for his own arrogant, complacent, stupid reasons, couldn't give a shit."

Roux's bloody face was lined with sorrow and fear. He shook his head. I stared around at the conflict, the death and ruin. So much pain, so much horror. Through it all a few goats and sinagries were battling on here and there with the remaining Men. The rest were down.

Over by the trees, Rose was still skirmishing, her horns low as she butted a fallen hantaumo. I'd seen her right there the other morning after I'd had the verity. Aherbelste had stood by her, and I'd thought he'd been a distortion of her pretty face. I'd seen so much in the past few days, and now this...

I made to drop down by Grampi's side, but an idea struck me. Slowly, I turned back to Rose. I'd seen Aherbelste here twice, plus once up on the slopes on the way to Fae. He was the god of goats and the home, even though he'd represented something much more terrible in recent religion. What had Roux said...? Gods would only help if they cared. They had to be invested in the cause... personally. Well, why had Aherbelste been here unless he had some kind of personal affinity or connection to the place? Perhaps the goats had drawn him.

"Roux," I called. "We have to do the ritual again." He drove a dagger into a writhing hantaumo. I ignored the urge to turn away. "Aherbelste, he's been here—he knows the farm. We have to try."

He raised his blood-spattered brow. "Alright. It's not like we've any other options. I'm low on herbs. What have you got?"

I fished in my pouch and handed him the bags. He rifled through the contents and passed some back. "Scatter these." We did so, almost hurling the stuff around. Lucas yelled as claws sliced down his arm. He kicked the wraith away and stomped on its head.

Roux raised his arms and linked with the substances, golden light building as it had before. "Aherbelste, god of goats, protector of home and hearth, dweller in this place, we call to—" The air grew thick with a blanket of hantaumo, raw hate bearing down. "We call to thee!" The light dissipated, only the cold glow of the hantaumo remaining.

"What the hell just happened?" I yelled.

"They're dampening the ritual. There's too many of them." Roux twisted his beard, his gaze despairing. "We'd need dragon's scale to get through this," he blabbered, "or a collude with a powerful animal... or golden alder leaves... possibly even Roland's sword... and as we don't have any of those things, we're..." He couldn't bring himself to voice the inevitable.

But I'd caught on something he'd said. It reminded me of a far-away dream... no, a memory. After Dame Blanche had helped me, she'd placed something in my hand... a golden leaf. But the recollection was distant. It had been a massive effort to recall the pit, and the rest had slipped away—but surely I'd tucked the leaf into my pouch...?

A hantaumo slammed into me from the side, knocking me to the ground. Slaughter and a group of men pounced and hacked the life out of it. I hauled myself up and dove into my pouch, but there was nothing there. If there had been, I would've noticed when I'd filled it or given herbs to Roux. I rummaged around desperately and caught a glint of gold. The lining had bunched at the bottom. I unfurled the fabric to reveal a superbly crafted golden alder leaf. Perhaps the gods hadn't abandoned us.

"If anyone has a last-ditch idea," Lucas shouted, "now might be the time. We're not going to be able to hold them for much longer."

I shot out my hand to Roux.

He goggled at the glinting gold. "What...? How...?"

Lucas caught a glimpse. "No time for questions. Get on with it."

Roux gathered the leaf into cupped hands and extended it before him. "Aherbelste, god of goats, protector of home and hearth, dweller in this place." A slight glow rose from the ring of herbs we'd scattered earlier. Sweat beaded on Roux's brow as he fought the hantaumo's blanket on his collude. Then he linked with the golden alder leaf. It vaporised to pure light that poured from his hands, blasting the miserable hantaumo away. "Aherbelste," Roux roared, "we call to thee!"

And from the trees arose a mighty beast. This time he stood as high as the farmhouse on two spindly goat legs, his head and horns a giant version of the herd's, although his chest rippled with a man's brawn—all apart from the Pyrenean goat hair across his pecs and down his middle. His horizontal irises glowed with an ethereal light as he surveyed the farm and roared.

As that awful bellow continued, light pulsed from him to the herd, infusing them with gold. The remaining goats paused to absorb his radiance as it shielded and strengthened them. Those slain in hairy heaps on the ground were brought to life. Daisy struggled up with a very mean glint in her eyes. As one, Aherbelste and the herd attacked.

If the shrieking had been bad before, it was worse now.

The hantaumo turned amass and dove for Aherbelste. He had the benefit of height—something none of us had down here between the buildings—and he swept his arms through the horde, casting them into trees and smashing them to the ground where waiting super-goats stamped and gouged them to death.

I drew my sword, then wondered why I'd bothered. Even so, the weight of it in my hand was comforting. Lucas finished off the last of the nearby hantaumo, but his movements were restricted. He was flagging or hurting. Probably both. I wasn't surprised after what he'd been through.

I returned to Grampi. "Best damned goats in the Pyrenees," he yelled. He was fine. Maybe... just maybe... we were almost through the worst. Aherbelste was making fast work of the wraiths.

A bloodless scream rent the air. I scoured the battlefield for the origin, my instincts howling that I had to protect myself from whatever released that splintering cry. A shadow rose from the valley, and my blood ran cold. I stared at it, numbed. It looked like a hantaumo, all shrouds and rotting flesh, though it was much larger, and a circlet of bone crowned its hooded skull. But the presence it brought with it... It was a nightmare beyond nightmares, absolute devastation.

"The hantaumo queen," Lucas muttered.

Something about her was familiar. Flickers came back... the pit, lifeless corpses, gaping mouths... and a presence looming above that my young mind couldn't face. My stomach pitched. The horror I'd not been able to see... the encounter I'd buried deep... it had been her, the hantaumo queen, I was sure of it. And now she was here, right in front of me. I couldn't move, couldn't breathe, the dread of that moment swamping me as though I'd never left the pit.

She rushed at Aherbelste and wrestled him to the ground. The wraiths, spurred by the sight of their leader mauling the enemy, stormed in, covering him entirely as they gnashed and tore at his skin.

And from Tarascon, more wraiths advanced. We'd wiped out so many, yet it hadn't been enough. Lucas and Slaughter rallied and met the new onslaught. Roux fell to the ground clutching a head wound. Riveted to the spot, I could only gape at the queen.

"We're not dead yet." Lucas managed to grin as he struck down another hantaumo.

"To the last man," Slaughter cried, slicing his axe into the bone foot of one that had flown too low.

A hantaumo rammed into me, hurtling me away from Grampi. I hit the ground and my blade went flying. The wraith positioned itself to strike, but someone took it out. I pushed up to my knees, unable to prevent my gaze returning to the queen, the vision of desolation.

She floated up from Aherbelste, who was overwhelmed by hantaumo. Unhurriedly, she turned to us—to Grampi—and approached. She'd wanted to take his life for years, and now she would. But as she glided closer, her leer settled on me, not him.

Pure terror rose, my heart hammering, my ears ringing. As she drifted toward me, she shrank to an almost human height. My instincts bawled to get the hell out—right now—yet something held me still. I caught Lucas's alarmed glance, but he and the others were barely managing to hold off their own attackers, never mind helping me.

The queen glided through our now ruined inner circle of defence. She drew near, her flesh dripping with putrid decay. An escort of wraiths closed in, a barrier against assistance.

"Camille Amiel." Her decomposing lips twisted with my name, her voice a delicate embrace before a disembowelling.

I wanted to scream, to back away, to run, but I could only tremble, just like in the pit. She smiled, if that warped grimace could be called a smile. "My dear, there's no point trying to escape. Our encounter all those years ago left you rather defenceless—unable to swing a blade if it meant a little blood." She tutted. "Monstrous rats weren't enough to spur you to action. And now, you can't even move. Truly, fear is the best restraint. Nothing more is needed."

She drifted closer, my nostrils full of her carrion reek, her gaze alone enough to rip me apart. "I've been watching you," she said, "listening from the dark lands."

The thought that the thing from the pit had somehow been tracking me... it was too much.

"You believe I'm here for Izak," she continued, "and that all my efforts are for him. My curse ruined his life in the most delightful way, and his death will be a bonus, but it isn't him I want. It never was." She dragged her bony talons down my cheek almost lovingly, her touch desolation. "No, Camille. I want you. Izak's granddaughter for my daughter's desertion. A fair exchange, don't you think?"

That's why I'd been taken as a child—she'd wanted me in revenge for Mathilde's betrayal. Somehow, back then she'd not succeeded, and she'd returned for me.

The queen shot forward and rammed her palms into my chest, thrusting me to the ground, my head striking something. Her talons clamped my upper arms, pinning them to my sides, her weight holding me down. I attempted to struggle, but I was as helpless as I'd been as a child.

She drew her bony hands inward, her claws piercing my chest. I tried to move, panic and pain fogging everything. There was no doubt, she would take my life. Yet through it all, I thought I heard something... a voice... a sweet voice... "Camille, reach out your hand. Come on, Camille, reach out to me. You can do it." But the queen's talons found residence between my ribs and agony prevailed. Even then, I couldn't scream.

She lowered her head to my neck, her lips brushing my skin.

"My dear," she whispered. "You will taste so good."

CHAPTER 35

THE QUEEN BURROWED INTO MY NECK, HER TEETH searing skewers, yet I was a passive lamb, my world pain and nothing more. Part of me roared that I had to get away from her, but the terror of years ago froze me.

My head spun as she sucked delicately, taking more than blood, taking my strength, my will, my essence. As she continued, the commotion of battle muffled, the carnage narrowing... blurring... until I could only see corpses—not broken Men and sinagries in the farmyard, but gaping mouths, faces frozen in torment, bodies decomposing. The pain dulled, and the memory of lying in the pit as a small child all those years ago filled my being.

Something hovered above me. This time I knew what. I recoiled, petrified. I'd been so small, I'd not known that something as awful as the queen could exist. The presence of oblivion that accompanied her was so diabolical, my young mind couldn't begin to process it. She sank lower, her tattered shrouds fluttering, her skull dripping with putrid flesh, her bony claws outstretched for me... She wanted me.

Closer she came, her talons encircling my bare arms. She screeched. I had the notion it was a shriek of joy, of claiming, but it took on an agonised edge. Her claws released me and she fell back, a spear in her middle. She pulled it free, registering a silhouette on the side of the pit. With an infernal howl she swooped away and battled the figure in a blur of slashes.

The next thing I knew, someone was calling my name. "Camille, give me your hand. Come on, Camille, reach out to me. You can do it..." Such a sweet sound amidst the nightmare. I couldn't imagine anything that lovely after this hell. In the corner of my eye, I noticed the queen slumped in a heap by the edge of the pit, her shrouds covering body after body.

The voice called again. "Come on, Camille, just reach out for me. I know you can." It was the woman who had battled the hantaumo with Grampi—Mathilde. She leant over the side of the pit, her hand outstretched across mangled remains. She was way off. If only I could wriggle toward her, but I was paralysed with fear.

Mathilde cursed. She rose and stepped on one of the bodies, trying her weight. It sank down, a deathly stench rising up. She returned to her front and tentatively shimmied across the corpses, her torso smearing with blood and entrails. Her fingers wrapped around my wrist and she crept back, pulling me with her. At the edge, she clutched me in her arms and set off, clambering up the scorched rock face at the pit's edge. All the time she muttered soothing, gentle words… words I'd longed to hear in that misery.

But as we rounded the top, something cast a shadow over us. The queen had risen. She hung in the air, huge and vengeful. Mathilde sprinted onward, almost crashing into an oncoming figure. Grampi. He took me, and Mathilde turned to face her mother as we pelted away.

The hantaumo descended from all around, and there were people—no, fae—with weapons, protecting us and heading for the queen. But, looking back over Grampi's shoulder, my gaze fixed on Mathilde as she grappled with her mother, then sank down, lifeless.

My child self couldn't understand what had happened— all she felt was terror. But my adult self was there too this time, reliving the memory with her, and something new began to ease through my body… a harrowing dismay for Mathilde, who'd given her life to rescue me. The tragedy was all too clear. Then the dismay grew tight and raw and firestorm hot.

I was angry.

Scratch that. I was fucking furious.

The queen had traumatised me, she'd caused indescribable misery to countless creatures, and she'd killed her own daughter. Not only that, but part of my hazy consciousness was still aware of the farm, of me being used as a tasty snack, and of everything I loved crumbling. I needed to do something about it.

Fury urged me on, a life force of its own. I groped through the reverie toward my awareness of the farm, desperate to clamber out of myself. As I got close, streaks of pain overwhelmed me, and I fell back, back to the pit, as though the queen was somehow holding me at bay. I tried to return again, but I couldn't push through.

Then, in a flood of agony, I was back, and the world reconfigured. The queen had released her bite hold and my sides, her blood-curdling shrieks filling the air. I tried to make sense of everything through the driving rain as I gritted my teeth against the pain. Lucas came into focus. He'd made it through the hantaumo and had driven his sword into the queen's side. As he pulled it out, wraiths closed in.

He thrust his blade into the hantaumo next to him, spun and speared two at the rear, then took out another with a roundhouse, but there were too many. They seized him and yanked his arms behind his back, one prying the sword from his hand.

The queen left me slumped on the ground and floated over. Lucas had given me an opportunity. My wounds were excruciating, but the pain was nothing compared to the indignation thrumming through my blood. I balled my hands into fists and squelched the debris of the soaked barn floor between my fingers. Even that small movement hurt. But... I'd moved. Fury had released me.

To be sure, I stirred my toes in my sodden boots then bunched and released the muscles in my limbs. The tiny movements, unnoticeable to the queen, brought me back to myself. I was free. I wasn't that small child, frozen in the face of the queen's indescribable horror. I was in charge of my own damned impulses. And I'd do whatever it took to guarantee she never raised her ugly head again.

She rose a little way in the air before Lucas, appearing no worse for wear after her impaling. "Lucas Rouseau. A pleasure to meet you," she drawled.

"The pleasure is all yours," he replied with a look almost as evil as hers. His captors stepped back, leaving him alone in front of the queen. He eyed their retreat suspiciously, assessing his next move. Before he had time to act, the queen slammed him to the ground and pinned him down as she had me. Lucas writhed against her.

I needed to make a move. And quick. The queen was convinced I was paralysed. I had my chance. Shifting only my gaze, I searched for my sword. There it was, a glimmer on my periphery—I'd struck my head on it when she'd attacked me. I assessed the distance between myself, the blade and the queen.

"Hmmm. You really are a heavy burden for your family to bear," she said to Lucas, stilling him with ease. "They will be overjoyed to hear I've broken you." She twisted his sword arm. The crack was audible, even in the din of battle. Lucas cried out then gritted his teeth.

Shit. I had to do something. But she was angled so she'd notice my slightest move. She'd be on me before I could do anything.

Two hantaumo forced Lucas's head and shoulders back. The queen pulled off his already ripped tunic and placed her bony claws at his clavicle. Her fingers splayed, she dragged her nails unhurriedly down his chest, skin and muscle springing open as she slashed. He screamed, arching against her. Damn it to hell. I needed something to ensure she wouldn't notice me move.

A flare of outrage jerked my sinews painfully tight. Was my apprehension just an excuse not to use my blade, like before? I was fast. I'd reach her before she could react. And if I didn't, well then, I'd deal with it.

As the queen stilled her claws, Lucas managed to turn his head a little, his glassy gaze meeting mine. Those dark eyes held suffering... and something more. Not a call for help. Perhaps just acknowledgement—a recognition of the crazy few days we'd spent together.

She turned to follow his gaze. "Oh yes, our dear Camille can't offer any assistance, the poor mite. Encountering me all those years ago has left her rather incapacitated. Not to worry. I'll make your death quick"—she wrapped her claws around Lucas's neck—"then I can get right back to her." She squeezed, crushing the life from him. He choked, his face red, his eyes bulging. Revelling in his agony, she grinned. One thing was for sure, it was now or never.

For a split second I paused, terror blanketing me once again, but rage wouldn't let it take hold. In a swift movement, I grabbed my blade, sprang up and leapt over. The queen turned, her ugly jaws parting as she registered my advance. Before she could move, I swung the sword up, grasped the hilt with both hands, and with a roar, drove the blade down on her neck.

Steel met bone and the blade freed. I stilled the momentum before it struck Lucas's chest. The queen's head rolled to the ground and her body slammed onto Lucas. Released, he gasped for air, his eyes wide with disbelief.

I balked at the severed neck, but it was merely a disgusting sight—the pit, the queen and the rest of it a fraction of the horror it had been. Gathering myself, I brandished my blade at the surrounding wraiths, my breath heaving, but they were motionless, staring at their dead leader in horror.

A strange stillness descended upon the battlefield. Aherbelste, the goats and what remained of the Men fought on, but the storm abated and the hantaumo's shrieking dissipated. As if sensing the queen's death, the rest of the wraiths turned to gaze at her remains.

Aherbelste took advantage of the distraction and sprang up, pulling wraiths from his body then tearing them from the air, snapping and stamping with hands and hooves. The hantaumo around us edged away and rose, screeching to their sisters. The wraiths not currently being mauled by goats or kneecapped by Men joined them, and the evil throng soared out of sight. The eerie glow dissipated. For a moment it was pitch black, then the moon came out, illuminating the yard.

I scoured around for the others. Roux crouched in the back corner of the barn, his hands over his head. Slaughter and a number of Men had formed a protective prehistoric-man barrier around Grampi. In the stillness they disassembled, avoiding Grampi's flailing arms. He was clearly alright.

I hauled the queen's body from Lucas and dropped down beside him. His chest was a bloody mess, his arm lay at an unnatural angle and his eyes were glazed, but the corner of his mouth tugged up ever so slightly. With some difficulty he met my gaze. "You did it, Camille," he rasped.

But there were too many dead—Men and sinagries. Aherbelste appeared unscathed from his mauling and was stamping out the last of the wraiths that hadn't escaped. The goats followed his lead, still glowing from whatever Aherbelste had done to them. As I took in the destruction, my inaction galled, a rawness I couldn't begin to confront. Not to mention that everything had happened because the queen had wanted me.

But enough inertia for a lifetime. Lucas needed help. "Roux," I shouted.

He hobbled over with a limp and gawked at Lucas. "Well, well, well. We'll have to do something about that." He tucked his hand into his torn and blood-spattered cloak and pulled out a vial. "One of his healing potions. Should start the restorative process nicely."

As Roux tipped it gently to Lucas's lips, Slaughter appeared. "Honestly, boss, see what happens when we leave you for one second."

Lucas groaned. I couldn't tell if it was from his wounds or his obligatory sovereignty over the little guys.

Aherbelste strode up, shrinking to around twice my height. He lowered his head. "I will hunt down and kill the rest of the escaped hantaumo," he rumbled. "And I will ensure the fetters of those in the dark lands are secure." We all stared at him. No doubt everyone else was thinking the same as me—that giant goat mouth had just spoken.

"Uh," I managed, "thank you for everything."

He smiled—he actually smiled with those rubbery goat lips. "After all, it is my farm, on my land," he said, "and these are my goats. Although I am honoured to have the Amiels as custodians." Yep, I'd thought so. Grampi was the owner on paper, but the land itself belonged to forces much older than our family. Aherbelste bowed his head once again, then stalked off into the trees.

Some of the herd made to follow, but Delphine bleated. They returned to the yard and began grazing. Rose, resurrected Daisy and the rest of them were chomping and chewing the remains of the hantaumo. With that as goat fodder, there was no way we were going to make cheese for a long, long while.

The Men were already dealing with their dead and aiding wounded comrades and sinagries. A kerfuffle came from the group around Grampi. He'd managed to sit up. "Honestly, would you give a man the space to breathe? You've done a superb job protecting me, and I'm grateful—I truly am—but now I'm perfectly alright."

My mouth fell open. No goats. Not one mention of a goat or a goat-related subject.

He angled his head and grinned. "Damned good fight. One for the journals."

I ran over and threw my arms around his neck, then drew back, assessing him. His hands were a normal colour, and he looked better than he had in a very long time. "I can't believe it. The curse... it's gone."

He beamed. "Curses tend to go with the death of their creators."

"Well, say something else." I needed the reassurance he wasn't going to launch into goat-speak again.

"Camille," he murmured. My stomach flipped with joy. It was the first time he'd spoken my name in years, and it was warmth and home and love. "Camille." He brushed a strand of hair from my extremely grimy face. "I'm so proud of you, chérie."

CHAPTER 36

I PEERED THROUGH THE LOFT WINDOW, SCANNING THE yard for Grampi. The farm had an early-morning freshness about it, and from the looks of the sky, it would be a fine day.

Men's calls echoed around as they patched up the farm-house masonry, hanging from makeshift rope ladders that extended from the roof. After the battle, they'd cleared away the perished fac, returning them to their kind. In the week since, they'd done an amazing job repairing the wall of my loft, the barn and the part of the farmhouse that had been blasted to smithereens. Now they were putting the last touches to everything. I'd wondered how we were going to disguise the damage and the speedy restoration, but Roux had temporarily glamoured the place in case of unsuspecting visitors.

The Men's death toll had been high, very high. But Slaughter had explained that on their demise, the warriors returned to the Great Sorcerer of the Cave for an epic feast involving a lot of something that sounded rather like scrapelather. Once fortified and completely hammered, they would reincarnate to claim the honour of another life. Reincarnation, it seemed, didn't involve procreation. The Men just appeared fully formed and ready to dismember the foot of anyone who had a problem with that.

This meant there were fewer Men around to help as they were all partying in the cave. The knowledge that they wouldn't be gone forever made the horror of that night a little easier to bear. I'd already spotted a couple of the fallen rebuilding the place.

The goats were hale and hearty thanks to Aherbelste. The only real losses were the sinagries. One of the survivors had stayed at the farm, lurking in the trees. I'd fed it five macarons for breakfast this morning, the poor thing.

And considering everything the townsfolk had been through, they were doing remarkably well. The D&D gang had managed to deliver Lucas's potion far and wide, so the wraiths had struggled to feed on victims to the point of death. Once the hantaumo had been wiped out or fettered, recovery took a few days. In the end there had been three deaths in addition to Henri and Madame Bonnet, and all of them in the elderly and infirm. Lucas had orchestrated everything to look like a dysentery outbreak, and the severity of the storm was explained as a freak of nature.

There was no sign of Grampi in the yard. I'd pop into the farmhouse before work and catch him. I grabbed my sword and slung the scabbard over my shoulder. After the hantaumo, the blade was staying right by my side. I rubbed my neck where the queen's jaws had pierced my flesh, and the whole thing flashed before me once again. Lucas's healing potion had left nothing but a faint scar, though I'd had nightmares ever since. But... I'd killed her. I'd broken through my fears. And now I could damned well protect myself and others.

I took my bag from the sofa and paused, staring at the notepad underneath—the notes I'd made on the hantaumo and the queen. I now had masses of firsthand information on the creatures, but it was observational rather than anecdotal, and it fitted into anthropological study rather than pure folk lore. Anyway, there was nothing I could do with it. No one would believe me, and I'd be a laughing stock if I attempted publication.

I headed downstairs and stepped outside, tripping over a heap on the doorstep. I regained my balance and scanned the pile of random objects—a huge sheep's fleece, sheafs of freshly cut herbs, a root, mushrooms, a large cow's horn filled with a brown substance, a stunning woven blanket, a cured ham, a jar of honey.

Grampi strode over from the barn. "Payment," he said as he drew near.

"What?" I picked up the horn and smelled the contents, jerking it away as the odour hit.

He hung his arm around my shoulders, merry creases playing in the corners of his eyes. Since the curse had broken, he'd looked much better—and younger. He squeezed me to him. "Payment for services rendered."

I shook my head, still not understanding.

"For your work as a Keeper," he added. "Fae give a token of their appreciation, and this is a particularly fine hoard."

I stared at the pile then at Grampi. Roux had said the pay was good, but... "Uh... this is it? Nothing else... like money?" I was grateful—really, I was—the goods looked like they'd taken a lot of effort to make or produce. But I thought Roux meant gold or silver, or at least something with market value.

Grampi unhooked his arm and examined the root. "You could buy anything with this mandragore. It's very fresh. Probably best you hang it to dry." I could buy anything in Fae, perhaps, but it wouldn't help with the bills.

He placed the mandragore down and shook his head, his attention on my scabbard. His snowy beard quivered as he drew a shaky breath, then he met my gaze. "You know, I never meant for you to be a Keeper. I only taught you swordsmanship because you loved it so much. The last thing I wanted was to put you in danger."

I squeezed his hand. "I know that."

The regret on his face brought back our escape from the queen when I'd been a child, and it brought back Mathilde as she'd sunk down lifeless. The memory had harried me since the battle, and there was something I needed to ask. "Mathilde..." I struggled to find the words. "She died because of me." It was so unfair that one person should lose their life in exchange for another. "And the destruction the other night... I was the one the queen wanted."

Grampi grasped my shoulders and fixed me in the eye. "Mathilde chose to face her mother then and there. Not because of you, but because their confrontation was long overdue." I lowered my head. He shook my shoulders a little. "And don't ever blame yourself for the queen's deluded actions. You didn't do anything. She chose to come after you from a misguided sense of revenge."

I nodded. He was right, but it didn't lessen the pain.

His gaze hardened. "You know, you don't have to become a Keeper."

My lips tugged into a half-hearted smile. "Maybe I won't." Especially considering the danger and the pay. But one thing was for certain—I'd seen another realm, and I was completely and utterly fascinated.

He raised his bushy eyebrows. "Not that I have to worry. I know how lethal you are with that thing." He inclined his head to my blade.

"Deadly," I said with a grin.

———

"She's absolutely amazing. Maman says she's one of a kind." Alice was mid-clean of the espresso machine, the café's early-morning rush over. She nodded towards the kitchen, where a plump figure crowned with a pearly-white bun was deep in discussion with Inès about the amount of sourdough needed for a brioche leaven. "I mean, she bakes like an angel," Alice added. "I've never tasted anything so good, not even Maman's brioche, although don't you dare tell her I said that."

I finished putting through a payment. "She's great, isn't she?" Dame Blanche turned and met my gaze, her lips pursed, her eyes sparkling. I grinned back. When I'd first visited her, she'd been fervent about the integration of the fae and human realms and the benefit to all. So when I'd returned to thank her for the alder leaf, I'd asked if she was interested in the job. It had been a long shot, but she'd accepted.

And it wasn't only Dame Blanche. To encourage inter-mingling and help keep the borders firmly bound, Roux had put word out in Fae that all creatures were welcome in the human part of town, glamoured of course. Our current clien-tele, apart from a few humans, were two goblins and an elf. It was early days, but we were going to give the goblin boulanger in fae Tarascon a run for his money.

"It's the first time ever Maman has allowed anyone to take her place baking the brioche," Alice replied. "Now she can damned well put her feet up and take it easy. Where on earth did you find Blanche?"

"Uh..." How to answer that one? "Umm... she has a small cottage in the mountains... remote. I just... bumped into her one day."

"Stroke of luck..." Her voice trailed away as Lucas entered. "Hot doctor at nine o'clock," she whispered.

I'd told her about the huge mistake of a drunken hookup, and she'd berated me for not sharing sooner. I was glad she knew, but still that gulf loomed. I couldn't tell her about Fae or her boyfriend's secret identity, and I desperately wanted to.

"I'll leave you to it," she said with a smirk. She was

convinced there was more to our relationship. There was. Just not in the way she thought.

Lucas swaggered up to the counter, appearing all better thanks to a number of potions and a few colludes. "Hot," he said with a grin. "A perfect description of me." He clearly had paranormal hearing as well as everything else.

I hid the smile that wanted to emerge, revealing only an amused glare. He was way too attractive for his own good, that much was for sure—the fickle arrogance in his straight mouth, the shrewd intelligence in his gaze, the musculature hiding under his shirt. Not to mention he'd slain multiple beasts in my defence, put his life on the line for the town, and hadn't eaten Delphine. There was a lot in his favour right now, although spiking my drink was completely inexcusable, and I couldn't shake the memory of him in the cave—his hideous true form.

Anyway, I wasn't going to indulge him. "Good morning, Lucas," I said in my most polite voice. "What can I get you? Poisonous rat to go?"

His face screwed up. "Eurgh... don't remind me. I'll have a noisette instead. Hold the poison."

I began his order. "Dysentery alibi still holding?"

"Perfectly. And apparently they found some corroded pipework in René's boulangerie. The explosion has been put down to a gas leak."

I snorted. "How ironic." As I passed him the cup, our fingers brushed. Lucas swallowed and looked away, appearing almost vulnerable for a split second. Was he still processing everything that had happened?

Then he plastered on a megawatt smile. "Oh, and Nora opted to retain her memories of Gabe and the hantaumo."

"Really? I thought she would've been all too happy to forget."

He shrugged. "Nope. Said life made sense that way. She understands the necessity of keeping quiet, and the consequences if she speaks out."

Nora's elven kidnapper pushed through the door and hurried to the counter dressed in his usual cloak. I couldn't tell if he had his ear tips on or if I was seeing him as he truly was. "Hey, Doctor Rouseau... Camille..." He eyed us warily. The poor guy had been through so much, in addition to the years with his ass of a father. "Pain au chocolat, please," he said.

"Late for school?" Lucas asked with a grin.

Gabe cast a nervous glance between us as I bagged up the viennoiserie. "Very, very late. Overslept."

I passed the bag. He paid with his phone then glanced between us again. "I just wanted to say, uh... thank you... for everything."

"All in the job," Lucas replied. "We were glad to help."

I let the "we" sit with me for a moment. It was strange, like a couple, but not a couple. Partners-in-arms. I still wasn't sure about it, though I nodded. "Any time." Then I realised what I'd said. "Actually, scrap that. We'll be here anytime *you* need us, but I would rather not deal with rats or hantaumo ever again."

"What she said." Lucas took a swig of his noisette.

Gabe's face closed in and his lip quivered. "I have to say I feel a bit bad about blowing up Papa's boulangerie." He looked down at his feet.

He'd said a bit, so not fully. I chuckled to myself. "Maybe it was your way of standing up to him, and perhaps that's not such a bad thing."

"Yeah," Gabe replied. "He seems kind of mellow since the explosion. Like on some level, he knows. Anyway, thanks for being there. I, uh… really appreciate it." With an apprehensive smile, he headed out.

Lucas's mouth quirked. "So now you're advising kids to blow up real estate to gain their parents' respect?"

"René is a jerk. And at least I don't go around spiking drinks. The doctor is truly the perfect role model."

He scraped his hand through his hair. "You're not going to forgive me for that, are you?"

"Never."

He stared at me, shaking his head, then said, "We'll have the rest of the week off, time to recuperate, then we need to get on with your training."

That was rather presumptuous. "I haven't agreed to be a Keeper yet."

"Either way, if you're going into Fae, you'll need guidance."

I couldn't argue with that, and I couldn't wait to get back there. Full folkloric immersion. "Sounds good," I said. "Any plans for your break?"

"I have to check on the bounds. Roux says the cracks are getting worse. And I have a date with a water nymph tonight. Not one of Naïs's daughters, you'll be glad to hear."

"Which only confirms my suspicion that you're a complete player." I shook my head. "Well, have a good time."

"I most definitely will." He bumped his brow and made his way out with a handful of customers.

A holler rose from outside. In the car park a hulk of a figure leered at a group of girls across the road. The girls looked like they might be in one of the upper years at school, their outfits skimpy for the sun. I wasn't going to ask why they weren't in class.

"A load of whores," Max yelled. "Dress like that and you'll get some, and no man will be to blame for his actions." Every part of me clenched tight. I truly couldn't believe that oaf of a troll, and I'd had enough.

As Max barged through the door, the girls made various gestures at his back. He settled at his usual table and released a breath, satisfied with his morning's abuse.

I hauled my blade from the shelf at the bottom of the counter, drew it from the scabbard then assessed the room. Only the troll and the elf remained—no humans. A quiet morning, but it would pick up shortly. Alice was still in the office, and Inès and Dame Blanche were chatting animatedly in the kitchen, out of sight of the door. Guy and José were also busy in there.

Max sat a little way back from his table, allowing space for his large girth and his legs. Before he knew what had happened, I crossed the room, swung my blade and slammed the point into Max's seat, millimetres from his prize jewels.

His jaw dropped as he goggled at the sword. With a tug, I pulled it out then raised the tip to his neck. "This is my patch now," I growled. "There will be no insulting or sexually objectifying women, or anyone else for that matter. And you, my old friend, are completely responsible for each one of your actions, as is every man... troll... fae."

He made a grunting noise. "Camille, be reasonable."

"And while I'm at it, stop insulting my grandfather and... stop being such a jerk." I pressed the blade closer and his eyes actually bulged. I had to admit, his discomfort was more than a little entertaining. I released him and sauntered to the counter, the blade on my shoulder. The elf and the goblin shifted nervously in their seats. I sent them my best enjoy your-coffee grin.

Max's face set in shock, he scuttled out without a word. Job done.

I wiped my blade on a tea towel, then tucked it away on its shelf. When I rose, René had come in. "How can I help you?" I said stiffly. Surely it wasn't about the gas again, not after the explosion?

"Camille. Just the person I wanted to see." Strange. His tone was actually pleasant, his chest not quite so puffed out. "I've been in communication with the folklore department of Toulouse University. They're coming to town in a couple of weeks for their summer research project, and they're looking for someone to assist them—a keen volunteer."

I gaped at him. He was being nice, and the folklore department of one of the most prestigious universities in France would be here. "Uh... project? What sort of project?"

"Oh, I have absolutely no idea, but I immediately thought of you. Interested?"

Was I interested? Yes, I was interested. I was one hundred percent, downright interested. I caught sight of a white head moving in the kitchen. But hell, I had Dame Blanche working at the café, Lucas was a drac, Roux had invited the whole of Fae to the town, and there was the fae version of Tarascon behind the car park. But it was all glamoured, right? What on earth could go wrong?

I met René's eager gaze. "Yep. Tell them I'm in."

FIND OUT HOW LUCAS GOT HOLD OF FICKLETURN'S
BREECHES AND MORE...

Get Folkloric Fae,
the Folkloric prequel novella, FREE at:
www.karenzagrant.com

Perfect for reading at any point during the series.

A message from Slaughter...

The Men of Bédeilhac would be exceedingly grateful if you would leave a star rating for the book on Amazon to signal your appreciation for their little-known fae race of fearless, violent and only occasionally inebriated warriors.

Thank you very much!

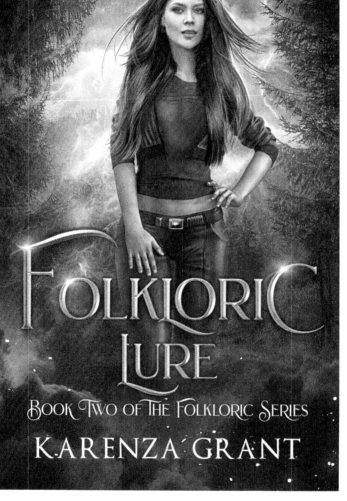

FOLKLORIC
LURE

Book Two of The Folkloric Series

KARENZA GRANT

Chapter 1

Today was important to me.

On a one-to-ten scale of importance, it had started at a nine, then shot way past a hundred, to the point where my stomach swam and my hands would actually be shaking if I wasn't forcing myself still. And all of it because a team from the University of Toulouse's folklore department was coming to town for their summer research project. Today. In a matter of hours.

They needed someone to help out—an assistant to run errands and organise everything. That person was me, and it would mean I'd be working with Professor Margot Joly, one of the most renowned folklorists in France, if not the world. I'd be in a position to run my paper, *Recent Experiences of Ancient Folkloric Phenomena*, by her, and I'd be in the company of fourteen folklore enthusiasts, from degree students to industry experts, who I could geek out with the whole week long.

With the folklore department arriving imminently, one might wonder, then, why I was hiking toward the rounded summit of Les Calbières at dawn, dressed in semi-medieval leathers, a sword strapped to my back. One might also wonder why I was following up said hill the perfectly proportioned, ridiculously intriguing and stunningly sculpted frame of a drac—a fae that Margot Joly would insist emphatically was a folkloric concoction of the area's collective psyche, and was definitely, absolutely and completely not real.

I'd needed to get out of my loft to get away from the project preparations spooling through my mind. They'd kept me awake for most of the night. When Lucas's text had come in at five a.m. asking if I wanted to join him on a hike to investigate the recent spate of acid attacks on cattle, I'd agreed. Either that or my head would explode.

Now I came to think of it, though, there was a chance Alice hadn't ordered extra strawberries for the brioche goûter we were serving the team at midmorning. The café's famous dish of light brioche wrapped around sticks of homemade dark chocolate, served with crème fraîche, wouldn't be the same without strawberries. Saturday was busy, so Alice might have forgotten. I'd have to check as soon as I got back. If the worse came to the worst, someone could pop out to Super U and pick up a few cartons. They might not be the best quality but—

"So, is it working?" Lucas asked over his shoulder, the bronze rays of dawn delineating his jaw, his sword swaying a little in its back scabbard as he walked.

"What?" I snapped. How was I supposed to remember anything with him interrupting?

"The distraction. Are you managing to take your mind off today?" His lips clamped tight then quirked.

Damn it. I'd gone right back to obsessing over the arrangements again. "Nope. It's not working. But being up here is definitely better than being stuck in my loft." Exercise and the outdoors always reduced my stress levels. I drew in a deep breath and absorbed the sunlight that trickled over the distant peaks. The glow brightened from bronze to gold that suffused the rocky, cattle-cropped grassland, the scattering of trees and the flock of sheep in the distance loitering around the Pons farm.

"You've been avoiding me," Lucas said as he took a bend in the path, the sun silhouetting the angles of his face.

Yes, I'd avoided him. I'd been too busy to make his morning noisette at the café, and I'd purposely not entered fae Tarascon, even though I was burning to explore—not that I would've had the time with all the preparations for the project. "What makes you think that?" I said nonchalantly.

"We haven't spoken for the last two weeks, since the whole hantaumo thing wrapped up. It's careless."

"What?" It wasn't the fact we hadn't spoken—that was true enough—but the careless part...

He gripped the chest strap of his scabbard with one hand and glanced at me with that shrewd gaze. "You know exactly what. You're spending all your time on the project preparations, but your Keeper training must come first. There's so much out there that's a threat. It's beyond careless—it's downright dangerous."

Irritation prickled through me, making the too-hot air hotter still. Mornings were usually cool in the mountains, even in the summer months. It wouldn't be midsummer for a few days, and yet it was sweltering. I stomped ahead and turned to Lucas, stopping him mid-stride. For once, due to the rising ground, I stood almost level with him. "I'm not a Keeper," I said into his face. "So I don't need to train." Becoming a Keeper of the Bounds between the fae and human realms was a big deal, and I wasn't sure it was for me.

"Come on, Camille, you can't resist the lure of Fae, the mystery, the adventure." His eyes sparkled with something that looked a lot like mischief. "And you saw the hantaumo. Having access to Fae necessitates learning about it. Or are you going to be one of those humans who wander across the bounds never to be seen again?"

I jabbed my finger at him. "This!"

"What?" He narrowed his eyes.

"This crap that you've started on. This 'You must learn everything about fae right now, and you must become a Keeper for your own good because I want you to.'" I mimicked his voice pitifully, shaking my finger some more. It was one of the reasons I'd been avoiding him. But we'd been through so much together with the hantaumo, my avoidance felt petty, and I'd hoped I'd heard the last of it. Some stupid hope.

He caught my wrist. My angry pulse throbbed under his grip. I couldn't help but shiver as his thumb ran over my skin.

"You can't hide from it," he said.

But truth be told, my irritation originated from more than his presumption that I'd become a Keeper. The attack on Tarascon—on all of us—was a lot to take on board. Not only had the queen of a bunch of lethal witchy wraiths been hell-bent on taking my life, but since the breakneck few days when we'd faced the hantaumo, I'd had to come to terms with the actual existence of fae. In a weird, counterintuitive way, spending time with one of them didn't help. It just left me reeling, and I needed time to process this new reality.

There was something else, too. Now Grampi was better, the possibility of attending university had come up again. We could probably just about manage the farm's bills if I kept working, and assisting with the summer project would help me decide if it was what I really wanted. Plus, I'd have the chance to make a good first impression on my potential tutors. But going to university would also mean I wouldn't have as much opportunity to learn about fae, and I'd have to turn down the role of Keeper. But those options were pretty overwhelming right now. It was easier not to think of them.

I yanked my wrist back. "I'm not hiding. And I'll investigate, train, learn, whatever, when I'm good and ready, and not a moment before."

His lips curved into an ungodly grin, his pupils glinting. "Made you forget about today, though, didn't I?"

It took me a second to catch up. He'd been doing it on purpose. "You sod. You absolute git."

He laughed, the ring deep and beguiling.

I pulled myself from the sound and strode toward the

summit, working my annoyance into my pace, the low sun bright in my eyes. He was such a... such a what, exactly? He'd behaved so far out of line, giving me verity without my knowledge to reveal the hidden world, and sleeping with me when he'd known what lay ahead of us, and yet he'd saved my life multiple times. He'd believed in me when I hadn't a hope left, and he'd been willing to sacrifice himself for the town, for Grampi, for me. But the threat was over, and I needed to get used to the fact that this man, the town's new doctor, wasn't human. He was other, an enigma, something I'd never had to deal with before.

And now, in his infuriating way, he'd managed to distract me. I wasn't going to admit it, but I felt a little better. Squinting against the glare, I sidestepped around a rock. Lucas darted forward and shoved his palm into my ribs, thrusting me off the path.

I stumbled, then gained my footing. "What the hell did you do that for?"

He angled himself to block the blaze of the sun and nodded to the ground. Something glinted in the path where I would've stepped. My vision adjusted. Thick bright green liquid pooled on the dry earth.

"The acid?" Everyone was talking about the attacks of the past few days. Some sicko was spraying animals with an extremely corrosive chemical, causing them slow and agonising deaths.

"Looks like it." Lucas crouched down and sniffed the substance, then took a coin from his pocket and dropped it in the gunk. It sizzled and dissolved in seconds, bubbling.

Definitely not something I needed to step in.

He rummaged in his pouch, put on gloves, drew out a glass vial and plastic lab spatula, then took a sample. To our side, more acid pooled amidst the rocks.

"Spraying acid is one thing, but why would some idiot leave the stuff around like this? The sheep would probably just avoid it, anyway."

"My thoughts exactly." Lucas tucked the sample into his pouch then placed the spatula into another vial and stashed it with his gloves.

"We have to be close to the bounds." We were roughly on the other side of the mountain to Lucas's house, where I'd entered Fae for the first time. "So is it fae related?"

"Possibly..." He rose and headed off the path. I followed, and we passed another patch of acid... and another. "Look." He indicated to a heap on the brow of the summit that, in the awkward light, I'd taken for a rock. We walked over, circumnavigating more gunk on the way.

The heap was a very dead Black-Face Manech ewe, one of the dairy breeds of the region with black legs and face, a white body and curly white horns. Its skin, muscle and bone had been deeply corroded across its chest, shoulder and abdomen. The sheep's intestines were visible, patches of acid pooling around them, eating away at the creature. A little vapour rose, the smell acrid. My stomach turned. It wasn't so much the goriness—after defeating the hantaumo queen, I was coping a lot better with that sort of thing. I'd say my reactions were pretty normal, rather than the complete freeze and overwhelm they had been. But what got me was the pain the animal must have gone through.

Lucas bent down and placed his hand on the ewe's acid-free throat. He stilled, his eyes locked on the creature. "It's still warm. This happened recently." His voice was rough, his features darkening, twisting, his skin shrivelling tight against bone. Lethal, saw-like teeth flashed as his lips retracted.

My heart rate spiked. I wanted to step away, but my feet were rooted to the spot. Apart from his initial introduction, Lucas had kept his other form well hidden. I shuddered at his warped features—his true self. He was an abomination from hell, so completely other to his suave and too-hot-for-his-own-good everyday self. He drew a sharp breath, and the man returned.

"Beautiful," I said, barely hiding my revulsion.

He glanced from the corner of his eye and grinned. "It's the flesh. I've not eaten fresh kill since that goat."

"How could I forget?" Not my most cherished memory.

"Though it's probably best I don't indulge. The acid would give me indigestion."

I snorted.

A similar heap lay a little way off beside a gorse bush. On the lookout for more gunk, I walked over. Acid had worked into this ewe's gut and reproductive organs. Its body quivered and its eyelids flickered, its eyes dull with pain. The poor thing. "This one's still alive," I called.

Lucas strode over and scowled as he took in the mess, then he met my gaze. "Nothing can replace that amount of tissue loss. With the weapons we have, the most humane end will be stunning the sheep by cutting the nerves behind the eye, followed by decapitation." He drew his blade with a slick scrape.

I nodded and faced the other way. There was scuffling, then a thunk and a thwack. I turned back. The ewe's head lay on the ground. I breathed through the sight. He wiped his blade on the grass and sheathed it.

"The attacks are absolutely hideous," I said. "Who could be doing—"

A holler came from the direction of the farm, and a shot blasted out.

We spun toward the source.

Blood drained from my face. Even from here I could make out the lumbering gait of Monsieur Pons, but the shotgun took most of my attention. That and Ripper, his giant bear-eating Pyrenean Mountain Dog, charging toward us, his shaggy white coat and meaty chops flopping as he ran.

The story continues in *Folkloric Lure...*

Afterword

It's been such a wild experience writing Folkloric—the series has given me so many laughs already, and I'm eager to venture into more antics.

I'm guessing some of you, if you're anything like me, like to embark on armchair voyages, googling locations, or perhaps you like to geek out on folklore. So here are a few notes on the setting and local mythology. After all, Camille would never forgive me if I didn't give you the lowdown.

Most of the series locations in the human realm exist. Tarascon (its full name is Tarascon-sur-Ariège) is a stunning town in the South of France, nestled in the Ariège valley in the foothills of the Pyrenees mountains. Despite its beauty, it's no tourist town. It's situated on one of the major routes through the mountains between France and Spain, and it's an industrial centre with quite a history.

I fell in love with the area at first sight. Forest-clad mountains shelter the valley, castles perch high on remote crags, and caves descend far into the depths of the earth. The poetry and artistry of the troubadours that blossomed here in the 12th century laid the foundation for the novel as we know it, and way back in prehistoric times, the first modern humans (the Aurignacians) emerged here—the region is known as the cradle of civilisation. It's also a place associated with Arab invasion and Charlemagne, not to mention rebellion, heretic religions and the grail. As you can see, there is plenty of fuel for urban fantasy.

Above all, though, it bears a wildness and a mysterious otherness. It's not difficult to imagine other realms nearby—that an entrance might lie behind an old gnarled box tree or within a stalagmite-filled cavern. And it doesn't take much to envisage a fae town under the slopes of Coustarous.

As to the folklore, I try to draw as much as possible from the actual mythology of the region, and many of the creatures in the Folkloric series are noted in local lore. As in other places, it has its fair share of fae, goblins, trolls, dragons and giants. However, the specifics get very interesting. Think of dracs, the fae of Bédeilhac (known in Folkloric as the Men), Dame Blanche, the croquembouche, the hantaumo, Count Estruch, and many other examples—too many to mention here. Curiously, Count Estruch was a real count and the origin of the earliest European vampire myth. If you want to google what he got up to, be warned, it isn't pleasant.

The Pyrenees mountain range also has its own pantheon of gods, ruled over by Abellion, a sun god akin to Apollo. Baeserte and Aherbelste are other examples. What very little is known about them has been obtained from roman excavations. Roman gods gradually replaced the old pantheon, and more recently, Christian saints supplanted the Roman deities. In spite of that, the traits of the old gods live on in more recent personifications, so there is something to be gleaned.

Having said all this, there's not a whole load of lore to go on for the purpose of creating characters. A couple of paragraphs on how dracs shift into gold cups, luring people to their watery graves, isn't much to shape into a wily doctor with rather mischievous tendencies. I have two words for you: artistic licence. Yet when I can stick to the lore, I do so.

If you want to find out more, there's not much published in English, although Martin Locker's *The Tears of Pyrene* is superb. If you read French, try one of Olivier de Marliave's excellent tomes on the subject, for example, *Trésor de la Mythology Pyrénéenne*.

Before I finish, there are a few people I'd like to mention who have been instrumental in getting this series off the ground. Octavia Denning, my gratitude to you is unending. Dorine Maine, thank you for everything from the bottom of my heart. A special shout-out goes to my writing group: Viktoria Dahill, Katie Mouallek, Rachel Cooper and Abhivyakti Singh, for always being honest and saying what needs to be said. You keep me on my toes and striving to do my best. Jack Barrow and P.M. Gilbert, it's been great working with you. Many thanks to Toby Selwyn, my super editor, and to Deranged Doctor Designs for the top-notch covers despite my terrible cover specs. I'm indebted to my superb ARC and Street Team. You guys rock. Massive thanks goes to L.A. McBride for answering question after question with angelic patience. Rillian Grant and Minerva Grant, you make it all worthwhile. And last of all, thanks to you, the intrepid reader, for daring to delve into this utterly crazy world.

About the Author

Karenza Grant writes fun and feisty urban fantasy with plenty of humour and a little slow-burn romance.

Her early years in Cornwall were largely the source of her fascination with all things mysterious. She lived below a hill reputed to be the Cornish residence of the Unseelie Court, and the local myths got their claws in. Now she's inspired by a broad range of creators from Jim Henson, Arthur Rackham, and Olivier de Marliave, to a whole host of amazing authors on the urban fantasy scene. Currently, she's enjoying weaving her love of France into page-turning stories.

She has three black cats known as The Three Guardians, and a crazy lab x spaniel who is just about the only thing that can extract Karenza from her writing desk—if the pooch isn't walked, the legions of hell will be released.

Connect

There's nothing better than hearing from readers. Drop me a line or join me on social media. I hang around on Facebook on a daily basis and would love to see you there.

You can find all the links on my website:
www.karenzagrant.com

Printed in Great Britain
by Amazon